SWEPT INTO A VOLCANO OF SENSUALITY AND DEATH . . .

BARTHOLOMEW—Despotic ruler of Soufriere, he possessed a savagery as hot as the overhead sun—and a touch as cold as death.

COLIN—Returning from self-imposed exile in America, this true son of Soufriere watched in mounting anger as his homecoming turned into a nightmare.

WENDY—A Chinese beauty from San Francisco, she came to Soufriere for a holiday—and stayed for an experience that blew her life wide open.

PIERRE—Selfless revolutionary, he saw but one way to Soufriere's freedom—the death of Bartholomew.

PEARL—Bartholomew's ravishing mistress, she paid for her devotion in Soufriere's flaming holocaust.

THEY GAMBLED THEIR LIVES IN A SEETHING DRAMA OF THE WEST INDIES . . .

SACRIFICE PLAY

SACRIFICE PLAY

John Ballem

FAWCETT GOLD MEDAL ● NEW YORK

*This book is dedicated to the
Grenadines—exquisite isles
dreaming on a turquoise sea.*

The Island of Soufriere is not to be found on any map of the Caribbean. However, its topography, history, and people are common to many of these enchanting subtropical islands.

During the tumultuous 16th and 17th centuries, Soufriere changed hands between the French and British no less than seven times. Finally, in 1778 British troops stormed ashore to recapture the island and set the stage for two centuries of uninterrupted English rule. The British Colonial Office, wearying of the search for new names for this flyspeck of an island, contented itself with removing the accent from "Soufrière." The name commemorates the island's most spectacular feature—one of the very few still active volcanoes in the Caribbean.

The frequent turnovers of power made the ordinary citizens singularly indifferent to the identity of their political rulers; they asked only to be left alone to pursue their way of life undisturbed. This ostrich-like attitude served them ill when Soufriere was granted Independence and became one of the world's smallest sovereign states. Bartholomew, a charismatic black union leader who had been elected premier two years before, declared himself President for Life and began his harsh dictatorial regime.

Chapter One

A fat, oily bubble formed on the surface and then a geyser of black water erupted. A few scalding drops touched the skin of the youth dangling at the end of the rope, and he screamed with mingled fear and pain. His frantic attempts to draw his legs out of range were obscured by the cloud of steam that billowed up as the geyser subsided. The air was filled with the rotten-egg smell of hydrogen sulfide.

Carl Dykstra, standing on the wet, slippery crust of sulfur that rimmed the cauldron, waited for the curtain of noxious steam to drift away. Then he called out, "You'll be boiled alive, Tommy. Like a fucking lobster. Tell us what we want to know and put an end to this."

Dykstra thumbed a lighter to his cigarette and squinted through the smoke at the teen-aged mulatto. Blood dribbled down Tommy Demaret's chin where his teeth had bitten through his lower lip to keep from crying out. Carl's strange eyes traced the raw yellow rope from the knot cutting into Tommy's wrists, up through the block and tackle on the crossbeam and along to the two uniformed thugs anchoring it on the far side of the bubbling pit.

Leisurely, Dykstra pivoted on his heel and surveyed the floor of the slumbering volcano. Pockmarked with cones of crystalline sulfur and fumaroles leaking sulfurous steam, it looked like the antechamber of hell. It

7

was deserted except for the interrogation squad and the sentries posted around its perimeter. All the men were members of Bartholomew's secret police, cynically named the Institute for Social Research by Tony Mallabone, the dictator's white adviser. The ordinary people who suffered their cruel harassment dubbed them the "Mongoose Gang," a name entirely in keeping with their true nature. Carl flipped the cigarette butt away and nodded to the two men on the rope.

The block and tackle squealed rustily as the wretched youth was lowered to within scant centimeters of the roiling surface. With an ominous sucking sound the turbid water prepared itself for its next leap skyward. Tommy was sobbing now, an incoherent gibbering of terror as another deadly bubble grew beneath him. It vented a telltale wisp of steam and Carl gave a quick hand signal. His men tugged on the rope, yanking Tommy out of range as the superheated jet shot up.

"The next time's for real. Nobody is worth dying this kind of death for, Tommy. Tell us the name of the bastard who runs the S.F.U.—that's all I want."

The leader of the interrogation team ran a hand through his thatch of blond hair, sunbleached the color of straw, and smiled expectantly up at his victim. Seen at a distance, Carl Dykstra looked like the very model of American youth, California style, equally at home on a tennis court or luxury yacht. Up close, however, the absence of either eyebrows or lashes made his eyes look like two poached blue eggs. Usually he kept the unsettling orbs hidden behind dark sunglasses, except on missions of violence when he reveled in their shock value.

"This is it, Tommy," he said softly and began a slow countdown from ten.

For a microsecond that seemed to stretch into a

hushed eternity, the boy made no sound after his legs were immersed. Then his reflexes took over and he began to thrash, pushing his bare limbs deeper into the liquid inferno and bellowing a primordial scream of agony torn from his very guts.

The terrible sound echoed around the crater as he was slowly raised out of the boiling water. Blackened patches of skin peeled away from his writhing legs, and two long strips hung down from the soles of his feet. When the screams finally broke into exhausted sobs, Dykstra said in a loud voice, "Lower away, men."

"No, No! Oh, God. I'll talk. Anything!"

"Good boy. The name of your leader . . . No tricks!"

"Pierre . . . my . . . my brother."

The blond interrogator exhaled a long sigh of satisfaction and murmured, "It fits." He fell silent for a moment then glanced sideways at the two Mongoose thugs. "You know what to do," he said quietly.

The bright blade of a machete flashed and the severed rope whipped through the pulley, plunging Tommy Demaret into the molten pit. He died instantly, but his head, the *café au lait* skin now a livid scarlet, mouth open in a silent scream, floated above the surface for a long moment. Then he slowly sank from view, dragging the coil of rope down with him. The youngest member of the Mongoose squad retched helplessly and was violently sick.

Carl looked at him with contempt. "You better shape up, soldier, or you'll pull latrine duty."

Dykstra's expression was thoughtful as he stepped back to let his men dismantle the wooden frame. His elation at bringing this vital piece of information to Bartholomew was tempered with uncertainty about the dictator's reaction. Pearl Demaret was a favored member of Bartholomew's court, and he might not be too thrilled to discover it was her eldest brother who was the leader of the troublesome Soufriere Freedom Union. On the other hand, Pearl had cut herself off from her family years ago, and Carl knew Bartholomew still stuck his black cock into her every now and then. Most likely it would never cross the president's egotistic mind to doubt her loyalty.

Reassured, Carl walked beside his men as they carried the wooden timbers over to the storage shed. The fading sign above the door grandly proclaimed it was the site of "The Soufriere Experimental Geothermal Project," but the interior of the small brick building was dusty with disuse, and the only evidence of any geothermal "experiments" was an untidy pile of galvanized pipes in the yard. Bartholomew liked to boast that someday the volcanic springs would be harnessed to supply all the island's electrical needs. Until that unlikely event, the project provided the perfect excuse for closing down what had been a prime tourist attraction and using it for other, more sinister, purposes.

Carl's face wore a contented smile as the jeep carried him back to the tiny nation's capital. Once he had briefed Bartholomew on the success of the interrogation, he would be free to set out on the hijacking mission. A couple of relaxing days cruising the Grenadines and then the quick pounce on an unsuspecting yacht. This was the way to live!

Chapter Two

Antilles Rose ghosted downwind with only her jib raised to catch the trades. Up ahead a light blinked once. It was slightly inshore of the schooner, closer to the dark hump of the land. Standing behind the deckhouse, Capt'n Johnny eased the wheel and the ship swung slowly to port. They were running without lights, and the small wave curling out from the bow gleamed with phosphorescence on the dark sea.

Three native pirogues, their flour-sack sails furled, bobbed silently on the water as *Antilles Rose* glided up to them. Capt'n Johnny made a chopping motion with his arm and the crewmen in the bow cast off the jib halyard and lowered the sail noiselessly to the deck. A strong pull of the oars brought the first boat alongside. Colin Townsend bent down to pick up her painter and secure it to a cleat.

"You doan' want no part of this night's work," Capt'n Johnny warned in a hoarse whisper. "You jes' a passenger and best you stay that way."

He was right, of course. If, by some wild chance, a customs launch happened on the scene, Colin should be able to claim that he was just along for the ride. He handed the rope to one of the crew and crossed over to the starboard side. There was no railing, just a low planking that extended calf-high above the deck.

The contraband was offloaded with the smooth efficiency of long practice. Wooden crates, their sides boldly labeled "White Horse Scotch Whisky," came up through the forward hatch. The black arms that lifted the containers up from the hold were invisible in the darkness, imparting an eerie quality to their smooth ascent. Within thirty minutes all three of the fishing boats were creeping back toward their home island of Carriacou, stacked so high with whisky crates that their gunwales barely cleared the water.

Capt'n Johnny crouched beside Colin as he waited for the night to swallow the last of the sharp-prowed pirogues. "I's been in the bubble trade since befoah I can remember, but I's still mighty happy to see that stuff off the boat," he whispered.

Colin grinned in the darkness. "That happy feeling is what keeps you in the game, Johnny."

For a moment Colin found himself almost envying the black man's lifestyle. The *Antilles Rose* was an ancient wooden sailing vessel with patched sails, a leaky hull and a balky, stinking engine. But Capt'n Johnny owned every piece of her twenty-two meter length. And the "bubble trade"—so called because sparkling wine often formed part of the contraband cargoes—was an honored calling in the West Indies.

When Capt'n Johnny was satisfied the current had pushed them well south of Carriacou, he signaled for the mainsail to be raised. The bare feet of the three crewmen padded across the deck as they moved into position near the mast.

"Hold it," the captain hissed. "Somethin's out there."

The only sound was the slap and gurgle of the sea against the hull. Capt'n Johnny held his hand cupped to his ear but now they all heard it; a faint mewing wail coming from somewhere out in the water. The

12

whites of their eyes shone in the darkness as the crew stared nervously at their skipper.

"It *could* be a seagull," Colin ventured.

"No seabird call like that."

The sound came again, a quavering call that was quickly choked off.

"Somebody's in trouble out there, Johnny."

"Yeah, mon." The captain handed him a flashlight and went below to start the engine.

The switch of the flashlight was sticky with corroded metal, and Colin had to fumble with it before he was rewarded with a feeble beam. There were no whitecaps to distract the eye, only the dark swell of the sea. On the third pass with the rapidly failing light, Colin caught a flash of movement.

"Whatever it is, it's just off the starboard bow," he called out, and the schooner changed course obediently.

"My God, it's a girl!" Colin muttered as he spotted her white bikini top.

She was half floating on her back, her arms moving feebly. A wave splashed out from the schooner's hull and filled her open mouth. Her arms went slack and her head sank beneath the surface, the long black hair trailing behind.

Aiming at the spot where she had gone under, Colin launched himself over the side. He dove deep but not deep enough; the dark shape of the girl was below him and sinking with the fatal speed of the totally water-logged. If he returned to the surface for air he would never be able to reach her. He jackknifed in the water and scissors-kicked in pursuit until his outstretched fingers finally touched that blessedly long hair. Twisting the strands in a firm handhold he struggled back to the surface. Even as his bursting lungs were sucking in a great gulp of air, his free hand was under her armpit to

13

raise her head above the water. Capt'n Johnny was playing the flashlight on them and, just before it flickered and died out, Colin saw that the girl was Chinese.

Treading water and with his hands under her small rump, he pushed her limp body up the schooner's hull until the sailors could grasp her and lift her on board. They stretched her on the deck and stood back while Colin knelt beside her. She was unconscious and her breathing had stopped. Forcing her lips open, he placed his mouth against hers and blew his breath into her lungs. On the fifth ventilation she coughed and her chest began to heave as she fought for air.

She retched and turned on her side to let the sea water gush from her mouth and nostrils. Her eyelids fluttered and she began to shiver uncontrollably.

"She's coming round but shock could still finish her off. She's got to be kept warm." Colin scooped up her slight form and headed for the wheelhouse.

Squatting beside the bunk in the cramped cabin, Colin felt *Antilles Rose* heel under the full weight of her canvas, and the asthmatic wheeze of the engine died away. The girl choked and pushed the mug away, hugging the woollen blanket around her bare shoulders. Her enormous almond eyes looked at him gravely, and Colin saw that she was exquisite. Her face was just slightly heart-shaped with high cheekbones above a softly rounded chin. Her hair was already beginning to gleam as it dried.

He corked the rum bottle and asked, "Can you speak any English?"

A small, weary smile touched her lips. "Of course," she croaked. "I'm American."

14

"Sorry about that," Colin apologized lightly, then went on, "It seems you're going to make it."

"Thanks to you." She broke off as another fit of shaking seized her. When it had passed, she whispered, "Did you pick up any of the others?"

"What others?"

Colin heard Capt'n Johnny's rubber boots clumping down the companionway and spun around. "Did you hear what she said? About there being others? We'll have to come about and search the area."

"It's no use." The girl's voice had returned to normal; it was soft with each word carefully articulated. "I was just kidding myself. I know I'm the only survivor."

"You better start from the top," Colin said. "Beginning with your name."

"Wendy." She seemed about to add her surname but paused to gaze around the untidy, shabby interior. "What kind of boat is this?"

"An island trading schooner. She's not particularly elegant but she does seem to stay afloat."

"Is that what you do?" The dark eyes were studying him intently. "Run this boat, I mean?"

"*I* don't." Colin gestured at Capt'n Johnny. "He does. I'm just a passenger, like you."

The captain reached across Colin and silently handed her a fresh mug of coffee. She cupped both hands around its warmth and took a grateful sip. "Can we radio the Coast Guard?"

"The only radio on board is my Sony transistor," Colin told her.

"It wouldn't have done any good anyway," she sighed hopelessly.

Capt'n Johnny spoke for the first time. "You on a yacht, mistress?" She nodded and he muttered, "Pirates."

"Murderers is more like it." She sat up, one hand clutching the blanket against her breast. "Look, you're not part of them, are you?"

"Whoever 'them' may be," Colin replied, "no, we're not. My name is Colin Townsend; I'm a flying instructor from California on vacation on the island where I was born. The captain here is an old friend from childhood. I practically grew up on this schooner."

The girl seemed to be no longer listening. Tears welled from under tightly closed eyelids, and she was sobbing with a dry racking sound.

Colin looked at Capt'n Johnny. "You know what happened to her, don't you?"

The black man nooded somberly. "I can make a pretty good guess. But she tell us for sure."

"I'm sorry." Wendy sniffed noisily and wiped her eyes with the back of her hand. "It was so awful. I can't believe it really happened." She took a deep breath. "It was just after sundown."

Colin glanced at his waterproof Seiko; she had been in the water for five hours. She was tougher than she looked.

"The other boat seemed to come out of nowhere. We were 'motoring' and had our cockpit lights on, which may be why we didn't hear or see them. All of a sudden these men were jumping onto the deck and shooting. They didn't say anything; they just opened fire!"

"They only wan' the boat," Capt'n Johnny murmured.

"Were they locals?" asked Colin. "You know—blacks."

She frowned uncertainly. "Some of them were. But the leader was white. Even blonder than you," she glanced at Colin's sun-streaked hair. "There was something funny about his face though, like it was kind of unfinished." She shivered beneath the blanket. "It all happened so fast. I really didn't see much."

16

"How did you manage to escape?"

"I was up in the bow, on the far side of the deckhouse, scraping the supper plates into the sea. When I saw them gun Milt down in cold blood, I just slipped over the side. I guess they didn't notice in all the shooting and confusion."

"How many were on the boat?" Colin pressed on with his questions, figuring it was good therapy to keep her talking.

"Five of us. We are . . . were," her voice failed and she took a deep gulp before continuing in a rush, "from Baltimore. Milt's a doctor. He and his wife have been coming down here every winter for years. They were expert sailors and they would bareboat charter a yacht and spend two or three weeks cruising among the islands. This year they asked me and a couple of others to join them and share expenses. We picked up the boat in St. Lucia and spent the last week sailing down the Grenadines. It was super."

"What boat you charter?" Capt'n Johnny asked and nodded knowingly when Wendy replied, "*Sympatico.*"

"Fast, ver' fast. Which be why they wan' she."

Colin drew a sharp breath as the full realization of what they had stumbled into sank home. Ever since he had arrived back in the islands he had heard whispered tales of the merciless pirates who hijacked fast luxury yachts and used them to smuggle marijuana and cocaine into the United States. Their method was brutally effective. Having seized a yacht, they immediately killed everyone on board to eliminate witnesses. Then they would cram her full with bales of marijuana brought out from Colombia by motor launch and sail at top speed up the American coast to rendezvous with either a freighter or motorboats outside the twelve-mile limit. Each yacht would make only one trip, which usually was completed long before she was reported missing. The hijackers would open her sea cocks to scuttle her the moment the Colombia gold was on its way ashore, and one more pleasure craft would be listed as "missing at sea."

Colin was almost pitched on top of Wendy's bunk as *Antilles Rose* shuddered, then swooped down the trough of a wave. Capt'n Johnny kept his balance effortlessly and showed a gap-toothed smile.

"Pretty soon we pass by Kick 'em Jenny. You remember that rock?"

"God, yes! Like it was yesterday."

A sail flapped with a hollow boom as the schooner fell off once more. Capt'n Johnny went back up on deck to guide the old vessel through the stretch of turbulent water.

When Colin looked back at their castaway, her eyes had closed and she was breathing deeply and regularly. He felt her pulse, a little fast but steady. Sleep was the best cure for the exhaustion and trauma she had been through. He turned down the wick of the kerosene lantern hanging from the low ceiling and followed the captain out.

Antilles Rose was just poking her nose beyond the rocky islet that thrust its sheer cliffs above the waves that had rolled unchecked all the way from Africa. The trade winds bounced off the steep sides of Kick 'em Jenny, doubling in force and rattling the sail battens like machine-gun fire. Gusts of wind snatched the crests from oncoming seas and flung them on board.

"Shorten sail!" Capt'n Johnny shouted, and the crew hauled on the lines with alacrity. A savage squall beat against the taut sails and sent a torrent of white water crashing over the lee gunwale. Another sea surged on board and then they broke free of the miniature maelstrom that swirled around the volcanic outcropping.

Colin laughed with exhilaration and wiped the salt spume from his face. "That's the part I remember best about all the trips we made, Johnny."

The older man smiled, honest affection shining from his weathered features. Johnny Somerville had grown up with Colin's father at High Trees, the old Townsend plantation on the east coast of Soufriere. His boat had become a refuge for Colin when the youngster's world had been shattered by his father's alcoholism and the loss of the plantation that had been in the Townsend family for five generations.

The reminiscent smile faded from the seaman's face at the thought of the Chinese girl they had fished from the sea and the trouble she could bring. He motioned Colin to sit beside him.

"If them pirates find out that one got away, they'll be after her like starvin' sharks."

"That's just what I've been thinking," Colin agreed gloomily. "I didn't know the hijackers operated this far north. I thought they did their dirty work just off the South American coast so they'd be close to the source of supply."

"Mos' likely they already had one boat and found out that she was 'hot' so they have to grab another one."

"Figures." Colin suppressed an unexpected yawn. "I'm whacked. I'll look in on our passenger and then sack out for a couple of hours."

The girl was asleep, or pretending to be. Colin wasn't sure which. He blew out the lamp and went back topside.

Antilles Rose boasted one life jacket, a tattered, ragged affair that looked like it would float like a stone. Colin placed it under his head and curled up on the wooden planks of the deck. For a few minutes

19

thoughts of Wendy and what she had been through nibbled at the fringes of his consciousness, then the rhythmic motion of the ship sent him plummeting into sleep.

He was wakened by a shower of salt spray as *Antilles Rose* heeled over on a new tack and bowled westward before the wind. Colin blinked and stretched luxuriously. The sun was up and the cobalt sea was empty under a cloudless Caribbean sky. Capt'n Johnny turned the wheel over to one of the crew and let the patched mainsail out a notch to ease the strain on the rigging.

"When do you reckon we'll make Albertstown?" Colin asked.

"Three, mebbe four hours after sundown if the wind hol'."

"Any noises from our passenger this morning?"

Capt'n Johnny, who was propping himself against the side of the wheelhouse for a catnap, shook his head and Colin knocked gently on the companionway hatch.

"I've been lying here trying to convince myself that I've just had a horrible nightmare. But," Wendy swung her legs over the edge of the bunk, "it really did happen, and I've got to start living with it."

The tropical sun quickly turned the small cabin into a blistering sweatbox, and it was decided that Wendy could stay on the deck so long as no other craft approached within telescope range. Just before noon the crew rigged a tarpaulin awning aft of the wheelhouse and Wendy and Colin retreated to its shelter. After twelve years away from the Caribbean, Colin's light skin wasn't yet ready for a full day's exposure, although he had almost reached the golden toast shade which was as dark as he would ever get. Thin blue smoke drifted back from the stove made from an oil barrel as the cook grilled their noonday meal of flying fish.

"Were your friends, ah . . ." Colin began.

"Chinese?" Her smile was wintry. "No. They were all true-blue Caucasians."

"Hey, cool your jets on this race stuff," Colin protested. "You may have every reason in the world to be touchy; I have no way of knowing about that. But I'm just trying to get a piece of pretty important information."

"You're right, of course. I'm sorry." This time her smile was genuine. It was also, Colin decided, utterly breathtaking.

"I've already told you there were five of us," she went on, now seeming anxious to cooperate. "There was Milt Schuman and his wife Marion, and Ted, a close friend of theirs. He was an experienced yachtsman, like Milt. Then there was Susan who was the Schumans' first cousin and just about my best friend." She blinked and looked away.

"I'm sorry," Colin muttered uncomfortably, then pressed on. "I suppose that sooner or later the hijackers are bound to discover there were five people on that boat."

She shivered, despite the subtropical heat. "They can't help it. They'll find my clothes, and we took all kinds of Polaroids."

"So they'll know what you look like," Colin groaned softly. He tried to sound convincing as he added, "They'll figure that you drowned. After all, it was only by the wildest fluke that you didn't."

Before she could reply, Capt'n Johnny stooped under the awning to hand her a plate of flying fish. Colin noted with amusement that she rated the one plate on board that wasn't hopelessly chipped and cracked.

His fork cut into the tender flesh, and he paused with

21

the morsel halfway to his lips. "Do I get to know your last name now?"

"Wha-? Oh," she laughed and said, "It's Wong. Wendy Wong. My mother had a weakness for alliteration, I'm afraid. She always wanted a son so she could call him Walter."

"Do your parents live in Baltimore, too?"

She shook her head, the soft coils of dark hair swirling around her slender neck. "They're both dead. Killed in a car accident three years ago. That's why I left San Francisco and went east."

"I'm sorry," Colin muttered. "Brothers, sisters? Friends?"

Again she shook her head. "My closest friends were on that boat."

As though to change the subject she peered out from under the awning to watch a jet whine overhead, leaving a white contrail in the clear blue sky. "Where are we headed for, anyway?"

"Soufriere," Colin answered. "Ever heard of it?"

"Not until this trip. Milt said something about it not being a very healthy place to visit." She made a deprecatory gesture. "He was probably joking."

"He wasn't. It's no secret that some pretty strange things happen on Soufriere. But they stopped hassling the ordinary tourist a couple of years ago. After they started to stay away in droves."

The frayed cordage creaked as the schooner jibed. Then they heard the heavy reverberations of powerful engines and Colin saw the snow-white hull of a banana boat bearing down on them.

Hastily he and Wendy slipped down into the cabin. When the throb of the banana boat's engines died away, Capt'n Johnny called out, "Traffic gettin' heavy out there. Mistress bes' stay below."

"There's no point in both of us being miserable," Wendy said as Colin wiped the sweat from his forehead. There wasn't even the tiniest bead of moisture on her smooth skin. "You go back on top. It's me they'll be looking for."

"I'd like to talk some more if you don't mind," he said, and she made a little gesture with her hands that seemed to indicate he could suit himself. Nettled, he fell silent until she asked with the air of one making conversation, "You said you practically grew up on this boat. Is this some sort of nostalgia trip for you?"

"That's just what it is. When I heard that *Antilles Rose* was taking on cargo at St. Bart's, I flew up there on one of the local airlines to sail home with her. I don't know how many times I made this trip as a kid."

"And then I came along to upset your nice peaceful vacation."

"You can hardly be blamed for that. Anyhow, I'm not exactly on vacation." He looked directly at her. "I'm sort of in between careers. The flying school where I instructed closed down last month. Seems like the U.S. government finally decided they had enough private pilots and stopped the subsidy. So I came back home to rethink a few things."

Colin shifted uncomfortably on the creaky wooden stool. Wendy's white bikini left little to the imagination. She had the Oriental's trim bottom and slim waist, but she departed from the mold with long shapely legs and well developed breasts. He felt an almost irresistible urge to hold that delectable waist and to taste her lips, but the remote expression on her face held him in check. It was obvious her thoughts were still with her murdered companions.

He got to his feet, stooping under the low roof. "I

think I *will* get some air. Maybe you can manage to sleep in this furnace if I leave you alone."

The yacht traffic increased as they approached Soufriere. Most of it was heading into the wind back toward the Grenadines, and many of the boats, their amateur crews wearied by the incessant tacking, motored under bare poles. The pirates have it made, Colin mused as *Antilles Rose* changed course to avoid tangling with the four identical yawls. With so many pleasure boats cruising the Caribbean, they could reach out and grab one whenever they felt like it.

He stiffened as a white powerboat cut in front of their bow and then swung back toward them. He glanced anxiously over at Capt'n Johnny as the cabin cruiser's diesels were throttled back and her bow-wave subsided. Good Christ, were they going to be boarded? Then the powerful diesels rumbled back to life and the cruiser veered away to run parallel with them. Colin nearly shouted with relief when he saw the sunburned tourists lining her deck to aim their cameras at the quaint old sailing vessel.

The swift tropical night fell as they approached the narrow northern tip of the pear-shaped island. Soufriere was average for the Caribbean in size: twenty-five kilometers long and fourteen wide at its southern end. A spine of mountains ran down its center, with lush rain forests and green valleys on the western half and a high, flat plateau on the eastern Atlantic coast that was ideal for the cultivation of sugar.

It has so damn much going for it, Colin thought as a few scattered lights winked to life on the coastline. And with a population of just over 100,000 it didn't even have the usual Caribbean problem of overcrowding. But under the tender ministrations of Bartholomew and his henchmen, nearly half the work force was unemployed and most of the people lived at the bare subsistence level.

An orange glow suddenly began to grow halfway up the dark shoreline. Colin pointed at it. "What's that? Some sort of beacon?"

A look of repugnance crossed Capt'n Johnny's good-tempered face. "They burnin' down somebody's house. That Bartholomew, he hab a heavy hand."

The distant glow disappeared from sight as they rounded a headland and started to sail down the west coast of the island.

"What about your men?" Colin glanced in the direction of the three deckhands sprawled around the forward mast. One of them was softly strumming a battered guitar and a rum bottle was being passed from hand to hand. "Rescuing a beautiful girl from the sea makes a pretty exciting story to tell."

The skipper removed his dark blue, woollen cap and scratched his kinky hair, thick fingers making a rasping noise against his scalp.

"I's not worried about two of them. They wan' no part of them pirates." His heavy, black eyebrows drew together in a frown. "But that Jed's tongue wag worse than a woman when he get a bellyful of rum. Ah'll put the fear of the Lord in him before we lan'."

It was almost eleven o'clock when they entered the darkened harbor of Albertstown. The capital city of Soufriere, named in honor of Queen Victoria's beloved consort, was justly famed as having one of the best natural harbors in the Caribbean. The horseshoe-shaped bay was deep enough to accommodate the largest cruise ships and was sheltered by hills that surrounded it on three sides. In daylight it presented a colorful and picturesque sight with its tiny houses sprawling over the roller coaster hillsides. But at this hour only a few lights showed and the narrow streets were deserted. *Antilles Rose* docked at her customary berth in the middle of a long row of other stubby masted sailing vessels. The only sound was the creak of wooden hulls rubbing against fenders made from old truck tires. Colin and Wendy waited in the cabin with the lantern extinguished while Capt'n Johnny went ashore to collect his battered Vauxhall from the parking lot.

"Keep your head down and move smartly," Colin murmured as the car rattled toward them over the rough concrete deck of the wharf.

They drove directly to Colin's hotel, Treasure Lagoon, in the resort area just south of the city. The "lagoon" was a drainage ditch and the hotel was a long way from the beach. But it was cheaper than its ritzy neighbors and less of a drain on Colin's dwindling savings.

Capt'n Johnny waited in the car while Colin hurried Wendy up the outside staircase that led to his second-story unit. He pulled down the blinds before switching on the lights. She shrugged out of Colin's nylon windbreaker and asked, "Is it okay for me to have a hot tub?"

"Help yourself. I'm going back out for a few words with Johnny."

The interior of the small sedan was filled with the fug of Capt'n Johnny's pipe as Colin opened the door and slipped into the front passenger seat.

"No way that girl can go back stateside," the captain muttered around the pipe stem. "Them hijackers will be campin' on her doorstep."

"I know." Colin reached over the back of the seat for his duffel bag. "She's probably as safe here on Soufriere as anywhere."

"Mebbe so." Capt'n Johnny looked dubious. "You plan on telling Mistress Jill about she?"

"I'll have to give that one some thought," Colin grunted as he climbed out. He watched the captain drive off, noting that he headed back to the docks rather than to his neat little saltbox of a house up in the hills. At daybreak he and his crew would unload the schooner's legitimate cargo: sacks of cornmeal and cartons of soap and condensed milk.

Colin heard Wendy splashing in the bathtub as he unpacked the duffel bag, pitching the dirty laundry on the floor of the clothes closet. Then he rummaged in the closet until he found a short Japanese style kimono which he laid on the bed. The bathroom door opened and Wendy peered out. She had wrapped a towel around herself, and there was a faint flush to her cheeks and damp tendrils of hair curled entrancingly around her bare shoulders.

"I'm kind of guilty about it, but I'm beginning to feel almost human again," she announced.

"You may *feel* human, but you *look* divine," Colin smiled and handed her the kimono.

"Maybe we can contact the police in the morning," Wendy said as she reemerged from the bathroom, knotting the belt of the silken robe around her waist. "And get me off your hands."

"We'll see." Colin was noncommittal. No point in telling her that the capabilities of most Caribbean police forces didn't go much beyond directing traffic and posing for tourists, especially on Soufriere where Bartholomew's Mongoose Gang held sway. The ordinary police would be about as much protection against the hijacking ring as a pellet gun against a charging elephant.

"Which one is yours?" She waved a hand at the twin beds.

"I usually crawl into the one next to the window."

"Terrific." She pulled back the covers of the other bed and climbed in.

"Colin?" Wendy paused with her hand halfway to the bedside lamp.

"Hmm?" He looked across the room at her. The almond eyes were huge in her flowerlike face.

"Thank you for saving my life. And I'm sorry for being such a nuisance."

"A pleasure. And you couldn't be a nuisance if you tried. As you very well know."

Breathing deeply so she would think he was asleep, Colin lay staring up into the darkness, trying to decide on their best course of action. Then he remembered his appointment with Mallabone at eleven in the morning. There would be no time to make any arrangements until after that. He turned on his side and went to sleep.

Chapter Three

A gentle wave buoyed Colin up and he gazed back toward the land. The sun bounced off the white beach with a dazzling glare and the slate roofs of the beachfront hotels poked through the dark green of the palms. His morning swim had taken him a kilometer out from the shore, but he was still close enough to see little knots of tourists organizing beach chairs and settling themselves for a day in the sun. Although it was the height of the season, the hotels were far from full. It would take time for the tourist trade to recover from the violence and looting that had followed Bartholomew's seizure of power.

All Colin knew about that troubled period was what he had read in the American press. He had almost completely lost touch with Soufriere in the twelve years he had been away. His mother, who had never really adjusted to life in the West Indies, had returned to England within months of his father's death. She had remarried and now lived contentedly in Southampton.

It was almost a whim on Colin's part that had brought him back here when the flying school closed down. The California winter had been wet and dreary, and he had a sudden vision of sugar-sand beaches and lettuce-green water sparkling in the sunlight.

For the first couple of weeks he had done the tourist

bit; lazing about on the beach, swilling rum punches and cautiously renewing a few acquaintances. And meeting Jill Powell, who had been a mere child of ten when he left but was now an imperious, russet-haired young lady whose gray eyes darkened to mauve when the sun went down.

It was only in the last ten days that the idea of a small inter-island airline operating out of Soufriere began to take shape in Colin's mind. He had given it a lot of thought while the *Antilles Rose* coasted down the Grenadines. The idea would be to start small; one secondhand Islander should do it, and wait for the traffic to build up.

A speedboat, towing the day's first water-skier, roared past, rocking him with its wake. Colin spat out a mouthful of salt water and swam back to the shore with a smooth, powerful crawl.

Wendy opened the door to his knock and gestured in the direction of the small electric stove. "I was going to make breakfast, but I guess you cleaned everything out before your trip."

"Uh, huh." Colin toweled himself dry, deciding not to mention that he hadn't made so much as a cup of coffee since he arrived. "I'm afraid this place doesn't run to room service, but there's a coffee shop."

"I don't know about that." An uneasy expression flickered across Wendy's face.

"Feel sort of exposed?"

"Something like that. I can't forget that I'm the only witness to a multiple murder."

"You have a point," conceded Colin. He held an imaginary pencil over an imaginary pad of paper. "May I take your order, madam?"

"That's better." Colin swallowed the last piece of

bacon and wiped his mouth with the paper napkin. "Now, where do we go from here?"

"Well, for starters, this bikini is the only thing I own." She managed a weak smile. "All the cash I had was on the boat, apart from a few dollars to keep my bank account open."

"I can carry you for a while." Colin raised his hand as she started to protest. "Just a loan. You can keep track of it and pay me back. What do you do? In Baltimore, I mean?"

"Interior design. I work with a firm."

"Will they miss you? Start making inquiries?"

"Not for ages yet. I'd just finished a major project and I had five weeks off."

Colin helped her stack the few dishes on the counter beside the sink. He told her the chambermaid would show up at any time but that she wouldn't take any notice of Wendy. Then he checked his watch. "I've got an important meeting in town. It may last till after lunch. You'll be okay here?"

"Of course." Her grave face was transformed with another of those devastating smiles.

Thoughts of her still crowded Colin's mind as he drove the rented Skoda toward Albertstown. With an effort of will, he forced himself to concentrate on his upcoming interview with Tony Mallabone, the enigmatic Englishman who was Bartholomew's chief adviser. Jill had introduced him to Mallabone at a party a week ago, before he had flown up to Saint Bart's to join the schooner. The tall, languid Englishman had registered just enough of a reaction to show he was aware of the background between Colin and Jill's family. Then he had drawn Colin to one side, murmuring that he had heard some interesting rumors about his plans.

He was about the same height as Colin's 187 centimeters, but his shoulders were narrow and rounded, and his frame seemed almost boneless. The lank, blond-gray hair was combed back from a receding hairline, and his face was long and elliptical, like a football with the features stuck on as an afterthought.

He didn't detain Colin for long; too many other people were clamoring for the ear of the dictator's confidant. But he had set up the meeting for today.

Mallabone came directly to the point when Colin was ushered into his office. "I have taken the liberty of mentioning your project to the president," he said, fitting a cigarette into a long, jade lighter.

Colin drew back in alarm. "Hey," he protested, "it's not a *project*. It's just an idea that popped into my mind."

"Understood," Tony murmured smoothly. "Nonetheless it does have considerable appeal. The president was quite taken with the idea of Soufriere having its own airline. In fact—" Mallabone paused to tap his cigarette into a silver ashtray, and Colin noticed with a twinge of distaste that he had allowed the nails of his little fingers to grow into curved talons, "in fact," Tony repeated as he continued, "he even went so far as to say it was long overdue."

Colin, with the sinking feeling that events were rushing beyond his control, kept silent. The only sound in the spacious room was the hum of the air-conditioning unit in the corner window. Then Mallabone spoke again. "Of course, the right to operate the airline would be a very valuable concession," he purred.

Colin shook his head vehemently. "Hell, no. It could just as easily be a one-way ticket to bankruptcy. In the first place, it wouldn't be an *airline*. Not at first. Just one small airplane to see if the market is there."

Tony waved an airy hand. "The market is there, old

boy. Tourists are positively *flocking* back to Soufriere."
He shrugged. "However, if you're not interested, there
are others who . . ."

"I didn't say that," Colin interrupted. "Just that it's
anything but a sure thing."

"With the right kind of government support, it could
be a license to print money." Mallabone pressed a
buzzer and a white-jacketed attendant came in to re-
move the ashtray with its single mashed butt and
replace it with a gleaming new one.

"You are presently at liberty, I understand?" Mallabone resumed in his fluting English voice.

"The flying school where I worked closed down,"
Colin replied tersely.

"Just so. And you have the necessary capital?"

"I'm afraid not. Look," Colin got to his feet, "we're
going nowhere. Let's just forget it."

"Don't be so impetuous, dear boy. There's no reason
why something can't be worked out." Mallabone paused
for effect before continuing as though thinking out
loud. "There just may be a way for you to earn suffi-
cient funds to swing it and, even more important, earn
the goodwill of the government."

"And what does that involve?" Colin had a pretty
shrewd idea of what was coming.

"Just your flying skills, which I'm informed are very
impressive."

"If it's handling drugs, I don't want any part of it."

"Absolutely not." Mallabone's expression was pained.
"Oh, it may involve bending a few customs technicali-
ties, but no drugs."

He glanced up as a red light flashed on over the door.
"The master calls," he murmured, his bantering tone
tinged with irony.

"Tell you what," he said as he rose unhurriedly to his

33

feet. "I'm having a bit of a bash at my place on Friday. Eightish. Do come, and you'll find it more exciting if you come alone. We can talk some more." He extended a limp hand.

A public phone booth stood just outside the gates of the pink stucco building which housed Mallabone's suite of offices. Colin stopped the Skoda in front of it and left the motor running while he debated with himself. He had to check in with Jill anyway, and she could provide a safe haven for Wendy. He wasn't at all sure that he should involve her in Wendy's troubles; it was the realization that he had no place else to turn that finally decided him. He shut off the ignition and climbed out of the car, feeling in his pocket for change and hoping it wouldn't be Jill's father who answered the phone.

His luck was in; it was Mary Powell, Jill's mother, who came on the line. She sounded genuinely pleased to hear from him, asking about his trip and "that dear old rascal, Capt'n Johnny." She continued, "Is he still making a mint out of the bubble trade?" She hooted with laughter when Colin blandly replied he hadn't the foggiest notion of what she meant, then she told him to hang on while she had someone fetch Jill from the stables.

While they both waited, Mary told Colin that they had been up half the night before battling a cane fire.

"Accident or otherwise?" asked Colin.

"Definitely otherwise. They left the gasoline tins behind so there wouldn't be any doubt. It's all such a mess. We're due to start the harvest on Friday, and some of the other plantations should have started last week. But the cutters' union is still holding out." Mary broke off and said, "Here's Jill now."

"I was getting worried," Jill's breezy young voice

sounded anything but. "I was afraid that old boat had finally succumbed to a watery grave and I wouldn't have a date for the Sugar Cane Ball."

"She'll stay afloat as long as the worms keep holding hands," Colin laughed. "Anyway, I would have swum all the way to Soufriere rather than miss taking you to the Ball."

"Liar," Jill replied amiably. "When do I see you?"

"Right away, if you like. Can you drive in to the hotel?"

"I'm on my way. What's up, Colin? You sound a little strange."

"Nothing's up. Just somebody I want you to meet, that's all."

"Now, I *am* curious. See you."

Wendy cautiously opened the door when Colin gave the prearranged series of knocks. He knew from the look on her face that she had spent the morning grieving for her friends. She brightened considerably, however, when he told her about Jill.

"She *could* be a big help," she agreed with a show of enthusiasm. She even broke into spontaneous laughter when Colin, after saying it would be good for her to be with a girl her own age, added that Jill was twenty-two. "Hell, I'm an old lady of twenty-six," Wendy spluttered happily.

Jill's dark-fringed eyes widened when Colin stood aside to let her see Wendy standing beside the bed. Her look of puzzled irritation gradually disappeared as Colin related Wendy's experience.

"How awful for you." Impulsively Jill reached across and squeezed Wendy's hand when he got to the part about her sailing companions being gunned down.

"You'll stay at Palm Hill, of course," Jill said firmly when she had absorbed the whole story. "There's acres

35

of room, and," she added with a teasing smile, "I won't get all green-eyed at the thought of you and my sexy friend sharing the same room."

Colin winced inwardly; there were times when Jill could be too obvious. Almost gauche—a sharp contrast to her usual lady-of-the-manor style. He didn't care for the proprietary air much, either. But that was a problem for another day.

A look of puzzled distaste flitted quickly across Wendy's face, but she accepted Jill's offer with grave courtesy. "It certainly does seem like the ideal solution. If you're sure I won't be in the way. . . ?"

"They won't even know you're there," Colin assured her. "Palm Hill is the island's largest plantation and it has platoons of staff."

Jill and Wendy left soon after in Jill's bright yellow Honda. Wendy's face was almost totally hidden behind the enormous sunglasses Colin had brought back from town, and she wore his kimono over the bikini.

"I'll lend you some of my clothes until we can get you outfitted properly," Jill said as she drove out of the asphalted parking lot. "They'll be a little loose around the hips, I'm afraid," she added with a self-conscious little laugh.

"You're being very kind to me." Wendy snuggled down in the bucket seat until her face was below the windshield. She felt secure, and warmed by Jill's easy friendship.

The road crossed the wide southern portion of the island, skirting the last outliers of the mountain range. They drove past a banana plantation, the green stems neatly tied in blue plastic bags against insects. "That belongs to the president." Jill waved a hand. "And this doesn't," she added drily as another plantation came into view. The unharvested fruit hung brown and rotten on the stalks, and the tangled undergrowth sprouted unchecked.

Beyond the rolling hills the terrain abruptly flattened out and they were passing between fields of sugarcane, the dark green of the leaves burnished silver in the sunlight.

"If they don't start cutting soon, the whole damn crop will rot in the fields," Jill muttered.

She slowed as they came to a crossroad where the tall cane, growing right to the edge of the fields, completely blocked the view.

"That's High Trees." Jill pointed to an overgrown driveway between two adjoining fields. "It belonged to Colin's family for absolute centuries."

"But not any more?" Wendy straightened up in the seat and twisted her head to look for the plantation house as they went by, but the driveway disappeared from view over a small knoll.

"No. He didn't tell you about it?" Jill sounded surprised.

"Not a word. I know he was born on this island, but that's about all. He talks more about his flying."

Jill pulled out to squeeze past a tractor towing a train of empty cane wagons. It was a ticklish business, with the swaying, bouncing carts taking up most of the space between the limestone banks.

"He must have been about fourteen or fifteen when it happened," Jill said as she swung back to the left-hand side of the road. "I guess the bottom had dropped out of the price of sugar and all the plantations were in trouble. Most of them managed to survive, but Colin's dad was drinking heavily and signing IOUs all over the place. So they were evicted and forced to move into Albertstown. I gather Colin started to run wild not long after."

37

The green walls of the endless cane fields were making Wendy feel almost claustrophobic, while at the same time she welcomed their concealment. A tiny frown etched faint lines between her arching eyebrows. "That seems out of character, somehow," she said thoughtfully. "I think he comes across as very competent and professional."

"He does. Now. But I'm talking about when he was a kid." Jill gave Wendy a quick sideways glance. "I guess he didn't mention the 'accident' then?"

Wendy shook her head wordlessly, and Jill continued after a long pause. "I think you should know about it, since you'll be staying with my family. Colin and my brother, Robbie, were best friends. Always together. Daddy bought Robbie an MG sports car for his eighteenth birthday. Bright red. I can still see it. Well, there was an accident. Colin was driving and they took a corner too fast and went into the ditch. The car rolled over and Colin was thrown clear but Robbie was trapped underneath. Then the car burst into flames."

A slight tremble crept into Jill's voice, and she gunned the Honda unnecessarily as they passed a group of cyclists.

"It almost finished my parents," she went on after a pause. "Daddy still hasn't gotten over it. Even after all this time. Robbie was an only son; there were just the two of us. Sooo," she exhaled a long rueful sigh, "you can imagine that things have been a bit strained around the old homestead since I began seeing Colin. Mother does her best to smooth things over, but . . ." She didn't complete the sentence; instead she pointed through the windshield. "And, speaking of the old homestead, that's Palm Hill up ahead."

Wendy leaned forward. The weathered stone bulk of Palm Hill's Great House topped the rise, its mullioned

38

windows facing toward the sea. A long driveway flanked by a double row of towering royal palms curved gracefully up the side of the small bluff.

The dogs came down off the steps as the Honda pulled into the cobblestoned courtyard. Wendy sucked in her breath, relaxing slightly at the sight of the joyously wagging tails.

"The only danger is being slobbered over," Jill assured her. "But you'd better stay inside anyway." Jill climbed out of the car and patted each soft muzzle. The Palm Hill Great Danes were one of Mary Powell's many hobbies. At nightfall the pack of five giant hounds was the scourge of any would-be prowlers, and also waged a running battle with the tribe of monkeys who lived in the grove of mahogany trees next to the vegetable garden.

Mary Powell was working in the small plot of land set aside for her rare plant collection. It was fenced against the dogs, and she carefully latched the gate behind her. Jill's mother was a short, sturdy woman with friendly brown eyes and honey-colored hair frosted with gray.

"I thought Wendy could stay in Martin's quarters," Jill said after the introductions were over.

"What on earth for?" Mary Powell's pleasant features wore a look of mild amazement. "There's tons of room in the Great House; why pack her off to the stables?"

"Wendy's not anxious to advertise her whereabouts just now." Jill bent her head so Wendy could hear through the open car window. "Martin trains our race-horses," she explained. "He's moved down to the track for the meet and he won't set foot outside the grounds until it's over. He's so fussy he insists on doing his own housekeeping so nobody goes near the place. It's the perfect hideaway."

"And I'm not to know what she's hiding from?" Mary asked mildly.

"Not just yet, mums."

"I see." Mary eyed her daughter for a moment then gave a resigned shrug. "I'll get the key and meet you over there."

She turned and strode purposefully toward the house with the five dogs trailing after her.

Chapter Four

"Mother has it all figured out." Jill grinned at Wendy across the immaculate, austerely furnished room. "She thinks you're hiding from a jealous lover."

Wendy gave a little shiver. "If only that's all it was."

Colin got up and moved his chair out of a patch of morning sunlight. Wendy must have had a good night's sleep, he thought. Her skin glowed with a porcelain sheen and those enormous eyes were calmly alert. He shifted his gaze to Jill.

"Your father doesn't know about this, I trust?" he asked.

"Nope. It wasn't hard to persuade mother not to tell him. He's got so much on his mind with this union business. He's head of the owners' negotiating committee and it's really getting to him. The poor dear had to go into Albertstown early this morning for another all-day session. And," she paused for a quick glance at her watch, "I've got to make a trip in there myself. You wouldn't believe the list of things mother's given me to pick up for tonight."

"I'm kind of surprised at your parents going ahead with the Ball despite all the union problems," Colin said, adding for Wendy's benefit. "The Sugar Cane Ball is a Palm Hill tradition; it's always held on the night before the harvest starts."

Jill laughed. "It would take a lot more than a bunch

of cane cutters to make mother give up the Ball." She paused with her hand on the doorlatch and looked at Wendy. "I don't suppose it would be a good idea for you to attend?"

Wendy shrank back in alarm and shook her head vehemently.

"Too bad. It would have been fun to watch you bowl over the local stagline."

"I like her," Wendy said as the door closed behind Jill. "Do you two have a thing going?"

"No." Somehow it was desperately important to Colin that she understand. "We're just friends. She's great company and we've been making the scene together. That's all."

"I'm not so sure she would buy that," Wendy replied thoughtfully. "I have the feeling it means much more to her."

Colin, irritated by Wendy's impersonal attitude, shrugged impatiently and dropped the subject. He wanted to shake her. Almost as badly as he wanted to kiss her. Instead of doing either, he turned his back and gazed out the window at the deserted stableyard.

The trainer's apartment was over the old stables, unused now since the new ones had been built next to the training track. Colin jumped as something struck the shake roof with a loud crack. "Those damn monkeys," he muttered, another childhood memory clicking into place.

"You should have heard them just before dawn," Wendy said. "I woke up thinking the whole place was under attack before I remembered Jill warning me what to expect. Then," she smiled dreamily, "I fell back into the most delicious sleep."

"It's done wonders for you." Colin took advantage of

the moment to stare openly at her, drinking in her flawless, exotic beauty.

She gave a nervous little laugh, as though unnerved by the intensity of the gaze, and walked over to the kitchenette.

"It's lunchtime," she announced with forced gaiety. "Let's see what Jill brought."

He left soon after they had polished off the beautifully prepared seafood salad and most of the bottle of Moselle. He had parked the Skoda under the giant banyan in the courtyard of the Great House, and Mary Powell called him as he walked past the garden. She put down her shears, instructed the gardener to go on picking flowers for the Ball and joined Colin as he crossed the cobblestones to his car.

"That lovely girl is American," she murmured as she fell into step beside him. "Is she someone from your past, Colin?"

"Heavens, no. I met her for the first time a couple of days ago. She's just a gal who's in a bit of a scrape at the moment."

"I see. The less I know, the better. Is that it?" Mary Powell brushed a strand of graying hair from her forehead as they stopped beside the car. "Forgive me, Colin, for being such a nosey old goose. It's just that," a troubled look crossed her kindly face, "I don't want to see Jill hurt."

Her words stayed with Colin as he drove back to Treasure Lagoon. She had spelled it out pretty plainly and she was right. He didn't know what might have happened between Jill and himself if Wendy hadn't appeared on the scene. They might have drifted beyond friendship into something deeper, maybe even marriage. But there'd never be the heart-stopping reaction he got whenever he looked at Wendy. God knew he had brought enough pain to the Powell family without messing up their daughter. He'd let things simmer down, starting tonight at the Ball.

Colin sensed the air of excitement as soon as he came within earshot of the party. He was late and was forced to park the Skoda on the road and make the long climb up the driveway on foot. There was an excited buzz to the conversation and a constant swirl of movement as guests hurried from group to group.

"Isn't it wonderful?" Jill had obviously been on the lookout for him and hurried over as soon as he stepped onto the long gallery. Her dress set off the smooth tan of her bare shoulders and emphasized the full curve of her hips.

"You mean you haven't heard?" she cried when she saw his puzzled look. "The strike. It's over. The cutters start work in the fields tomorrow." She took his hand. "You can hear about it from Daddy."

Colin followed her reluctantly. Jill made a point of throwing him and her father together as much as possible on the theory that time and exposure would wear down the older man's resentment. Andrew Powell, who was by nature a mild-mannered person and who could deny his daughter nothing, managed to be distantly polite to Colin, but that was all.

With his sparse gray hair, brushed straight back from a receding hairline and mild blue eyes behind gold rimmed glasses, Jill's father looked like an accountant. Only the permanently roughened and sunburnt skin betrayed the outdoor life of a planter. He was speaking in his quiet, authoritative voice when Jill and Colin joined the group of plantation owners clustered around him.

"I'd feel a great deal better about it if it was a

genuine settlement," he was saying. "But it wasn't. Nobody would come right out and say anything, but the union leaders were frightened out of their skins." Andrew Powell paused while his eyes roved around his audience. He stiffened slightly when he saw Colin, but continued in a voice that was barely above a whisper. "Bartholomew's little playmates let it be known that there'd be some broken heads unless the cutters caved in. The economy is shot to hell anyway and even Bartholomew recognizes that losing the sugar crop means total bankruptcy."

His listeners muttered uneasy agreement. The relationship between the dictator and the planters was a curious one. So far Bartholomew had made no attempt to seize their lands or interfere with their affairs. But it was an uneasy truce and one which could be abruptly terminated at the whim of the capricious dictator.

Jill's father inclined his head to listen to what one of the men was saying, and Colin's glance strayed to another group of guests standing just inside the drawing room. David Henderson said something that drew a laugh from the two couples he was with. David, a few years older than Colin, was struggling to build up a mini-conglomerate based on an import business and a few general stores. He had told Colin something of the bizarre unreality of trying to conduct business under the Bartholomew regime.

Here again, probably because of his profound disinterest in matters commercial, the dictator mostly left the merchants to their own devices. True, he would impose special taxes whenever his personal coffers were empty, and the local businessmen were constantly being "invited" to the president's nightclub where they were expected to order bottle after bottle of fifty-dollar champagne. But he kept his hands off the actual operations.

"Except," David had added ruefully, "for ruining the economy so that nobody can pay for anything."

Colin wondered how long David would stick it. The mulatto businessman was exactly what the Caribbean needed; astute and ambitious while being at the same time a completely local product. But all the business acumen and energy in the world couldn't cope with the antics of a demented despot. And where in hell does that leave me? Colin wondered to himself. With my crazy scheme of trying to start a goddamn airline on Soufriere. Who needs the hassle?

David had spotted Colin and he and his wife were coming over to join him. Gail Henderson was a slim East Indian from Trinidad with a flashing smile and a mane of curly black hair.

David was quietly elated over the settlement of the cane cutters dispute, knowing that his little enterprise was doomed if the holdout had continued. "This way there's at least a chance that we can survive."

Colin, welcoming the diversion, led them down to the patio bar, saying they needed a drink to toast the settlement. Jill, amused at how neatly he had avoided a face-to-face meeting with her father, tagged along with them. The bar had been set up next to the small ornamental pool where two thin columns of water rose in the air and splashed back among the lily pads. Brown toads squatted around the concrete base like huge dog droppings. The younger crowd had congregated on the patio where they danced to the music of a four-piece group from Albertstown.

This was the Caribbean at its best, thought Colin as he danced with Jill, the soft tropic night like a balm on the skin and, high overhead, the fronds of a towering royal palm fluttering in the light breeze.

Nearly all the guests were white, although the dark skin and slightly thickened features of some betrayed an ancestor who had strayed across the color line. Here and there a black, or a *café au lait* mulatto like David, bobbed among the sea of white faces. But it was a planters' party and the Soufriere plantations were basically a white scene.

The music increased in volume and tempo as the evening wore on, and Colin wondered if Wendy could hear the sounds of the Ball from her hiding place.

She could. Faint strains of the music drifted in through the open window of the horse trainer's small apartment. Wendy sat in the dark, motionless on a hard wooden chair she had placed some distance back and to one side of the window. She could see the cobbled stableyard bathed in the thin light of the stars. Large bats made their erratic, darting sorties after insects. A whistling frog resumed its strident bleeping when the distant music stopped. The band was taking a break while a midnight supper was served.

The harsh call, so disproportionately loud from such a tiny frog, ceased as abruptly as if someone had pressed a switch. Wendy held her breath as she heard the low murmur of voices and two figures came into sight around a bend in the path. Their faces were hidden by the shadow of the mahogany grove, but their clothes were startlingly white against the dark background. There was the rumbling sound of a man's laughter and the two shapes merged into one.

Lovers looking for a place to be alone. Wendy relaxed and eased herself back into the chair from which she had half-risen. But then the thought struck her. Suppose they were coming here? She reminded herself

47

the door was locked; her thumb touching the outline of the key in the pocket of the slightly too-big jeans Jill had lent her.

The couple moved out from the shadow of the trees and began to cross the yard. The top part of the girl's dress had been pulled down and the man's head was bent over her exposed breasts. Wendy was trapped where she was; they were almost directly below the open window now and would hear the slightest sound if she tried to move. She heard the small sucking noise as the man released the woman's nipple. When he raised his head she saw he was wearing dark glasses; an incongruous sight in the velvety night.

His partner swayed slightly on her feet and brushed a strand of hair away from her damp forehead. She peered up at him, frowning with sudden drunken petulance. "What's with the shades? If you're gonna screw me, you're damn well gonna look at me!"

With a quick motion of her hand, she tore off his glasses, then whispered, "Oh, my God! I'm sorry. I didn't mean . . ."

She tottered backwards, he turned to grab her and a scream bubbled in Wendy's throat. Quickly she clamped her hand over her mouth to choke it back. She needn't have worried; the small sound was lost in the sharp smack of the man's open palm against the girl's face. With cold ferocity he slapped her three times, sending her sprawling on the cobblestones. Then he lifted her skirt and entered her, pumping himself to a quick grunting climax.

A tight little smile twisted his lips as he got to his feet and zipped up his pants. Frozen with horror, Wendy had another glimpse of the handsome blond face disfigured with those bulging eyes she had last seen on the deck of *Sympatico*. Then he put on the dark glasses and muttered to the sobbing woman with quiet menace, "Not one word to anyone. Or you're fish food. Understand?"

She nodded and clambered painfully to her feet. With the toe of his white patent shoe he pushed her purse toward her. "You got any makeup in there, you better use it."

Wendy's heart was hammering so violently she thought it would choke her. Instinctively her body moved slightly to ease the pressure. She went rigid with terror as a chair leg made a tiny scraping noise on the floor.

"What was that?" The woman paused in the act of applying powder to her stinging cheeks.

"Monkeys." The "s" was slurred. The blond killer glanced up into the looming mass of the trees. "We probably made some old stud horny." He gave a short bark of laughter and headed up the path, not bothering to glance behind at the girl who hurried after him, adjusting the shoulder straps of her gown as she stumbled over the cobblestones.

It was several long minutes after the girl's white dress had disappeared around a bend before Wendy moved. It was as though an electric current had shot through her body. She felt the prickle of sudden sweat in her armpits and a tingle ran unpleasantly down her arms and along her fingers. She got to her feet and stood clutching the smooth back of the chair.

The killer shouldn't be here. He should still be at sea, sailing toward the U.S. and his payoff. Still it was three days since that awful night. Plenty of time to reach Soufriere by another boat, or by plane. It didn't matter how he had managed it, he was here. A guest of Jill's family.

Groping her way into the bathroom she fumbled for

the toilet articles Jill had given her. Her sunglasses, the white bikini and an extra cotton shirt were her only other assets. Jill had planned to do some shopping for her tomorrow. She stuffed these few possessions into a paper bag and crept down the short flight of stairs that led to the outside.

The giant bat snapped her out of her trance. It was swooping in hot pursuit of a particularly succulent moth when she opened the door. Flaring up on silent wings it was a macabre shape in the pale starlight, making Wendy jump back. When her heart climbed down from her throat she was quietly furious with herself. It was damn well time she started acting like the cool professional woman she knew herself to be. Okay, so she had been through a traumatic experience that would bend anybody's mind and she was still in hideous danger; that was no reason to behave like some spineless Victorian heroine.

Hugging the wall Wendy made her way to the far end of the empty stables where she crouched and looked back over her right shoulder. The festive lights of the Great House cast a nimbus of orange light over the hilltop. It looked warm and inviting but death waited for her there.

Slowly she turned her head to peer at what lay beyond the stables. A faint track, little more than two indentations in the grass, skirted the edge of the trees and then was swallowed up by the darkness. At least it led in the opposite direction to that taken by the killer. She pushed herself away from the shelter of the building.

Earlier in the evening, just after sundown, she had heard the baying of the dogs. But not since. They must have been locked up for the party, she decided thankfully as she reached the end of the mahogany grove without being attacked. Just past the trees a white rail fence

50

bordered a wide meadow. The stone wall running along the far side looked as though it marked a boundary of the plantation.

A horse snorted almost in Wendy's ear as she placed a cautious foot on the bottom rail. Before she could react, he spun on his hocks and galloped toward the center of the pasture. Now Wendy saw the loosely grouped herd standing motionless in the shadow cast by the trees. A tall chestnut left the herd and walked toward her, its tail swishing from side to side. Its companions began to follow behind. Horses were outside Wendy's experience; she had no way of judging their moods or anticipating their actions. All she knew was that they looked terrifyingly large and menacing as they emerged from the shadows. But somehow she had to make it across to that stone wall and escape from Palm Hill.

Desperately she looked along the fence line. It stretched right to the edge of the lighted driveway where she would be spotted immediately. There was no other way. She had to cross the pasture. Once more she put her foot on the railing and this time she forced herself to climb over.

Standing on the ground inside the fence she waved her arms at the leading horse. It halted, then stretched its neck forward and neighed noisily, lips curled back from frighteningly large teeth. Emboldened by her success in stopping its advance, Wendy walked hesitantly over the close cropped turf. One by one the other horses dropped their heads and resumed grazing. Except for the chestnut. It began to follow her, tail swishing ominously. The stone wall was less than fifty meters away now, but she dared not break into a run.

The horse gave another snort, spraying her with a fine mist of saliva. She turned to face her nemesis. It stood stock-still for a moment then turned and trotted away, and she began to breathe again. But suddenly it wheeled and charged back toward her, ears flat against its skull. It let out a prodigious fart and kicked both heels in the air, missing her head by a wide margin. Then, suddenly bored with the sport, it trotted back to the herd, neighing triumphantly.

Wendy ran the remaining distance to the wall. It was over two meters high, and the smooth stones were joined with even layers of mortar that afforded no finger- or toe-holds.

She threw her bag over then leapt upward, frantically scrabbling for a grip, but her hands slid off the smooth stones and she fell back. Picking herself up, she retreated a few feet then ran forward to hurl herself at the wall. She felt a fingernail tear and a sharp twinge stabbed through a kneecap. Then she was lying on top of the wall, the sharp edge of a stone bruising her breast. She eased her position and peered down the other side. There was a shallow, weed-filled ditch beside a narrow, black-topped road and then the open countryside.

She rested for a moment on the cool stones to recover her breath. Both her knees were smarting; the jeans hadn't protected them against being scraped. She turned her head so that her right cheek rested on the wall and looked up at the house, now clearly visible in its pool of light. The band had started up once more, and she could see couples making their way to the patio. Colin would be there, probably dancing with Jill. The Powell girl was madly in love with him although he didn't seem to notice. Or pretended not to.

Gingerly, wincing as the rough cloth rubbed against her raw knees, Wendy lowered herself down from the wall and dropped onto the grassy verge bordering the ditch.

Chapter Five

"She's gone, Colin. Wendy's gone!" Jill leaned against the hotel room door, staring at him with apprehensive eyes.

Colin, his head throbbing with a slight hangover, ran his fingers through his tousled hair.

"Damn," he muttered finally. "Did she leave a note?"

"Nothing." Jill paused, tiny frown lines appearing between her eyebrows. "Colin, she has no money, no papers. What will she do?"

Colin, shaken by the way Wendy's disappearance was getting to him, grimaced silently. The possibility of never again seeing that gravely beautiful face was a dull ache somewhere inside his rib cage.

"How about making some coffee while I grab a shower?" he headed for the bathroom. "Then we'll sort out what we should do."

Jill did more than brew coffee. When he stepped out of the steamy bathroom she was setting their places for a full breakfast of fried eggs and bacon. The shower had cleared Colin's head. He ate quickly, gulped his coffee and stood up. "If she's wandering around in the country, the best way to spot her is from the air. Let's go!"

Jill set her cup down in its saucer and said quietly, "Colin, listen to me. You're free of it now. Honorably. You've saved Wendy's life and done everything you could to help her. If she's decided to go it alone . . ." The look on his face stopped her, and she got to her feet with a rueful smile. "Anyway, I tried."

"Look," he said earnestly. "What you just said makes all kinds of sense. For you. There's absolutely no need to involve you and your family any further."

"Who would be your spotter, then?" She opened the door and smiled up at him. "Wild blue yonder, here we come!"

"You know, Wendy *could* have been snatched," Colin reluctantly voiced the thought as the Skoda worked its way through the crowded, twisting streets of Albertstown. "You're sure there wasn't any sign of a struggle?"

"It was as though she had never been there," Jill replied. "Once I got over the shock of not finding her, I really looked around. Of course, the fact that nothing was disturbed doesn't necessarily mean anything."

"I'm not so sure about that. They couldn't have taken her completely by surprise, and Wendy is smart enough to think of some way to leave a clue."

They fell into a glum silence as Colin edged past the last of the donkey carts, and they left the outskirts of the smarmy little subtropical city behind them. Jill brightened momentarily at the sight of the harvesting crews working in the fields and the first truckloads of sugar cane heading for the mills.

"There may be something to be said for a strong government after all," she murmured. "The cutters certainly changed their tune when the 'man' started to lean on them."

"Yeah," Colin agreed dubiously. He took his foot off the accelerator; the line of slow-moving trucks ahead of them was too long to pass. "But there'll be a price. He

54

may just decide he can run things better than the planters and take over."

The cane trucks turned in at the entrance to a tall-chimneyed sugar factory, and the Skoda picked up speed. Soon they breasted a small rise, and the airport control tower came into view. The Pearl Demaret International Airport was a standing joke among airline pilots—its runways were too short to handle anything bigger than turboprops, its terminal was small and tumbledown and the navigational aids were minimal. Bartholomew had named it to honor Pearl Demaret when she had won the Miss World contest three years before.

The crowning of a beautiful West Indian girl as Miss World had rated a three-column photo in a San Francisco newspaper, and it had given Colin a start when he realized he knew her. She was Pierre Demaret's kid sister, probably no more than ten or twelve when he left the island, but even then budding into delicious young womanhood.

A blurred color photograph of her was mounted on the wall just inside the terminal entrance. Colin paused for a brief moment to study it. Like her brother, she had inherited the small, elegant features of her French forebears. Colin had made no attempt to look her up since his return to Soufriere; the word was that she was very much a part of Bartholomew's court.

The terminal was deserted except for a middle-aged couple sitting forlornly on a wooden bench and a bored LIAT passenger agent idly cleaning his nails behind the counter. He lifted his head at the sound of Colin's footsteps on the gritty floor. He wasn't sure, but it was possible Aero Services might have a plane Colin could rent. They would find Aero Services in the hangar just south of the terminal.

The manager-owner waved away Colin's proffered commercial license. "Hell, I know who you are, mon. You don't have to prove anything to me." He pushed the rental form across the waist-high counter. "Just sign here and I'll take you out to the airplane."

The little Cessna 152 was a high-wing job, ideal for the purpose. Colin was helping the proprietor undo the tie downs when he heard the sound of a taxiing plane.

The charter operator nudged Colin with his elbow and chortled, "Here comes the Black Baron himself."

Colin untied the last knot and looked up to behold an incredibly dilapidated Cessna 180 coming down the taxi strip. The fuselage had once been painted white, but the blowing sand of countless primitive landing strips had peeled it away until the original metal shone with a dull pewter color. The windscreen was cracked and pitted, but Colin's trained ear caught the sweet sound of a well-tuned engine.

With a final revving of the motor, the 180 swung to a stop and two passengers struggled out of the cabin, an obese black woman and her scrawny husband in a baggy brown suit and crumpled fedora. The pilot followed them out and opened the luggage compartment door. He stood haughtily by while the little brown man strained to lift out two straw suitcases, bound with rope, and a heavy cardboard carton.

"It's beneath the Baron's dignity to help with the luggage, of course." The charter owner's whisper was somewhere between laughter and contempt.

The pilot of the ramshackle plane was a striking figure. Tall and slim, he had the insolent grace of a young African male. His skin was rich mahogany, his nose aquiline with deeply incised nostrils and the full lips just avoided the rubbery thickness of the negroid

His eyes were hidden by wraparound shades, and he wore his hair in tight, "dréd" rolls.

With an abrupt gesture of his arm, he directed his two cowed passengers to a gate in the sagging fence. Then he pivoted on his heel to survey the little group standing by the wing tip of the 152. He gave the plane's owner the vestige of a nod, letting his eyes run slowly over Jill's figure until a blush darkened her tan. Unhurriedly, lips curled in a self-satisfied smirk, he shifted his gaze to Colin.

"You Townsend, ain't yah? Hear you're some kind of hotshot."

Colin shrugged and coiled the tiedown rope with exaggerated care. "I can drive an airplane, if that's what you mean," he said evenly.

The black pilot glowered at him for a moment, then swung himself into the Cessna's cabin. The propeller kicked over a few times before the exhaust belched a cloud of thin blue smoke and the motor settled into a steady rumble.

"Just who in hell is *that*?" asked Colin as the noise of the departing Cessna receded.

"Joshua Todd," the other man replied, adding with a significant look. "He's a Koramantee."

"Ah," Colin murmured with an air of sudden comprehension. The Koramantee was the one African tribe that had never accepted the shackles of slavery. Fiercely independent, they chose torture and death over servitude. In the years before emancipation many had escaped and succeeded in remaining at large, mainly because the planters were none too anxious to have those defiant troublemakers returned to spread unrest in their slave quarters.

The Koramantee's Cessna was nowhere in sight as

Colin advanced the throttle, and the little 152 hopped into the air.

"We'll start at the plantation and fan out from there," Colin shouted as he throttled back and turned inland in the direction of Palm Hill.

Jill nodded and made a grab for the edge of the instrument panel as they hit a patch of mild turbulence. The countryside was covered with a quilt of cane fields separated by grassy lanes or "intervals" for the trucks to drive along. Apart from the black ribbon of the road, the only breaks in the sea of green were little clusters of shacks with chickens scratching in the red dirt and the spires of parish churches.

They were flying at three hundred meters, and the tiny blue plane bounced in the warm air currents. Jill fought back waves of nausea as she was pressed against the seat belt one moment and then the world seemed to drop away the next. Doggedly she squinted through the side window, searching for a glimpse of Wendy's slight figure. Colin touched her arm and pointed ahead where the Palm Hill Great House stood on its lofty promontory.

He flew a series of ever-widening circles around the plantation. They saw the Danes sprawled on the front steps and Mrs. Powell working in her garden. She looked up briefly when Colin made a particularly low pass, then returned to her pruning.

"I never knew there were so damn many trees on this part of the island," Colin shouted in exasperation. "You think it's all cane fields until you start looking for something, and then all you can see are the bloody great trees."

He was exaggerating but in fact there were a surprising number of tall palms and casuarina pines scattered among the endless rows of cane.

"She could be hiding in a place like that and we'd never see her." Colin threw them into a tight circle around the Cotton Tower, a deserted landmark that once had been used to spot the arrival of the great sailing ships coming to carry the cotton crop across the Atlantic.

Fifteen minutes later, they flew over the northern tip of the island where a long line of Atlantic combers crashed against the black coral cliffs. Wordlessly, Colin banked the plane in a slow turn and began to pick up altitude to fly along the island's mountainous spine.

The mountains were low, not more than a thousand meters at their highest point, but their rain forest growth was a startling contrast to the flat monotony of the sugar cane country. Lush green valleys spilled down the steep slope of the ridge; banana plants provided leafy umbrellas for coffee and cacao bushes, and solitary *immortelle* trees held aloft cascading sprays of bright orange flowers.

Colin didn't waste time crisscrossing over the dense vegetation. Their only chance would be to spot Wendy on the corkscrew road that snaked along the top of the ridge. There was a fair amount of traffic, women trudging along in single file with their headloads of baskets and wooden trays, men bent under the weight of sacks of charcoal, and donkey carts and trucks loaded with bunches of green bananas. Soufriere has so much going for it, thought Colin as he automatically adjusted for a sudden downdraft. With its abundant rainfall and variety of crops, it was one of the few Caribbean ministates that had a chance of becoming economically viable. But not with Bartholomew's heavy hand on the throttle.

They flew within sight of Albertstown without catching a glimpse of anyone who remotely resembled

Wendy's slim, jean-clad form. Colin avoided flying over the city, picking up the coastline only when they reached the resort belt. The white sand beach was dotted with the sprawled forms of sunbathers. A few shielded their eyes to squint up lazily at the little blue plane.

"She may head for this area," Jill said. "To be with her own kind."

"They aren't exactly her own kind," Colin replied with a faint smile. "But I know what you mean."

"It won't be easy for her out in the country. The older folk don't want any truck with strangers, and the younger ones will be even more suspicious. If you're not one of them, you're against them. And news of a woman tourist wandering around on her own will travel with the speed of light."

"With the speed of sound, at least," Colin agreed as he set a course for the airport. "It's entirely possible your mother may have already got wind of her whereabouts."

He switched on carburetor heat as they turned on to the downwind leg parallel to the runway. "But I have an idea she'll avoid the locals and try and fall in with some sympathetic tourists. The only catch is," he muttered as he eased the yoke back for a kiss-soft landing, "how does she tell friendly tourists from pirates?"

"That was a super landing," Jill said as they turned on to a taxi strip. "And speaking of the local rumor mill, the word is that you're going to start your own airline. It's spreading around the island like a cane fire."

Colin was frowning as he switched off the engine and the stubby little propeller came to rest. "I didn't know you had heard about it." He shrugged and released his safety belt. "It's just an idea. It probably won't fly, if you'll forgive the pun."

"Daddy says that ordinarily it would be a natural." She was fumbling ineffectually with the buckle of her seat belt. "But . . ."

"The 'but' being Bartholomew." He leaned over and unfastened her belt. He grinned suddenly. "I've even thought of a name for it."

"What?"

"Sun Air."

"Oh, Colin. It's super. I love it!" She flung her arms around him and kissed him on the mouth.

Chapter Six

Wendy heard the faint drone of a low-flying aircraft and scurried back to the protection of the casuarinas. The tall pine trees lined both sides of an overgrown track that had once been the main driveway of a plantation. She pressed herself against the deeply furrowed bark and squinted up at the patches of blue sky that were visible through the feathery branches. A small plane, bright blue wings rocking in the updrafts, entered her field of vision.

It passed directly over the trees, in the general direction of Palm Hill. As the waspish buzz of its motor faded into silence, Wendy's stomach growled unexpectedly, reminding her that she had had nothing to eat since early the previous evening. She had spent the night in the open, propped against the trunk of one of the casuarinas and half-dozing for the last couple of hours before daybreak. The trees had been a welcome haven in her journey through the slumbering countryside.

After picking herself up from the bruising scramble over the wall, she had started to walk along the deserted country road. It led to a settlement of one-room wooden huts scattered up the side of a low hill. They were all tightly shuttered, although there was no chill in the subtropical night. It seemed incredible to Wendy that eight or nine people would willingly cram themselves inside each little sweatbox and secure the shutters against even the slightest suggestion of a night breeze. Maybe it was to keep out evil spirits.

A pack of undernourished brown curs darted into the roadway at her approach, barking furiously. A rooster ruffled its feathers and crowed sleepily, but every shutter remained tightly closed.

The snarling onrush of dogs stopped at the edge of the village as though an invisible barrier stretched across the road between the last two houses. Appalled by the uproar, Wendy looked over her shoulder at the road she had traveled. The dim lights of two bicycles slowly wavered around a curve. They could be Palm Hill servants coming off duty from the party.

A hurried glance to her right showed a grassy strip along the boundary of the cane field. From the background reading she had done for the trip, Wendy knew that nearly all the Caribbean islands were free of poisonous snakes. Fervently hoping that Soufriere was one of those so blessed, she gingerly stepped onto the coarse, prickly grass.

She was jerked back to the present by the sound of the blue plane returning. It was even lower now and heading toward the horizon where an orange sun had climbed out of the sea that morning. She watched the wing dip, and the plane turned back toward her belt of trees. It soon became obvious that it was carrying out a systematic series of sweeps. Once it flew directly over her hiding place, then gradually swung north.

Wendy knew with sickening certainty that she was the object of the search. Maybe it was Colin in the plane. But it was too late now to attract his attention besides, there was no getting around the fact that the killer had been a guest at the Palm Hill dance. His presence placed a big question mark against every-one's real motives.

By the time she had finished with these gloomy reflections, the plane was only a small moving dot low above the horizon. Another reproachful twinge from her stomach reminded her that she was famished. Just before the sound of the plane had driven her under cover, she had watched a young native boy amble down the road, munching on a piece of sugar cane. She had almost stepped out from the trees to ask him for it. Row upon row of that very same sugar cane waved in a field directly across a small clearing.

It was unbelievably hot amid the densely packed stand of canes. A rivulet of sweat ran down between her breasts as she vainly tugged at a stalk. It stubbornly refused to budge until she began to bend it back and forth. Finally it broke off in her hands, and she was able to peel back the old leaves encircling the stem. She chewed and sucked greedily at the syrupy stickiness inside and was soon sated with the cloying sweetness. How glorious a steaming hot bath would be! She scrubbed at her sticky lips with the back of an equally sticky hand. Cautiously she pushed the last row of canes aside to peer out at the clearing. Two pairs of dark eyes stared solemnly back at her.

The boy was the older of the two; he looked to be about five. They were both barefooted; he was clad only in a ragged pair of tan shorts while the little girl wore a T-top and a soiled gingham skirt. Suddenly the boy tugged at her hand and they scampered off, her short pigtails bouncing as she ran.

Wendy watched them go with dismay. Now the whole countryside would know that a strange woman was wandering around on her own. She had better get moving, but to where? Sighing, she plucked a few blades of coarse grass and absently wiped her hands.

The small wooden sign read *Four Cross Roads*. Helpful as hell! Wendy bit her lower lip in sheer frustration. Then she was scrambling down into the ditch as the sound of an approaching vehicle grew louder. The Mini-Moke was overloaded with three couples of laughing, beer guzzling tourists. When it had passed, she climbed out of the ditch and began walking along the road.

She didn't hear the ten-speeds until it was too late. They were almost upon her before her ears caught the whisper of tires on the asphalt. The two young blacks eyed her with insolent stares as they sped by. Wendy kept her gaze straight ahead and fought the impulse to flee blindly into the fields. A hundred meters down the road, the ten-speeds made a U-turn and pedaled leisurely back toward her.

"Yuh lost, puss gal?" The first one dismounted and propped the bicycle against an outthrust hip. He wore skintight, faded jeans with a wide, leather belt and a short-sleeved sweat shirt over a muscular chest. His thick lips curved downward as he let his eyes with their clouded yellow whites travel over her body. They came to rest on her bare midriff where she had knotted Jill's shirt.

"I'm just out for a walk, thank you." She took a step forward, but her path was blocked by the second rider. His heavy face leered with the vacant emptiness of a borderline retardate. His thick torso was set on a pair of stumpy, misshapen legs, and he stank with the sour reek of body odor.

"Tain't often a honky woman, even a Chinee-honky, goes walk about by hersel' around heah." The taller one slowly stretched out a hand toward her. "You ever had a black stud, China-baby?"

She shrank back. "You're mistaken. I'm *not* alone. I just got out of the car to be by myself for a while. My friends will be along any minute to pick me up. That's probably them now," she lied desperately as the heard the squeal of car's brakes at the crossroads.

"Mebbe," he grunted and swung a leg over the seat. "But if it ain't, don't you worry about bein' lonesome." He nodded at his companion, and they pedaled rapidly away.

The car slowed and veered to the right as Wendy planted herself in the middle of the road, frantically flagging it down. The thought that she might be making a gift of herself to the killers stirred uneasily in the back of her mind, but even that could be no worse than being in the hands of those two black horrors.

The car was not going to stop. The windows were rolled up, and it was edging forward as the driver attempted to pass her on the right. A middle-aged couple were the only occupants; they couldn't possibly be part of the drug-smuggling ring. Tears sprang to her eyes at the thought of safety so agonizingly close. At the sight of her tears the woman passenger said something to the driver and the U-drive Hillman shuddered to a halt, the man giving an embarrassed grin when the motor stalled. His wife cranked down the window a grudging few centimeters and asked, "You in some kind of trouble, dear?"

The accent was unmistakably American. Wendy gave a little sigh of thankfulness. "I'm from the States, too. Look, I had, well let's say a difference of opinion with a friend. I bailed out of his car and now I'm stranded out here. I don't even know where I am. All I want is a lift someplace before he comes back. Please."

"You poor thing," the woman murmured soothingly. "Let her in, Phil."

They told her they were on their way to Wrecker's Castle and wouldn't be returning to their hotel until late afternoon.

"That suits me fine," she murmured thankfully. "I'm not in any rush to go back to that scene."

When they had gone down the road for more than a kilometer with no sign of the two cyclists, Wendy uncrossed her fingers.

The woman had a Hertz road map open on her lap and, despite the bewildering maze of roads and intersections, brought them to Wrecker's Castle with only one wrong turn. There was a comfortable air between the man and wife, and Wendy was chatting easily with them by the time they pulled into the parking lot. They wanted her to tour the historic mansion and grounds with them, but she told them she'd be happier just staying in the car. Phil Johnson parked the Hillman in the shade of the old trees bordering the nearly empty lot.

While the Johnsons made their way to the ticket booth, Wendy slithered down in the seat until not even the top of her head was visible and tried to sort out her options. They were painfully bleak. Once more she thought about trying to make her way to the American Embassy, and once more she rejected the idea.

In the first place there probably wouldn't be one on a dinky little island like Soufriere. And they couldn't help her anyway. Just before she left the States, the newspapers had been full of the story of a woman who had been blown to eternity with a bomb rigged to the ignition of her car. She had been an informer, under the protection of the State Department for two years. The other side had got her within a week after she had surfaced and tried to live a normal existence. Even back then the grim story had made a powerful impression on

Wendy. Despite the suffocating heat inside the car, she shivered at the thought of spending a lifetime in hiding, always wondering when and how the attack would come. And that was all the authorities could offer: public exposure followed by never-ending fear.

The washrooms were over by the entrance, next to the ticket booth. Wendy ducked her head as she closed the car door and then held her hands to her face as though adjusting her sunglasses. The tap water was tepid, but it was sheer joy to wash the sticky grime from her skin. Her mood was almost buoyant as she made her way back to the Hillman.

By now she had come to believe it was probably nothing more than coincidence that the killer had attended the Ball. The guest list for that bash must have run into the hundreds. Maybe it had been a mistake on her part to have fled the plantation in such a blind panic. And Colin should be warned about the enemy within the Palm Hill circle.

She studied the road map for the name of a resort close to Treasure Lagoon where she could ask the Johnsons to drop her off. She would go the rest of the way on foot. After dark.

When the Johnsons returned, it was clear they had spent more time discussing her than inspecting the castellated mansion an early colonist had built, reputedly from the proceeds of luring ships to their doom on the deadly reef by hanging lanterns on the rocks.

"Look, Debby," Phil Johnson blurted out as they headed toward Albertstown. Wendy had told them her name was Debby Ching; God only knew what stories might finally hit the press, and she didn't want these pleasant, harmless people making the connection. "We'd like to help you anyway we can," Johnson was continuing. "Is there anything we can do for you? Talk to your friend? Lend you some money?" He glanced at his wife as he said the last bit.

"You're sweet. Both of you. I hate to admit it, but if you could lend me just a little money it would really help," Wendy said uncomfortably. "In case things are still grim. It would only be a loan, of course." She was acutely embarrassed, but she would need some cash if she failed to link up with Colin.

Phil handed her fifty EC dollars and let her off at the gate of Coral Lodge, a middle-priced hotel on the same side of the highway as Treasure Lagoon and, if she had read the map correctly, less than a half a kilometer north of it.

Here in the center of the tourist area she felt much less conspicuous. Hotel guests returning from the beach glanced at her as they came through the gate, but the glances seemed to be nothing more than those an attractive female can always expect. Wendy put in time at a fast-food outlet until the abrupt tropical night descended. She stood at the counter with her back to the other customers and forced herself to dawdle over a hamburger and glass of papaya juice. Her long hair was tied in a knot on top of her head, and her shirttails dangled over her jeans. If "rumpled chic" is in, then I'm the height of fashion, she told herself ruefully.

Apart from a narrow strip of grass in front of the main building, Treasure Lagoon was surrounded by an asphalted parking lot. A solitary whistling frog called from the sparse shrubbery outside the office. Wendy knew Colin's room was in the section closest to the road, about midway along the second floor. She had been able to observe that much when Colin and Jill had hurried her down the outside staircase to the yellow Honda. Lights showed in most of the windows, and cigarette tips traced patterns in the dark as the hotel guests sat out on the balconies to enjoy the soft night air.

She would just have to climb that staircase and walk along the open air corridor as though she hadn't a care in the world. Damn, she wished she had counted the number of windows his room was from the staircase. But under the circumstances she couldn't really blame herself. Maybe she could spot him through the window, or she could always mumble an excuse if a stranger answered her knock. She was nerving herself to cross over to the stairs when a door opened and Colin appeared.

The killer, wearing dark shades and a wide grin, followed him onto the gallery. There was a third man there, too, but Wendy was barely conscious of his tall, indistinct form. Her attention was riveted on the tanned face and white blond hair of the hijacker. He was laughing at his own joke as he shook hands with Colin and then strode along the passageway. Sick with terror, Wendy retreated into the shadow of the parked automobiles.

Chapter Seven

After his unexpected callers had left, Colin frowned thoughtfully down at the *kuskus* rug. He supposed he should feel flattered having Mallabone come by in person to renew his invitation for the party that night. The Englishman had made it abundantly clear that Colin could do his airline project a lot of good by attending.

He couldn't figure out just where Carl Dykstra fitted into the picture. Mallabone seemed to treat him like a glorified bodyguard; but he had been a guest at the Sugar Cane Ball last night. Colin remembered seeing him there, making time with some chick in a clinging white dress. They had both gotten progressively more bombed as the hours passed. He made a mental note to ask Jill about him.

He was at loose ends tonight. The bumpy flight had given Jill a pounding headache, and she had gone back to Palm Hill to crawl into bed.

He stripped off his shirt and poured himself a short Scotch and water. Sipping it slowly, he let his thoughts return to Wendy. It sure looked like she had deliberately given them the slip. She was probably on her way back to the States right now. A drop of condensation from the glass landed on his bare skin. Absently, he flicked it off with his fingernail. The smart thing to do was to forget about Ms. Wendy Wong. The chemistry was there for him, God knew, but apparently not for her. He knew he was being irrational, but he couldn't help the feeling of resentment that swept through him at the thought of her cool indifference. He had no reason to expect anything different, but that didn't seem to matter. He was in a defiant, reckless mood when he drove away from the hotel.

Mallabone's place was an imposing limestone manor at the end of a long line of casuarinas. Double bronze doors swung open just as Colin reached for the horse's-head knocker. The party was in full blast. Directly in front of him, a plump, purple-faced man perspired in a comic attempt to match steps with a nubile black girl. Across the expanse of tiled floor, Carl Dykstra and a pouty-faced blonde rubbed pelvises, Carl's hands clasping his partner's bottom. The host suddenly appeared at Colin's elbow.

"Sorry about the racket," he shouted above the noise of the taped disco music. "Come into the library and have a quiet drink before you join our little frolic."

It was eerily quiet in the long, vaulted room. The walls were untreated limestone lined with low bookcases and hung with rich tapestries at either end. A black servant in a short-sleeved white shirt presided over a portable bar. He handed Colin a brown drink in a cut-glass tumbler as the latter sank into a leather tub chair.

"Chivas Regal," Tony Mallabone murmured. "Your favorite brand, I believe?"

"When I can afford it," Colin replied. "I'm impressed that you know."

"It is my business to know." Mallabone fingered the pendant dangling from his gold necklace. Colin realized with a start of surprise that it was a tiny gold spoon, the kind cocaine-sniffers use. "May I ask if you know anything about me?" Mallabone drawled in his pear-shaped tones.

"Well, I've just learned one thing about your habits," Colin replied.

"*Touché.*" Mallabone's smile was complacent. "Anything else?"

"You are known to be the power behind Bartholomew's throne. *Éminence grise,* I believe it's called."

Tony raised a wispy eyebrow at Colin's unexpected turn of phrase. "You flatter me," he murmured after a pause. "But I can tell you the president is very much his own man and acts on his own initiative. Or whim," he added with a faint smile. Then he put his glass down on a marble table, saying, "Let me tell you a little bit about tonight. It is really a small, intimate gathering despite the appalling noise. It is also in two parts. You saw the overheated American gentleman as you came in?"

Colin grinned knowingly and Mallabone continued. "We are doing our best to persuade him to make a substantial investment on the island. In an hour or so he will grow tired and leave, probably taking that luscious young girl with him. The few other guests in his age-group will also depart. Then the real party will begin for you."

He pressed a button under the rim of the table. "Now, I want you to meet the gracious lady who is acting as my hostess tonight. I understand you are old friends."

She was tall and copper-colored and fashion-model slender. Her face with its slightly retroussé nose, high cheekbones and wide full-lipped mouth, was perfectly framed by the short Afro curls that clung to her elegant head.

Mallabone kissed the air above her hand and led her

into the room with a flourish. "The pride of Soufriere—
the lovely Miss World!"

"Do you remember me, Colin?"

"Of course." He held her slim cool hand. "Pierre
Demaret's kid sister. You always tagged along when
we went down to the beach to play soccer." He released
her hand. "It knocked me out when I read about your
winning the title."

Her smile was dazzling. "It's so wonderful to see you
again."

Mallabone gave a delicate cough. "*Allons, mes enfants,*
it's party time!"

"The way I see it, the world press has given Bartholomew a bum rap," the American businessman
growled. He had given up on the dancing but kept a
firm hold on the girl. "They make out like he's some
kind of a crazy, but the minute you meet the guy you
can tell he's got lots of smarts. Hell, he talks like a
goddamn college professor." He squinted at Colin
through a cloud of smoke. "You from Soufriere, son?"

"Used to be, but now I live in California," Colin
replied. "Or at least, I did," he surprised himself by
adding.

The American gave him a puzzled look then lost
interest and wandered off, his meaty hand kneading
the girl's saucy rump.

Tony Mallabone frowned and shook his head when
Dykstra and the blonde started for the bedroom wing.
"We're supposed to be good until that old fart leaves,
baby," Carl muttered as he changed direction and led
the girl over to where Colin and the beauty queen were
standing.

"Danny's got himself a live one this time." Carl gave
a sneering laugh and pointed across the room at a
black beachboy sitting on a couch next to a pudgy

76

white woman. She had blue hair and was dressed in a cloud of pink tulle. "That one should be good for a nice present when she goes back home."

"Is she another potential investor in Soufriere?" asked Colin.

"Hell, no," Carl snorted. "She's just a tourist that Danny picked up. Tony likes to have Danny around occasionally. They were lovers until a few months ago when Tony found himself a new boyfriend—the pretty one passing around the drinks. Our host believes in putting his playmates to work. Poor old Danny gets all green-eyed."

"Attention, everyone. Your attention, please." Tony Mallabone stood in the center of the living room and clapped his hands. His habitually vacuous face showed a mixture of elation and apprehension. "I have just been informed that we are to be honored by the presence of His Excellency!"

An excited murmur rippled through the room, and the voice of the American businessman boomed self-importantly, "It'll be real nice to meet him again. He's a fine fella."

Mallabone stationed himself by the double bronze doors to greet his leader. Conversation died away as the doors slowly opened and Bartholomew made his appearance. Colin had seen the dictator's photo splashed across the front pages of *The Patriot,* the local weekly paper that danced to the government's tune, so he knew what to expect. Nonetheless, he was still taken aback by the *ordinariness* of the man.

In many ways, Bartholomew, with his broad features, neat mustache and alert, intelligent eyes, was the picture of an upwardly mobile, middle-class black man. In his mid-fifties, his close-cropped kinky hair had retreated halfway up his scalp. But the image was

77

shattered by the three-piece, white silk suit of impeccable cut and the gold-topped swagger stick. He held the stick in the fingers of his right hand, gently tapping it against the palm of his left. It was understood that one did not offer to shake hands with the president.

He was graciousness itself to Pearl, treating her with the exaggerated old-world gallantry of a *boulevardier* to a former mistress. Then he surprised Colin by speaking of the important role the Townsend family had played in Soufriere's history.

"May we hope that you will write another chapter in that saga?"

Colin shifted uncomfortably, not sure how he wanted to respond. "It's possible," he said finally. "If an opportunity comes along."

"We must do our best to provide such an opportunity." Bartholomew smiled before turning his charm on the American entrepreneur.

Dykstra, obviously making an effort to appear sober, stood at rigid attention throughout Bartholomew's short visit. The dictator nodded at him briefly, but otherwise ignored him. Within a half hour, Mallabone, bowing obsequiously, was escorting a beaming Bartholomew to the door. Most of the others, including the American and the teen-aged girl, left shortly after.

"It's playtime, dollface." Carl Dykstra's hand gripped the blonde's arm. She looked momentarily shocked at the painful pressure of his fingers, then smiled gamely and followed him.

The copperish skin of Pearl's thigh flashed through the long slit in her skirt as she walked across to a settee at the far end of the room. "Do you smoke?" She opened a platinum case.

"Me? No," Colin answered.

"I didn't mean tobacco." She lit what looked like a stubby, loosely rolled cigarette and drew the smoke deep into her lungs. When she finally began to talk only a thin trickle of gray smoke escaped from her mouth. "God, that feels good! I've been aching to light up all night."

"What is it? Colombia gold?"

"Better than that. It's a *pistolero*. Coco paste mixed with marijuana. It gives you a super high. Sure you don't want one?"

He shook his head. "I've got a pretty good buzz from the Scotch. I'll stay with that."

Colin looked around; they were alone in the huge room. He turned back to Pearl; her delicate face was raised invitingly. A momentary image of Wendy tugged at the edge of his mind, but he pushed it away, almost angrily. He was a nonstarter with that lady. He bent down and kissed Pearl on the mouth, catching the strong, sweet smell of the drug. She responded for a long moment then gently pushed him away. "Let me finish the smoke. Everything is much better then. Why don't you fix yourself a drink?"

When he came back with a stiff whisky, she was standing on the patio with one hand resting against a coral stone column as she gazed out at the sea. He touched her shoulder and she turned to come eagerly into his arms.

Her body was excitingly slender and firm. His right hand almost spanned her waist as he drew her close. She moaned softly and pushed her leg between his.

When his tongue began to seek hers, she broke off the embrace. "Let's go inside," she whispered. She took his hand and led him through the silent house to a large, airy bedroom. The gentle smack of surf against the beach came through an open window, and a lamp glowed softly beside a canopied bed.

Her breasts were narrow elegant cones ending in dark nipples that entirely covered their tips. At first he thought it was a birthmark, but as he lowered his head he saw she had a small tattoo on her left bosom: a black pearl inside an open seashell. The dark nipples hardened at the touch of his tongue, and she sank back on the bed, her hand reaching for him.

Pearl writhed under him like a snake, her breath coming in short, harsh gasps. Colin spread his legs and pressed his weight against her hips to force her frenzied rhythm to match his own thrusts. He was plunging deeper now, the tempo quickening as he mounted to a climax. She shuddered as she felt the warm sperm throbbing into her, then her long fingernails raked down his back.

"Don't stop. Please, don't stop now!" she whispered, pumping her hips up and down. At first she was doing all the work, her warm moistness riding his still erect penis like a piston until he felt the renewal of tension in his groin. Her fingers grasped his erection and rubbed the tip of his penis against her clitoris. "Lovely. Oh, so lovely," she moaned and slowly slipped him back inside. He placed his open lips over her mouth as their bodies moved in unison. They were sweating and biting and kissing each other as they strained and raced to orgasm. Her left hand groped for a small dish on the night table, and then she touched her nostrils with her thumb and forefinger and sniffed the pinch of white powder. Her back arched, lifting them both from the bed, as the spasms shook her. She gave a small cry somewhere between a scream and a moan and finally let her taut body go limp.

Pearl dipped her finger in the tiny pool of sweat that

formed in her navel. Licking her fingertip, she whispered, "I can taste both of us."

She settled back against the pillows and lit up a joint of marijuana. When the sweetish smell filled the room, she sighed with content. "You really should do up some smoke. It makes the sex thing so great. It just seems to go on and on with all those warm little explosions inside you."

"Sex with you doesn't need any help." Colin's hands were clasped behind his head while his eyes casually searched for signs of a hidden camera. The setup called for it, but he was immune to that kind of blackmail. He had no ties, no wife or fiancée to be hurt by his enjoying casual sex with a lovely mulatto.

Pearl sat up and stretched luxuriously, the dark-tipped breasts swaying with the movement of her arms. "Oh, I feel so good! I don't want to sleep, not ever. Let's walk on the beach."

Their ears were assailed by a pounding disco beat when they opened the patio doors. Carl and the blonde, both naked, stood in the shallow end of the pool, swaying to the rhythm.

"Does he always wear those?" Colin asked as they skirted the edge of the pool. Carl kept on dancing, but his head swiveled to follow Pearl.

"The dark glasses?" She pulled the flowing beach robe tighter around her shoulders. "They're sort of a trademark with him."

A security guard materialized from the darkness to unlock the metal grille gate. They stepped barefoot onto the sand and walked hand in hand along the deserted beach. The night was windless with a full moon riding high in the southern sky. Manchineel trees crowded the edge of the silvery sand, casting a shadow so black it seemed to have a weight and substance of its own.

Pearl turned and the classic lines of her face in the moonlight made Colin catch his breath. He held her by the elbows and slowly shook his head. "The others wouldn't have a chance."

"What others? What are you talking about?"

"The other contestants in the Miss World contest."

"You're sweet." She stood on tiptoe to kiss him. "But the reign of a beauty queen is over almost before it begins. One brief burst of publicity and a phony kind of fame, then . . ." She perched on a driftwood log, its trunk bleached white and polished satin smooth by the sea. "It's back to the oblivion you came from."

She lit a cigarette, this time a normal filter-tip Rothman's, and gave a bitter laugh when Colin asked, "And what does oblivion mean to Pearl Demaret?"

"It means," she answered slowly, "being one of 'Bartholomew's girls.' It all started when I was chosen Miss Carnival. I had just turned eighteen. I didn't find out until after I won, but Miss Carnival automatically becomes a 'special public relations assistant' to the president. Until the next one is crowned. Then she may end up working in his nightclub, or be turned over to one of his cronies."

She bent down and mashed her cigarette butt into the sand. Waves made little chuckling sounds as they ran over the reef. "That didn't happen to me because Bartholomew found out a contestant from the West Indies was due to win the next Miss World title. He had me elected Miss Soufriere, and things sort of went on from there."

She paused, then said, "He liked you. I could tell."

"Who?"

"The president. He meant all that stuff about your

family. The idea of hobnobbing with a Townsend really turns him on."

"You've got to be kidding," Colin scoffed. "You know what happened to my family."

"Some things die hard."

"Speaking of families, what about yours? I've been meaning to look up Pierre, but . . ." He let the sentence trail away.

"I never see my family. *Never*. They don't think much of my lifestyle." She fell silent for a moment, then said, "I'm starting to come down. Let's go back.

"I had a mad crush on you when you used to hang around with Pierre," Pearl murmured as they retraced their steps across the sand. "The blond, handsome Townsend boy. I used to dream that one day I would be grown up and you would suddenly realize you had been in love with me all along."

Colin was still struggling to frame a reply to that one when Mallabone's elongated frame emerged from under the manchineels. "Ah, Townsend," he purred. "I was hoping for a word with you tonight. After we see Pearl to the gate, we might stroll a little further down the beach."

"You and the delectable Miss World seemed to hit it off famously," Tony murmured as the gate closed behind Pearl.

"Childhood friends," Colin smiled.

A tiny crab froze as their shadow fell over it, then scuttled frantically back toward its hole. Tony's sandaled foot stamped it into the sand.

"Horrid things," he muttered, ignoring Colin's look of revulsion. "I assume you have given some more thought to the airline proposition?"

"Some."

"Just so. Well, I believe I may safely promise you

that if you were to carry out the assignment you and I discussed in my office, your project would fall into place."

"What's involved in the flying end of this assignment?" Colin skipped a pebble across the small waves.

Tony turned around and they began to walk back to the villa.

"Long overwater flights, close to the limits of the aircraft's range. Night landings and takeoffs under marginal conditions. I understand you have logged considerable time in the Twin Otter?"

"That's right." Colin's eyebrows lifted. The sturdy Canadian workhorse could pack one hell of a payload. It wasn't the sort of equipment you found at a flying school, but he had flown one every other weekend for a feeder line that ferried passengers between San Francisco and Stockton.

"Excellent. There's a guaranteed minimum of five trips at $10,000 U.S. per trip."

"At those prices, it's got to be drugs."

"It's something that pays even better than drugs. Art. Pre-Colombian art, to be precise. Stone carvings that have been moldering away for centuries in some South American jungle. Collectors pay the moon for them, dear boy."

Colin felt deflated. Mallabone's outfit seemed to be running an entirely different caper from the bunch Wendy had tangled with. "I'd have thought you'd use boats for something like that," he said.

"Oh, boats come into it as well. But we require a plane for the initial stages."

"When do you need my answer?"

"Now, preferably. Noon today at the latest. We want to be operational by Saturday."

"Jesus. You don't fool around, do you?"

"We do not." Tony showed large, slightly yellow teeth as he motioned Colin to precede him through the iron gate. "May I assume you are interested?"

"You may. But I won't say for sure until noon. God knows, that's not much time to think this one through. And my head space isn't exactly crystal clear at the moment, either."

"We know you can bring it off." They were walking through the empty rooms now, and for the first time Tony let a note of urgency creep into his voice. "Look, old boy, Twin Otter pilots are rather thin on the ground in these parts. If you complete all five flights, we'll throw in a fifty percent bonus. Then if you don't want your own airline you can lie on the beach for a year. Whatever."

The green Skoda, parked under a wrought-iron lamppost, was the only vehicle left in the paved courtyard.

"I'm afraid you've spent too much time in America," Mallabone chuckled as he watched Colin approach the car from the wrong side.

Colin shook his head sheepishly and turned around to cross over to the driver's door. The figure lurking beside the multi-car garage ducked back, but not before Colin had recognized Joshua Todd. The Koramantee's handsome features were set in a murderous scowl.

Chapter Eight

Colin woke with the knowledge that he was going to accept Mallabone's assignment. He also woke with the cobwebs of another hangover. A run on the beach and an invigorating swim took care of that, but he'd better cut back on the booze and high living or he'd end up flunking his next flight medical. He was reassured to find that the prospect of some dicey flying banished any temptation to continue with the party circuit.

Mallabone moved with swift, unruffled efficiency. By noon Colin was on board a sports fisherman threading its way through the narrow Careenage to the outer harbor and the open sea.

There had been barely time for a guarded telephone conversation with Jill. No word of Wendy's whereabouts had trickled back to Palm Hill. There was silence on the line when Colin mentioned that he might be out of touch for a few days. "I've got a chance to get in some deep-sea fishing," he explained.

"Are you after the same kind of fish you caught on the schooner?" she finally asked.

"No. We'll be fishing in different waters." He hung up with the promise to be in touch as soon as he returned.

They spent the afternoon trolling for fish. Colin's mind wasn't on it, but they boated several kingfish and a bonito. After dark they would head north for Jumbie

Island, the larger of the two outlying islands that were dependencies of Soufriere. The name had evoked a flood of vivid memories for Colin. "Jumbie" was the West Indian name for zombie, and the uninhabited, volcanic islet was reputed to be the home of the undead. Local fishermen and sailors gave it a wide berth. On a dare, Colin, Robbie Powell and Pierre Demaret had once tried to camp out overnight there, but had to give it up when they couldn't land their boat through the reefs and thundering surf.

Years later those same reefs looked just as impregnable. The bow of the fishing boat dipped sharply as the operator cut the engine. In the sudden silence Colin heard the booming crack of surf. Off to the right the curl of breakers was startlingly white against a black volcanic cliff. The solitary crewman was listening intently, brown forehead furrowed as he strained to hear above the roar of the surf.

The dugout was almost bumping their gunwale before Colin became aware of it. The boatman steadied him by the arm as he gingerly stepped on board the primitive craft. Handing Colin his small cloth satchel, he grinned widely and said, "Bes' you hang on real tight, sar."

Then the two rowers made a reverse sweep of their oars to pull away from the launch. The third crew member left the steering oar to take the satchel from Colin. He stuffed it into what looked like a small oil barrel and pointed at Colin's watch. "It hurt dat t'ing if it git wet?"

Colin shook his head but fished out his wallet from a rear pocket and handed it over. The man clamped a lid on the can and scrambled back to the stern. The noise of the surf was a continuous rolling thunder now, and Colin could see long fingers of spray shooting up the side of the cliff. What he couldn't see, however, was any sign of a break in the line of combers crashing over the reef. He tightened his white-knuckled grip on the gunwales and twisted around on the plank seat for an uneasy glance at the steersman. The black face was impassive, but the whites of his eyes rolled as they switched back and forth from the reef to the waves piling up behind the dugout. Then the two oarsmen stopped rowing and sat with their backs to the land and their gaze fixed unwaveringly on the man crouched in the stern. The oncoming waves were driving them inexorably shoreward. The steersman glanced over his shoulder at a wave, larger than its fellows and just beginning to crest, then faced forward and shouted something that was lost in the wild concussion of the surf. The long oars dug into the boiling water, and the frail boat hurtled toward the reef.

They must know what they're doing. Probably make this trip at least three times a day, Colin kept telling himself as the wave lifted them up as though to dash them on the rocks. The two men were rowing furiously, trying to keep the dugout abreast of the leading edge of the wave while the steersman leaned into his oar and fought to prevent them from turning broadside and capsizing in the smothering foam. Colin clung desperately to the gunwales, unable to see anything beyond the blinding sheet of white water. He felt, rather than saw, the oars being shipped, and then the thick hull was jarred with a rapid succession of hammer blows. It was like driving at speed over the world's worst washboard road.

The pounding ceased abruptly and they were gliding across the calm surface of a lagoon. Colin was drenched and his eyes burned from the salt spray. The crew furiously back-watered their oars to keep from crashing into the far side of the small lagoon. Despite their efforts the dugout grounded on the narrow strip of sand with a bump that almost fetched Colin over the side.

A dense stand of manchineel trees bordered the pocket-sized beach, and their poisonous yellow-green fruit littered the sand. A man, his cutoff pants startlingly white against his ebony skin, waded out and held the thwart steady as Colin jumped over the side.

The dugout pushed off immediately, and the man, who introduced himself simply as Leon, walked backward across the sand behind Colin, smoothing out their footprints with a long-handled rake. Shoving the rake out of sight in the underbrush, he led the way up the side of a volcanic outcropping. There was no discernible path even where clumps of vegetation sprouted among large patches of bare black rock. The trees, rooted in the crumbling volcanic soil, grew taller as they climbed. Leon, broad face glistening with sweat, signaled for Colin to halt at the edge of the trees.

"Dere be your runway, mon," he said, pointing to a stretch of barren ground extending to the edge of a cliff. It was littered with boulders, like ancient gods brooding in the fading light of the stars.

"And what am I supposed to do about those bloody great stones? Steer around them?"

"Dey be moved when it time. Dis way, nobody guess it be a landin' strip."

"No one would anyway," Colin assured him gloomily as he eyed its appallingly short length. The Twin Otter was the world's best STOL aircraft, but this was asking too much. He wished he'd had some experience handling her in tight situations, but there was hardly a need for STOL procedures on the jet runways of California airports. With an inward shudder, he averted his eyes and asked, "Where's the airplane?"

"Over here." Leon took him through a grove of coconut palms, their ridged boles elephant gray in the dim light.

The blunt, no-nonsense shape of a Twin Otter squatted on balloon tires under a canopy of trees. Discouraged as he was over his chances of surviving the takeoff, Colin nevertheless felt a surge of affection for the gallant old bird—it wouldn't be her fault if they ended up in the drink. This one was painted a dull, nonreflecting black, even including the propellers and landing gear. There was something else about it, something eerie, and it took Colin a moment to pin it down. It was the first time in his flying career that he had seen a civilian airplane without the ever-present registration markings on the wings and fuselage. Their absence had an even more sinister effect than the black paint job. She was a real stray, no question about that.

Filing the thought away for future reference, he paced off the distance from the parked plane to the edge of the clearing. That gave him an extra eight meters. Rev her up to maximum power, use STOL flap setting . . . shaking his head, he began to step off the remainder of the takeoff run. One hundred and ten meters later he was peering over a cliff that dropped with dizzying abruptness into the sea.

"Dey say dat drop help you pick up speed befoah you hit de water." Leon remained a cautious distance back from the edge.

"Thanks a bunch." A sudden sense of mischief prompted Colin to add, "You'll be with me, of course?"

Leon took a hasty step backward. "Not me, boss. You on your own."

In the shuttered light of a battery lantern, Colin studied the flight plan Leon had handed him. He was to be airborne at 1930 hours, fly without navigation lights at an altitude of fifteen meters to avoid radar. For the same reason he was not to switch on the transponder. He would tune the ADF to 1274 megacycles and fly a course of 263 degrees to radio station KIRO, Curaçao. That was followed by a short northern leg, and after four hours' flying time he was to turn the ADF to the 1172 frequency and home in on the beacon.

Thoughtfully, Colin switched off the lantern and slipped further down into the tropical sleeping bag. The instructions were certainly clear enough. The only thing was that when he landed, he wouldn't have the foggiest notion of where in hell he was.

Chapter Nine

"Danny's here, Tony. Wanting to see you." Carl stood in the doorway of the bedroom, not troubling to conceal his disdain.

"He bores me." Tony toyed with the gold earring dangling from the houseboy's ear. "Tell him to go back to that dreadful woman."

"You better talk to him. He won't tell me anything, but he's all wound up like he's onto something big."

"Oh?" Mallabone slipped his arms into a silk kimono. "Well, it's a fact those beach bums find out about things before they even happen."

"Tony, I don' wanna play no games wit' you. I tell you what I know straight out and you look after me. Okay, mon?" The beachboy's voice quavered with excitement.

"Very sensible, Danny. Do carry on."

"It about a Chinee woman." Danny paused to gauge the effect of his words.

"Continue," Mallabone said softly, his expression unchanged except for an involuntary pursing of his lips.

"One of de boys see dis chick by hersel' and he make known he available if she wan' some company. She come on all skeered and run off. Me friend say she choice, but don' look lak she got any tin."

"Where did your friend see her, and when?"

93

"Within de hour. Buyin' fruit from de ole woman at de banyan tree."

Mallabone's eyes narrowed. The little stand where the two wrinkled old ladies peddled garden produce was only a couple of kilometers down the road.

"Excellent, Danny. We can't be sure she is the one, of course. But it does sound promising. You haven't discussed this with anyone?"

"No, boss. I come here direct. Can I get some tin now?" Danny asked and added lugubriously, "Dat tourist lady, she try me sore."

Tony laughed. "Carl will give you a hundred. If this turns out right, there'll be more."

Wendy leaned against the rickety wooden fence that bordered the public path leading to the beach. Gradually her labored breathing slowed and the stitch in her side went away. The beach was almost deserted as the setting sun spread layers of rosy pink across the western sky. Native vendors closed their cardboard suitcaes filled with shells and trinkets, draped their stock of colorful cotton prints over their shoulders and began to trudge home across the darkening sand.

She had overreacted. That phony macho native had nothing more sinister on his mind than a harmless pickup. But she had dropped the papaya back into the crone's basket like it was a hand grenade and frantically picked her way through the small group of people shopping at the open-air stand. Beautiful, Wendy scolded herself, just beautiful! The only way you could have attracted more attention would have been to rent a billboard.

The beach, populated with only a few isolated groups of stragglers, was no place for her. Not until dark when she could slip along the edge of the sand and find a soft place among the rocks. That's where she had spent last night, crouched on a tiny patch of sand in a jumbled pile of water-smoothed stones. But the shelter of night was a full hour away. Reluctantly she turned and made her way back to the road where tourists and locals mixed in a leisurely promenade.

The dogs found her shortly after midnight. The sound of their nails clicking on the rocks wakened her from an uneasy doze. At first she thought it was foraging crabs, until she heard the panting, snuffling sound of their breathing. Simultaneously the moon emerged from behind a wisp of cloud to illuminate the dark, bearlike shapes loping toward her. Petrified, knowing it was useless to try and escape, she watched them approach. Maybe they were somebody's pets let out for a midnight airing. The forlorn hope died with the realization that they were Doberman pinschers. There were two of them; the one in front whined with excitement as he drew closer to his quarry. Wendy raised her hands to protect her throat, but they didn't attack. Instead they halted a few paces away from her, raised their triangular heads and set up a fierce barking that sent an electric shock along Wendy's spine.

A jubilant grin creased the handler's face as he flashed the light from Wendy to the Polaroid print in the palm of his hand. "Jackpot!" he breathed and snapped the leash on the Doberman's collar.

His partner pulled Wendy to her feet and ran his hand roughly over her body, letting it linger on her crotch. "She ain't packing nuthin'," he announced finally and gave her arm a painful jerk. "Move it."

"Where are you taking me?" She found her voice but it came out in a squeaky stammer.

"Just up the beach a ways." Hot rancid breath washed

over her as his deep laugh boomed out. "Dey got a little bacchanal goin' an' you invited. Special like."

They marched her along the beach and through a fragrant garden with a swimming pool to the columned entrance of a mansion where two uniformed guards took over and escorted her to a long, cool room. The guards withdrew just as another door opened and the killer of her friends entered. With his tanned skin and sun-bleached hair he was the model of healthy, carefree American youth. Except for those pale, poached-egg eyes.

"I'm glad to see you again, Wendy," he said in a conversational tone.

She contrived to look politely puzzled. "I'm sorry, but I don't remember meeting you. Look, just what is going on? The police take a pretty serious view of kidnaping, you know."

"Maybe we haven't been introduced, but you have *seen* me before, haven't you?" He pulled some photos out of his shirt pocket and held them in front of her. "Remember those fun days on *Sympatico?*"

One of the shots showed her in a bikini standing between Milt and Susan. Milt had a can of beer in his hand and was laughing down at her. Wendy swallowed painfully to clear the sudden lump in her throat.

Carl Dykstra studied the photo with an air of critical detachment. "You got more in the way of boobs than most Chinese broads. I like that." Those unsettling orbs studied her. "There's not much point in denying that you're Wendy Wong and that you were on that yacht. Is there now?"

Wendy met his stare without flinching and said nothing. The palm of his open hand smashed against the side of her head and sent her sprawling on the floor. "When I ask a question I want an answer," he snarled. "Get on your feet."

Her head was ringing and she wondered if the eardrum had been ruptured. She wanted to lie there on the cool, tiled floor, but his foot was poised to kick her in the midsection. Painfully she dragged herself to her hands and knees and slowly stood up. They were going to kill her, of course. She was a witness to the cold-blooded murder of four innocent people.

"Who helped you, Wendy? Who brought you to Soufriere?"

This is what they were really after. They had to know if she told anyone else about the killings. She bit her lip and braced herself for the next blow.

"You'll tell us all right. Before we're through you'll beg for the chance to spill your guts. But," his voice thickened, "I'm going to have a piece of you before the goods get spoiled."

He pulled her to him and crushed his mouth against hers. For a moment she was too startled to react, then her fists beat ineffectually against his chest. His thumb pressed on the hinge of her jaw, forcing her mouth open. She bit his probing tongue, hard, and he drew back with a snarl.

Grinning, he spat blood on the floor and came after her. Buttons flew from her borrowed skirt as he tore it open. He cupped her left breast and sucked at her nipple. She tried to knee him in the groin and then screamed in agony as his teeth clamped down.

Her scream exploded in his ear, causing his grip to loosen momentarily. Wendy tore herself free and ran for the door. The heavy brass knob refused to turn in her hands. Sobbing, she looked frantically around the room, searching for something to throw. It was hopeless: the few pieces of furniture were massive. She couldn't even lift a corner of those leather chairs, let alone throw one. There were no ashtrays, no tabletop knickknacks. Nothing.

Carl lunged at her and twisted her arm behind her back until she knew it would snap with the slightest additional pressure. His other hand tugged at her jeans and then he flung her onto the sofa with so much force that she bounced.

He quickly stripped off his pants and mounted her, lips pulled back from his even white teeth in a savage leer. She struggled to throw him off, rolling and twisting in a vain attempt to pitch them both to the floor.

"That's what I like," he bellowed as her struggles drove him deeper into her. "Keep it up. Fight me, baby."

Her frenzied thrashing abruptly ceased and her body went slack. The velvet brown eyes opened up to look up at him with withering contempt.

"Bitch!" he snarled, furiously pumping himself into her motionless and unresisting flesh. The breath rasped in his throat and his eyes were screwed shut as he neared a climax. Wendy pushed hard against his chest with both hands and pivoted her hips to the side, throwing the startled rapist onto the floor.

Stunned, Carl lay on his face while his ejaculation spent itself. "You fucking bitch!" he roared as he scrambled to his feet, hands balled into fists. "I'm going to take you apart!"

He stopped in mid-stride as a buzzer sounded and a small red light began to flash over the door. "Shit!" he muttered and wiped his penis with the tattered remains of Wendy's shirt.

"Okay, doll, the fun part's over," he said, zipping up his fly. "Why don't you make it easy on yourself and tell me who fished you out of the ocean?"

Wendy, sensing that the flashing light was a signal Dykstra had no choice but to obey, rolled over on the couch and turned her naked back to him. He glared down at her, snorted something unintelligible and strode to the door.

"That was extremely self-indulgent of you, Carl," Mallabone reproved mildly.

Carl looked puzzled, then shrugged. "I might have known. What is it, closed-circuit TV or old-fashioned peepholes?"

"It doesn't matter. What does matter is that you can't extract information from the modern female by sexual abuse. I'm inclined to believe they enjoy it. Pain and fear are the only effective tools."

Mallabone paused, then drawled thoughtfully, "She *is* remarkably lovely. So exotic. The president has been rather jaded recently, and this delectable morsel might be just the tonic he needs." He shot Carl a meaningful glance. "He would not be amused to discover you had been there before him."

"He doesn't have to know," Carl protested, trying to recall if he had marked her. Damn, his teeth marks would probably show up on her breast. He felt a sense of reprieve when Mallabone murmured, "However, all that will have to wait. The president is resting. He is quite exhausted after last night's religious exertions."

Bartholomew was a voodoo adept, a houngan who, years ago, had been initiated at a ceremony in a *tonnelle* in the Haitian hills above Port-au-Prince. It was whispered that the initiation had been accompanied by the dread Petro rites where the gods received their ancient offering of "hornless goat." The rumors of ritualistic cannibalism only added fuel to Bartholomew's aura of sinister power.

When Bartholomew presided at a voodoo ceremony,

Baron Samedi, Lord of the Cemeteries and Chief of the Legion of the Dead, was the *loa* who most frequently appeared. As the pounding drums sent the first of the worshipers into paroxysms, the possessed one's face was contorted into a diabolical leer, and he began to shoot an imaginary pistol at the roof. Recognizing the incarnation of the ghoulish Baron, his fellow initiates grabbed him and forced his arms into a frayed morning coat. A battered top hat was jammed over his ears and a pair of horn-rimmed dark glasses placed on his nose to complete the Baron's undertaker costume. Thus attired, the initiate was released to run and bounce around the *tonelle*, rubbing his groin against every person and object he encountered.

As the possessed dancer jerked and shrieked, Bartholomew traced Baron Samedi's symbol on the dirt floor of the peristyle with maize flour. Other *loas* dropped from the shadows to mount the writhing congregation until the temple was filled with gyrating, yelling celebrants brandishing colossal bamboo phalli. At some point in the wild melee a goat would be led in to be castrated and have its throat slashed with a cutlass. Bartholomew shrewdly did nothing to suppress the whispers that sometimes the goat walked on its hind legs and wore no horns.

Realizing how it strengthened his hold over his credulous subjects, Bartholomew several times a year held a ceremony in a palm-thatched *tonnelle* deep in the hills. The following day he spent in a trance of sleep.

Carl knew enough about the dictator's voodoo activities to realize it would be suicidal to disturb him on the day following a ceremony. But his initial relief over Bartholomew not finding out he had been dealt a wet deck with the Chinese broad was replaced with a fear that right at this very moment, some unknown bastard might be talking to the American or Interpol police about the murders. Of course Bartholomew could protect him from any foreign authorities, but only so long as he remained on Soufriere, and Carl had no intention of spending the rest of his life cooped up on this crummy little island—he wanted to roam the fleshpots of the world.

"Look," he said, "it's my ass that's in the sling. I've got to find out if that broad has told anybody else about me. It's for sure she didn't swim here herself. The boss won't care if she's had the shit scared out of her as long as she still looks good. Right?"

Tony nodded slowly. "All right. Do what you have to do. Just remember if you ruin that piece, the jumbies may have you for midnight supper."

Wendy was bewildered, but not about to object. She had been allowed to soak in a fragrant bath and told to put on a smart jump suit that was folded over the back of the dressing-room chair. Although the waistband was elasticized, it was still much too loose, and she had to roll the cuffs up a good four inches. Never mind, the suit felt deliciously clean and fresh. Her nipple throbbed abominably, but at least the brute hadn't bitten it off.

It was still dark when they bundled her into the back seat of a Toyota and drove past the shuttered shacks. The blond killer, she had heard one of the others call him Carl, rode in the front with the driver, dark glasses once more covering those revolting eyes. A thin mulatto sat beside her, a silenced handgun resting on his knees. After a few kilometers the car turned away from the sea and began to climb a rough, red dirt road. The fiery rim of the sun was just visible over the horizon when the Toyota bumped to a stop beside the dilapidated Cessna. Its propeller was already ticking over, and the Koramantee pilot gestured impatiently for them to hurry. He started his takeoff run as soon as the cabin door was clamped shut.

The early morning air was dead calm as they climbed to 1700 meters. Joshua Todd throttled back, looked somberly over his right shoulder at Dykstra and nodded. Wendy heard Carl suck in a deep breath. Then he reached across and depressed the doorlatch. The small cabin was suddenly filled with the sound of the motor and rushing wind.

Struggling to hold the door open against the propwash, Carl shouted, "Tell us who you talked to, or you go out the door."

He unsnapped her seat belt and Todd banked to the right. Wendy screamed as she felt herself sliding on the worn, smooth fabric. Frantically she grabbed for the headrest of the front seat.

Todd righted the plane while Carl dangled the buckle of her safety belt tantalizingly before her. The third man reached across the pilot's lap to prop open the door.

"It's a long way down, Wendy," Carl yelled. "Just give us the names and we close the door."

Wendy's jaw was clenched shut against the nausea crawling up her throat. There must be something she could tell them. But they probably meant to kill her anyway.

"I guess she needs to be convinced," Carl shouted in the pilot's ear. Todd nodded but his face wore a worried frown as he adjusted the plane's trim. "Be careful how you move around. This thing ain't no jetliner."

Wendy whimpered with unbelieving horror as she dangled helplessly one and a half kilometers above the quicksilver sea. It couldn't be happening to her, but it was. Her lips silently formed the word "Please" as she stared up at her tormentors.

Carl gripped her left wrist and the thin man crouched on the floor to hold her other one. His leg was hooked around one of the seat supports to keep from being pulled out.

The propwash tore at her, ballooning the pants of her too-big jump suit and pushing her back against the fuselage. She prayed for the blessed release of unconsciousness, but the instinctive will to survive was pumping adrenalin into her bloodstream. She closed her eyes, telling herself over and over that they couldn't afford to let her die until they had found out the identity of everyone she had spoken to since the massacre.

Without warning Carl released his hold and Wendy felt herself dropping. Then her right arm was almost torn from its socket as it took all the strain. The plane was in a gentle bank to the right, and she was dangling away from it, the top of her head level with the broken brace for a missing cabin step. Would she remain conscious until she smashed into the water? She had read somewhere that people blacked out before the end. She looked up at the two men, her eyes imploring them to put a stop to the nightmare. The face of the guard holding her was contorted with strain, and he was yelling something at Carl. Like he was telling him that he couldn't hold her much longer. Her flailing hand caught the edge of the open doorway and she hung on grimly. Carl moved his foot as though to stamp on her fingers, but the other one shook his head violently. She could feel the palm of his hand growing slick with sweat against her skin.

The sadistic pleasure on Carl's face was replaced with a worried scowl as he leaned out and grasped her arm. He nodded at the other man, and they began the struggle to lift her back in. Wendy's racing heart turned over as she felt her hand starting to slip through the mulatto's sweaty grip. With his other hand he grabbed the flesh of her upper arm. He nodded at Carl and slowly they heaved her up until her left knee found the edge of the door. With a sob she propelled herself sprawling into the cabin.

The Cessna was rocking wildly, but the Koramantee rode the controls with an expert touch. Wendy heard the doorlatch click home, shutting out the awful scream of the wind. Her arms were aching painfully, but that didn't matter. Nothing mattered except the sheer bliss of feeling something solid underneath her. Even when Carl picked her up and slammed her down on the seat beside him, she still felt an irrational sense of gratitude that he had brought her in from that terrifying void.

Her euphoria evaporated, however, when he placed his sneering face close to hers and barked, "Who else knows about the *Sympatico* raid?"

Wendy looked back at him with a glazed, uncomprehending expression. He shook her and yelled in a white fury, "You talk or we'll open the door again and this time we'll throw you out!"

Wendy's eyes closed and she collapsed against him with a small sigh of expelled breath. Dykstra pulled her upright and slapped her two stinging blows to the cheek. "You're just faking it, you stupid cunt! Snap out of it!"

"Knock it off, Carl," the Koramantee pilot snapped. "You mark that chick before the man sees her and all of us are in deep shit."

Hearing this, Wendy knew that she was not fated to plummet to her death. Not this trip, at least. She drew strength from the reprieve, regardless of the other terrors that loomed ahead. If survival meant living from moment to moment, then that was what she would do.

The pilot's earphones suddenly crackled with instructions, and he spoke a terse acknowledgment into the mike.

"They want us to stay clear of the city, so we'll put down at the strip near Louisville. There'll be a car to meet you."

"Shit," Carl muttered. The hamlet of Louisville was near the northern tip of the island, and it meant a long drive over the bone-crushing roads. "What's the problem?"

"I just drive an airplane." Todd throttled back and started a gradual descent as they approached the black coral cliffs.

Ten minutes later the Cessna was rumbling across a patch of rough grass toward two black Mercedes limousines.

The guards wore the green, short-sleeved uniforms of the Mongoose Gang with heavy black revolvers protruding from open holsters. Wendy was hurried into the second car, and with a quiet thunking of doors the little cavalcade got under way.

They thundered through the small village, horns blaring, people and dogs fleeing before them. A donkey stood stubbornly in the middle of the narrow street as the lead car bore down on it. There was a crunch as the Mercedes flung it through the air, its load of firewood raining down in their wake.

Carl, hooting with laughter, turned around in the front passenger seat for a final glimpse of the turmoil in their wake. Wendy realized with a small unpleasant jolt that apart from those dreadful eyes, he was remarkably good looking. Shock absorbers thrummed as a rear wheel dropped into a gaping pothole.

"You know what the president says?" Carl glanced

back at Wendy as though inviting her to share the joke. "He says Soufriere has so many roads he can't be expected to maintain them all. How about that?"

The sergeant sitting next to Wendy sucked in his breath at this heresy. Then they were all pitched forward as the driver stood on the brakes. The car in front had slowed to a stop underneath a banner whose crudely-painted letters spelled out a defiant message: DOWN WITH BARTHOLOMEW! DEATH TO THE TYRANT!

Carl swore as he saw a door start to open in the lead car. The bloody fools were going to haul down the sign. Grabbing up the transceiver, he barked, "Stay in the car. It may be an ambush. Get moving. Hit it!"

Both cars accelerated furiously, flinging up a rattling hail of loose stones and chunks of crumbling asphalt. Carl pulled Wendy off the seat, yelling at her to stay down. After two kilometers of wild bouncing from pothole to pothole, he thumbed the transceiver switch and ordered the lead car to resume normal speed.

"I want the driver of that car put on report," he told the sergeant. "We were sitting ducks back there."

The sergeant nodded grimly. After a few minutes he swallowed and said, "I wonder why those S.F.U. bastards didn't open fire?"

"Who knows?" Carl picked up the transceiver and gave an order to turn at the next crossing. "Maybe there was nobody there. That's happened before. Or," he glanced at Wendy, "they might have held back because of her. S.F.U. mean anything to you, doll?"

She shook her head and he grunted, "This time I believe you."

They drove swiftly through the narrow, congested streets of Albertstown, pedestrians scurrying out of the path of the black cars, and other vehicles hastily pulling off to the side. Then they swept up a smooth circular driveway flanked by velvety lawns. The first car pulled to a stop beside an open garage door, but the second one bearing Wendy and Dykstra drove right inside. The metal door immediately rumbled down behind them. Two members of the Mongoose Gang, both cradling submachine guns, waited for them inside the echoing, cavernous space. There was room for at least five automobiles, but the Mercedes stood alone on the spotless concrete floor.

Dykstra held Wendy back for a moment as they climbed out. "You're going to meet the guy who runs this country. If he finds out you and I had it on, things will happen to you that will make dying a privilege."

"And what will he do to you?" she asked defiantly.

"Not one damn thing. I'm too valuable." Despite his bluster, Wendy sensed the underlying fear.

Chapter Ten

The Twin Otter thrummed and vibrated as though bent on tearing herself apart, and the control panel jiggled and danced in front of Colin's eyes. He had the propellers on full fine and both torque gauges registered 180 centimeters. There was nothing more to do except pray. He released the toe brakes and the balloon tires began to roll, sluggishly at first as the maximum thirty degrees of take-off flap held them back.

"Come on, baby, move!" he muttered through clenched teeth as the palm trees went by with agonizing slowness. The yoke was heavy and unresponsive in his hands as he came up to the last point where he could chop the power and brake to a halt. Now he was past the boulder which marked the point of no return; he was committed and the end of the makeshift runway was much too close. He firewalled the power levers.

It took all his flying discipline not to yank back on the controls as they went over the edge. The turbines whined at emergency power, laboring to keep the plane and its heavy load of fuel aloft. For a heartbeat it looked as though they might succeed, then the Twin Otter began to sink inexorably down to the waiting sea. Colin held the yoke forward, his eyes riveted on the airspeed indicator. At the last possible split second he leveled off; he found himself pulling up on the yoke as though to hold the struggling craft in the air by physical force. The air speed was still too low, and he held his breath as he waited for her to mush down into the whitecaps. From somewhere she found enough lift to stay above their curling manes. Spindrift was splattering against the windshield by the time Colin felt the increasing response of the controls.

"You old sweetheart!" he shouted with exuberant relief as he eased the black plane into a gentle climb.

The swift tropic dusk soon caught up to the monoplane as it droned almost directly west fifteen meters above the surging waves. Colin's world was reduced to the dim and shrouded instrument lights and the occasional gleam of a whitecap. Flying this low and with the transponder not sending out its little blip, they were free from radar surveillance. The shape of a schooner running without lights suddenly appeared from out of nowhere on the dark sea. He pulled back on the yoke and zoomed skyward.

Those poor devils have just had the fright of their lives; Colin was briefly amused by the thought as he dropped down to his assigned altitude. He wondered if it could have been *Antilles Rose,* but decided not. Capt'n Johnny pretty well stuck to the Grenadian chain; he wouldn't be this far south and west. The encounter made Colin yearn for even another ten meters of altitude; he didn't relish the possibility of tangling with the masts and rigging of some schooner blacked out for a smuggling run. But his instructions were specific. He took what comfort he could from the fact that the inter-island boats didn't run to soaring masts; the rotting hulls simply couldn't carry much canvas.

According to his flight plan, it was time to tune in A.T.I.S. He twisted a knob and a taped voice, speaking in heavily accented English, recited information on the weather and gave landing instructions for the Willemstad airport. He was just north of Curaçao, one of the Netherlands Antilles. As he flew on he could see the lights of scattered settlements off his port wing and beyond that the dark bulk of Aruba. He had a vague recollection that the latter island boasted a small mountain, but he had no way of checking it since there were no maps on board. He had complained about this to Leon, but all he got was a shrug and, "What you wan' me to do, mon? *Draw* you one?"

There was no need to worry about the mountain; his assigned course was taking the Twin Otter directly along the channel that divided the two islands, hugging the almost uninhabited northern tip of Curaçao and giving a wide berth to the town of Sint Nicolaas on the south coast of Aruba.

For the first and probably the last time Colin knew exactly where he was, and he was not enthralled with the idea of wave hopping this close to land. A few kilometers further west and the course veered slightly north to avoid a peninsula jutting out from the coastline. He had no choice but to trust his flight instructions and follow them to the last detail. Obediently he turned south, climbed to ninety meters and dialed the ADF to the new frequency. The signal came in immediately, and he set a course to home in on the beacon 240 kilometers away. He was sure now that his landfall would be somewhere in the northeast part of Colombia, but that was all he knew.

He made a final check of the fuel. Fat city, there was a good thirty-minute reserve. Colin tightened up again as they crossed over the coastline. There were no lights, just white furrows of breaking surf. It was nothing short of suicidal, flying this low at night over unknown terrain.

The coast was well behind him when he saw the lights—four flarepots placed in a long rectangle. The flames were going straight up, indicating a no-wind condition, but the strip was long enough so it didn't matter. He came in fast and dropped her in hard. As he had expected, it was a rough grass strip, nothing more than an open field. But the Twin Otter had been built for just such conditions, and she rumbled to a full stop well short of the last two flarepots. They were extinguished immediately, and then somebody was pounding on the door with the palm of his hand. Colin opened it and a khaki clad man clambered in. He spoke English with a strong Spanish accent as he instructed Colin to follow the man with the flashlight.

Colin revved up and bumped over the hillocky ground until the bobbing light brought them to a grove of coconut palms. The light signaled him to turn 180 degrees, and then a horizontal slashing movement told him to cut his engines.

The hot humid air wrapped itself around Colin as he stepped down into the midst of a motley group of men. They were *mestizos,* a mixture of Indian and Spanish blood with some showing a strong dash of black ancestry. Without exception they were dressed in faded and stained shirts, pants cut off raggedly just below the knees and floppy straw hats. The one who had ridden with Colin and who was plainly in charge said something in Spanish, and the small army began to push the Twin Otter into a clearing in the palm grove. When the leader was satisfied with its position, he hissed another order and the outlines of the airplane were quickly hidden under a covering of palm fronds, already cut and stacked for that purpose.

Once everything was secured, they led Colin to a rude adobe hut where a bent-shouldered woman served him a glass of neat rum and a plate of charred beef chunks with refried beans. Then he sacked out on a wooden bunk with a mattress made from burlap sacks stuffed with straw, and slept heavily until the morning sun made the little hut intolerable. He stepped outside to be greeted with an arid, amber-hued landscape dotted with groves of palm trees. He was to be thoroughly weary of that monotonous view before the long day was through.

With nothing to do but wait, he could no longer suppress thoughts of Wendy. His subconscious must have been at work because he started with the certain knowledge that he was going to try and find her. If she had made her way back to the States, he would follow her. Baltimore was the place to start. Even if she was afraid to surface, there must be someone that she would contact. If that didn't work, he'd try San Francisco. It meant abandoning the Sun Air project, but there was no way he could stay hitched to the Bartholomew team anyhow. He'd take the ten thou' for this trip and cut out. They wouldn't take too kindly to the idea, but he'd deal with that when the time came.

The sudden memory of his passionate coupling with Pearl Demaret made him wince. But not for long. He recognized it for what it was—a pleasant interlude brought on by mutual attraction and his own rebellion at how much Wendy had come to mean to him. The important thing was to find out if he and the delectable Ms. Wong had a future.

It was late afternoon when the threadbare caravan struggled over the desiccated land. Colin stared with mounting consternation at the two long crates on the flatbed wagon hitched to a pair of scrawny mules. It was in the middle of the procession of pack mules and spindly-legged burros, and a half-dozen sweating *mestizos* shoved and tugged to help the straining beasts pull it up a small knoll.

"Do not worry, *amigo.*" The leader was standing at Colin's elbow. "Your magnificent *avion* can surely carry more than two half-starved mules."

"They're pulling and that's a lot different from lifting," Colin muttered and hurried over to supervise the loading. The wagon was backed up to the cargo door, and the two crates were carefully levered on board with planks and long poles, and then firmly roped to the eyebolts in the aircraft's frame. Checking the lashings, Colin was forced to acknowledge that the ragged native crew had done a professional job. Next the boxes and wicker cartons were loaded and piled on top of the long crates. Colin insisted on hefting each one to check its weight. He grunted as a particularly heavy one almost toppled him off his feet. "Jesus, what's in this anyway? Gold bricks?"

The leader shot him a sideways glance and ordered the wooden cover to be pried off. "It is more precious than gold, *senor,*" he murmured and stepped aside to let Colin look down at the stone head resting on its bed of straw. Its large nose was chipped and a section of the headdress was missing, but there was an unmistakable aura of nobility about the heavy-featured, full-lipped visage.

"The *guaqueros*—" the leader paused to explain, "our word for grave robbers—dug this fine fellow up at San Augustin only last week. It grieves me to see such treasures leave my country." He put on a doleful expression as he motioned a worker to nail the top back in place, "but what is a poor peon to do when he must feed his family?"

Colin couldn't figure out whether the man was serious or not, so he busied himself with rigging the metal grating that sealed off the cargo compartment. Then they began the tedious job of refueling with a hand pump from drums of JP-4. When that chore was at last finished, he was given another heavy meal of meat and rice and then presented with his instructions in an envelope sealed with an ornate wax impression.

Colin waited until he was alone in the cockpit before opening the envelope. Reading the single sheet of typescript in the light of the instrument panel, he found that it was almost the reciprocal of his outbound course. He was to fly a bit further north before turning east, but he would give odds that the final beacon would lead him back to that postage stamp of a strip on Jumbie. Somewhat to his own surprise, he found the challenge exhilarating, and he was whistling under his breath as he hit the start selector. When the noise of the engines swelled to a turbo shriek the four flarepots were lit and the heavily laden plane began its takeoff run.

Colin was in a state of euphoria on the long return leg. He had no reason whatsoever to expect Wendy to fall into his arms, but at least he would *know*. Anything was better than going through life wondering what might have been. And the thought of actually seeing her again sent a tingle racing through his blood.

Flares flickered to life below him, and Colin knew he had been right about Jumbie being his destination. The area the four lights outlined looked more like a helicopter pad than a landing place for fixed-wing aircraft. He deployed the flaps, and the Twin Otter slowed until it was almost hanging in midair. Following his instructions he had climbed to 150 meters, and from that height he took a quick look at the island below him. The night was clear and the western half stood out in bold relief against the mercury gray of the sea. The lights were about three-quarters of the way up the slope of a long extinct volcano whose flattened cone blocked his view of the eastern coast. The island was larger than he had thought; it must be nearly two kilometers in length.

His propwash set the palms swaying and dipping as he floated in barely above a stall. He slammed the props into reverse the instant the wheels made contact with the coarse surface of the lava bed. The blunt nose pitched forward when he tramped on the brakes, and smoke poured from the tortured tires as he slewed the Otter around in a near ground loop. In the fitful light of the flares he saw that they had erected a wire mesh barrier at the edge of the precipice.

"One hell of a landin', boss," Leon, visibly impressed, shouted as Colin opened the door.

"That was no landing. That was a controlled crash." Colin grinned as he lowered himself to the ground and gratefully stretched muscles cramped from the long flight.

Leon was carrying a rifle, and the dark shapes of a squad of laborers loomed behind him. Two of them climbed inside the cabin as soon as Colin opened the cargo doors and began to pass out the smaller boxes.

The grunting and sweating started when they reached the two long crates. The first one made it without mishap, but the man supporting the left front corner of the second one suddenly screamed in pain and doubled over with the agony of a popped disc. The overbalanced crate teetered for a moment while the man on the opposite corner struggled to hold it back. But he couldn't stop its momentum, and it toppled to the ground, landing on its front end and tipping over on its back.

The wooden sides split open, and the bottom half of a stone idol struck the ground with a sharp crack. A carved foot fell off, and two clear plastic packages filled with a white crystalline powder slid out.

Chapter Eleven

"You are exquisite, my dear," Bartholomew murmured as he held his hands under the hot-water tap.

From the bed, Wendy glanced fearfully in his direction. He was washing his hands with all the care of a surgeon preparing for an operation. She cringed as he dried his hands and walked toward her. He was naked and his penis was still limp. He was smiling with sublime confidence as he eased himself onto the bed and stretched out beside her.

His lips were surprisingly gentle as he brushed them over the hollows below her cheekbones and down the curve of her neck. "You realize you must do everything I want, don't you?"

Wendy nodded wordlessly. His fingers were between her thighs, lightly stroking her sex. She forced her rigid body to relax and his smile widened. "That's the way. You know Bartholomew will not hurt you. Let yourself feel.

"Now you must do something for me," he murmured and rolled over on his back. "Take me in your mouth."

"No," she whimpered.

"The alternative will be exceedingly painful." He spoke with calm detachment.

Screwing her eyes shut she ran her tongue lightly along his wrinkled organ. He had been circumcised, and the fleshy head of his cock was a purplish black.

119

"I said *in* your mouth." Bartholomew's voice was steely. He gave a deep grunt of pleasure as her lips opened. When he was fully erect, he entered her and came quickly to a climax, making no sound except for a soft sigh as his ejaculation began.

Bartholomew wore a self-satisfied smirk as he rolled off the bed and stood by the headboard.

"There is nothing I enjoy quite as much as a beautiful woman." He sighed with an air of faint regret. "You know, my dear, if we could clear up one little matter between us, we could enjoy a long and pleasant relationship. One which would be very profitable for you." He paused for effect. "Now I want you to tell Bartholomew who else knows about that little incident on the yacht."

Wendy swallowed, then croaked, "Nobody."

"Indeed?" Bartholomew's attention seemed to be focused entirely on lighting a cigar. He was oblivious to the few drops of semen oozing from his phallus and dripping onto the bright red rug. "You expect us to believe that you *swam* all the way from the Grenadines to Soufriere?"

He inhaled deeply until the end of the cigar flared red hot and took a step toward the bed. Wendy's gaze was riveted on the cigar. He raised it as if to brand her with its glowing tip. Instinctively she reached out and grabbed his hand. His skin was icy cold with a chill that burned its way through her terror. She gasped and released her grip. Now she knew the reason behind the hand washing routine—once the effect of the hot water had worn off, his touch was as cold as death.

Not daring to look up, Wendy cowered on the bed waiting for his wrath to rain down. Instead a maidservant, carrying a basin of warm soapy water, crept into the room and knelt to wash Bartholomew's private parts. His face was expressionless as he looked down at Wendy through a blue haze of cigar smoke.

"Bartholomew will give you a little time to think over what I have said." He accepted a silken robe from the servant and swung it around his shoulders with a flourish. The door opened as he stalked toward it.

Wendy heard the bath water being run, but she remained motionless on the rumpled bed and stared unseeingly up at the overhead mirror. If only she could will her mind to become a blank screen. She was brought back to reality by the murmur of a velvety voice. "I know it's rough, honey, but you'll feel better after a hot bath."

Slowly Wendy turned her head on the pillow and the face of a ravishingly beautiful mulatto woman swam into focus. As though in a trance Wendy let the stranger, who said her name was Pearl, assist her from the bed and guide her to the sybaritic bathroom. The same maid who had attended Bartholomew crouched on the marble floor, emptying a vial of bath oil into a steaming sunken tub.

Pearl was stubbing out a cigarette when Wendy, wrapped in a terrycloth robe, emerged from the bathroom. "It does help, doesn't it?" she asked in her throaty voice.

"Some," Wendy acknowledged. Soaking in the fragrant tub, Wendy had steeled herself to look at rape as merely an incident of her capture. Somehow, she must depersonalize it, like any other form of physical violence that might be done to her.

She perched on the freshly made bed and looked directly at her beautiful companion. "What's in store for me? Really."

The involuntary look of compassion that flickered across Pearl's face made Wendy shiver.

"That bad, huh?"

"It could be." Pearl's painted eyelids dropped as she busied herself lighting another cigarette.

She stayed for nearly two hours, smoking innumerable cigarettes as they talked in fits and starts. The room must have been superbly air-conditioned since the smoke was whisked away almost as it left her lips. Pearl didn't press Wendy to talk; she seemed content just to sit there and let the frequent silences grow. Wendy found her presence strangely comforting and once was almost tempted to break down and confide in her.

In self-defense she blurted, "This is the old bad guy, good guy ploy, isn't it? And you're the sympathetic friend I'm supposed to spill my guts to. Right?" She plunged on without waiting for an answer. "Well, there's nothing to tell. I was pulled out of the water just before I went under for the last time and dumped ashore by a bunch of natives speaking some kind of gibberish I couldn't understand a word of. And that's all there is."

Pearl gave her a commiserating look. "You'll have to do better than that, Wendy. And you're wrong about why I'm here. I just thought you could use a little moral support from another woman. If there *is* something you want to tell me, though, I'll pass it on and things might work out for you."

"I don't believe you. They'll never let me out of here alive."

"That's not true. Bartholomew really likes you. He can be very generous to those who cooperate with him."

Wendy made no reply and Pearl left soon after, in obedience to a red light that suddenly glowed above the door. She went directly to the dictator's office suite. Mallabone looked away from the TV screen and its picture of a confused and frightened Wendy. "Nice try, Pearl," he murmured. "But the only way to get the truth out of that lady is to tear it out."

"That's what I've been saying all along, for Christ's sake," Carl Dykstra raged. He was about to add something more but broke off at Bartholomew's frown.

"That's one pretty lady," Bartholomew smacked his thick lips. "I think she liked what Bartholomew gave her."

"Without a doubt," Mallabone murmured. "She just doesn't want to admit it."

"Very good! You are a very funny man, Tony!" The dictator laughed uproariously, squeezing Mallabone's arm in appreciation of the joke. Almost fainting from the pain, his victim managed to keep a sickly smile in place.

Carl watched the byplay with undisguised glee. It did him good to see the supercilious Englishman humiliated. Emboldened, he snarled, "Let's cut out the horseshit and really go to work on that broad. A little session over at the volcano will loosen her tongue."

"We need to talk alone, Excellency." Somehow Mallabone refrained from rubbing the throbbing ache in his stringy bicep. "Urgently."

Bartholomew dismissed the others with a wave of his arm. He thumbed a remote control switch and Wendy's image faded from the screen. With a look grown suddenly shrewd, he indicated his chief adviser was to speak.

"That girl is an American citizen. And so were those others on the yacht. If your name gets linked with this operation, it'll be the kiss of death for the economic aid program."

Bartholomew stirred uneasily in his chair and opened his mouth as though to protest.

Mallabone raised his hand. "Hear me out. The program is in extreme jeopardy already. If we didn't have the Chairman of the Appropriations Committee in our hip pocket it would have been cut off two years ago. It's lasted this long only because it's peanuts by U.S. standards and Nesbitt has played the anti-commie card every time it's been questioned. And remember the worthy senator is about to pay us a visit. If Nesbitt gets a whiff of the hijacking caper, he'll turn off the tap on all those lovely dollars overnight."

"We don't need their goddamn charity," Bartholomew growled, but without conviction.

"That's bullshit," Mallabone replied equably, sure of his ground. "Those American dollars are what pay the army and the Mongoose boys. Lose the support of the military and you lose the country. It's that simple."

"He'd never find out," Bartholomew protested.

"You don't really believe that. There are times when this administration has more leaks than a West Indies schooner."

"It's those S.F.U. bastards," Bartholomew snarled. "Okay, what'll we do?"

"Get her off the island. At least until Senator Nesbitt has come and gone."

"Jumbie?"

Mallabone nodded.

"Okay. Set it up." The intercom buzzed and Bartholomew pressed a button.

"Colonel Stroud is here with a report about that S.F.U. placard on the Louisville road," Pearl's voice was saying. "You wanted to know right away, Excellency."

"Send him in," Bartholomew ordered, black fingers drumming on the desk.

The commandant of the Mongoose gang snapped a

palm-out, British-type salute and stood rigidly at attention as he delivered his report in terse, staccato sentences.

"Prisoner Holmes has identified his accomplices. There were six of them, all well known to us as troublemakers. They are from the Grand Etang area, and he has revealed their hiding place. They are being rounded up now, Excellency."

"Satisfactory," Bartholomew said, and the room fell silent while he pondered. "They are to be executed at noon tomorrow. In the square at Louisville where they will be an example to some of the other hotheads. They will beat each other to death with truck axles. The survivor will be garroted. slowly."

He raised his eyes from the desk and looked at the colonel. "The prisoner Holmes. Is that young Adrian Holmes from Grand Etang?"

"Yes, Excellency."

"I am not surprised. And how is he?"

"The subject did not survive interrogation, Excellency."

"You have done well, Colonel."

Another salute quivered at the rim of the colonel's green beret and he withdrew.

"A dedicated man, the colonel," Bartholomew murmured.

"A dedicated *mercenary,*" Mallabone amended. "Like the rest of your troops."

Bartholomew shot him an uneasy glance and heaved himself out of the chair. "I'll drop in at the nightclub and glad-hand a few tourists."

Chapter Twelve

The trip back out through the reef was even wilder and wetter than the ride in, but this time Colin knew it was a routine operation for the surfboat. It was still necessary to grip the plank seat with both hands, but there was no longer the heart-banging fear that they would turn turtle with every wave. He welcomed the drenching spray of salt water because it meant they were leaving Jumbie behind and there had been a moment when he seriously doubted if he would do so alive.

Leon's gun had come up when the two packets of dope had spilled onto the runway, his eyes searching Colin's face for a reaction. Colin had played it cool, saying with a shrug, "I knew damn well it wasn't works of art we were packing. Guess my flying pay has just gone up."

"Doan' know nuttin' about dat," Leon muttered, but the worried scowl left his face and he signaled his men to go back to work with a jerk of his rifle.

"It ain't all drugs," he volunteered. "Some of dem heathen t'ings," an unmistakable quiver of superstition crept into his voice, "be for real. Seem like some guv'munt folks won' touch de drug trade, but doan' mind makin' some tin wit dese debbils."

There was no doubt that Leon had come to admire Colin's style. Already awestruck by his dazzling airmanship, the pilot's nonchalant acceptance of the situation put the final seal on Leon's approval. He had been friendly and talkative as they slipped and slid in the darkness down the rocky slope to the lagoon to keep their rendezvous with the surfboat.

The abrupt equatorial dawn was lacquering the ocean with bronze enamel when the dugout surged through the last breaker to ride easily on the calm waters of the open sea. The sports fishing boat kicked up an arcing bow-wave as it raced toward them.

Now that they were heading away from the forbidden island, the launch wasted no time in pretending to fish, but set a course directly back to Albertstown. Colin sat in the open rear cockpit and watched the wake thrown up by the twin screws. He had been royally conned. If he had known about the drugs, he would have turned that fruit Mallabone down flat. He didn't know enough to be sure what kind of drug the white powder was. Coming from South America it should be cocaine, but it also could have been heroin on a roundabout route into the American market. Well, he had decided to quit the operation anyway. He frowned with the realization that his discovery of the true nature of the trade wouldn't make Mallabone any happier to see him go. But Leon's report of his reaction should reassure them and buy him some time to prepare his exit.

Colin was half-expecting a reception committee, but no one accosted him as the motor launch slid up to a ramshackle jetty and he stepped ashore. The boatman told him Treasure Lagoon was just along the beach, around the first point of land. He was probably being followed, but there was nothing he could do about that, so he put it out of his mind as he trudged across the powdery sand.

A slip of paper with a message to call Jill immediately had been stuffed under his door. Her voice was casual when she came on the phone, but she made it clear that she needed to see him right away.

"What's coming down, Jill?" Colin kept his voice low. They were standing in the yard outside the Palm Hill kitchen where Jill and her mother were supervising the final preparations of the midday meal for the cane field crews.

Jill brushed a strand of red brown hair back from her eyes. "I'm afraid the hijackers have got Wendy," she replied miserably.

"No!" Colin breathed; he could almost feel the blood draining from his face. He swallowed hard. "How did you find out? Bush telegraph?"

She nodded. "The cutters are whispering about this beautiful Chinese girl who was hiding out on the beach and got carried off by some men. Naturally they're convinced that she's been abducted by white slavers and is already on her way to the harem of some Middle Eastern sheik."

Colin forced himself to concentrate. "Any clue as to who the men were, or where they came from?"

"Just one. They used tracking dogs. Dobermans from what I could make out. But nobody seems to know anyone who has dogs like that."

"I do," Colin said softly, remembering the dark shape padding around Mallabone's garden the night he and Pearl had walked on the beach.

"Who?" Jill squinted in the sun as she looked up at him.

Mary Powell, having seen the last wicker hamper loaded on the Land Rover, made as though to join them, until she caught sight of the stricken look on Colin's face and heard the sound of their fierce whis-

129

pers. She turned away and disappeared into the cavernous, old-fashioned kitchen, leaving them alone in the yard.

Colin scuffed the toe of his sandals on the paving stones worn smooth by a century of traffic.

"Want to know something funny?" his voice was thick with impotent rage. "When I brought Wendy to Soufriere, I was handing her over to her enemies. This damn island is the headquarters of that hijacking ring. Bartholomew—that's who's got Wendy! She'd be better off if I'd never pulled her out of the water!"

"Colin," Jill said sharply. "Get hold of yourself! You had no possible way of knowing all this at the time."

"Thanks, Jill." He gave her arm a gentle squeeze. "I guess I *was* overreacting. It's just the thought of her and what those bastards will . . ." he choked and didn't complete the sentence.

Jill gave him a moment to recover before asking, "What are you going to do? There's no point in talking to the police."

"That's for damn sure," he said bitterly. "There'd be an all out race to be the first one to turn me over to Bartholomew." Over by the old stables something fell to the ground with a loud plop. He paused and raised an inquiring eyebrow.

"It's just the monkeys," Jill told him. "They're always throwing things down from the trees. You were about to tell me what you planned to do. Remember?"

"It's a little hazy at the moment, I'm afraid. But I do have some kind of an 'in' with that crowd. . . ."

"I know," she interrupted. "I heard about that party at Mallabone's."

"Oh?" he wondered just how much she had heard, but decided not to pursue the matter.

"It's a bit more than that," he went on after a pause.

"But the point is, I can snoop around and maybe come across something that will lead to her."

"Oh, Colin, can't you see how insane that is? They're bound to force your name out of her, and then they'll turn on you."

"It's the only shot we have."

Jill started to protest but the stubborn look on his face told her it would be useless. She gave in gracefully. "Stay and have lunch with us, at least, before you go charging back to town."

It was a hasty meal, filled with long awkward pauses. Andrew Powell was absent; he would stay out in the cane fields until nightfall. Mary took one look at their worried faces and said, "Something terrible has happened to that lovely girl and you're not going to tell me."

"Right. On both counts." Colin managed a wintry smile.

He held Jill briefly in his arms before he climbed into the Skoda. "Oh, Colin, everything's gone so helplessly wrong," she whispered against his shoulder.

The road was littered with cane stalks that had fallen from the overloaded wagons, and clogged with trucks and tractor trains plying back and forth between the fields and sugar factories. Whole families labored in the fields, cutting and loading the green cane. It was a scene from another century. For a fleeting moment Colin's thoughts strayed from Wendy to wonder how long this white plantocracy could last. If not Bartholomew, then the winds of change would surely blow it into the limbo of history.

Three bulky brown envelopes were neatly arranged on his hotel room bed. Each one was stuffed with well-used American currency in denominations of one hundred dollars or less. The first envelope also contained a brief typewritten note: "Understand we have to talk. Please call 0749." The message was signed with the initial "M."

Rapidly, Colin counted the bills. Mallabone hadn't shortchanged him; there was excatly ten thousand dollars. Colin looked down at the small mountain of money on the bedspread then reached for the phone. The call would have to go through the hotel switchboard, but Mallabone would be aware of that. He was put through with a minimum of delay. The conversation was terse; mainly instructions from Tony on how to get to the government building where they would meet.

The air-conditioning unit in the window of Mallabone's office dripped and wheezed asthmatically, but it brought some relief from the stifling midafternoon heat. Tony opened with compliments that were obviously sincere about the way Colin had brought off his assignment. Then he came directly to the point.

"I gather you discovered something you weren't supposed to know, and got a bit of a shock?"

"You could say that."

"Pity. Well, what can I say, old man? You were misled, but only partially. The main function of that operation is to bring out artifacts, just as I told you. In fact the system was already in place when the opportunity came along to move some shipments of heroin from the Middle East through it. It was, quite simply, too lucrative to pass up. There, now you know everything."

Not by a damn sight, Colin thought to himself, but he said, "The key word is 'lucrative.' I'm the one who's taking the risks, so I want part of the action."

"Ah." Tony didn't bother to hide his relief as he tilted back in the swivel chair and murmured, "Well, I must concede that your contribution is vital. Why don't we just double the previous figure. Including the bonus, of course."

"And including the first trip?"

"You drive a hard bargain." Tony sighed and stood up. "Very well. The money will be delivered tonight."

"When's the next flight?" asked Colin as Mallabone escorted him to the door.

"It all depends on how quickly they can organize things at the other end. There are a lot of delicate arrangements that must be completed before a caravan can be assembled. But it will be soon."

He opened the door and accompanied Colin down a wide corridor dappled with patches of sunlight and shadow where the shutters had been half-opened to catch the faint whisper of the trades. Bartholomew, unmistakable in his white suit, was coming toward them. He seemed preoccupied; he gave Mallabone a jerky nod, stared blankly at Colin, who had opened his mouth to speak, and hurried on.

"You must forgive His Excellency," Tony murmured as he placed a hand on Colin's elbow to indicate that they should turn down the next corridor. "He has much on his mind, as I am sure you can appreciate. Affairs of state and all that."

Colin had heard stories of Bartholomew's voodoo activities and privately decided that the man was in some kind of trance. But aloud, he said, "Sure, I understand. Give him my regards, will you?"

"Of course." Mallabone remained just inside the entrance door as Colin walked out into the hot sun. Two Mongoose sentries presented arms with a great clashing of their assault rifles.

Chapter Thirteen

Wendy coughed and spat out a mouthful of salt water. Her stomach gave a sickening lurch as the cresting wave lifted the pirogue and catapulted it forward in a foaming cascade. She started to shut her eyes but changed her mind when she saw Dykstra looking at her. He was sitting with his back to the bow, facing her, and he actually seemed to be enjoying the wild ride.

Waiting for the inevitable moment when they would be spilled out and smashed against the black reef, Wendy comforted herself with the thought that death by drowning was preferable to survival at the mercy of Carl. Then, miraculously, they were gliding across a peaceful, palm-fringed lagoon to fetch up on a beach with a sudden bump.

"I've brought you a new guest, Leon." Carl used both hands to wipe the spray from his eyes. "She's really looking forward to your hospitality."

Leon muttered something unintelligible and busied himself with raking their footprints from the sand. It was clear he had little use for the white sadist.

Wendy was soaked from the drenching ride through the surf, but the noonday sun rapidly dried her out, leaving a residue of salt caking her skin. Their route skirted the base of the volcanic cone, through clumps of thick foliage still wet from a brief tropical shower. She broke off a cluster of leaves and rubbed their wet freshness against her cheeks.

The mournful *cuaco-coo-coo* of a wood dove called from the trees part way up the volcanic slope and was answered by another doleful refrain somewhere in front of them. The sounds were astonishingly lifelike, but she suspected they were signals from unseen watchers.

Leon angled to the left and they began to descend into a narrow ravine. The roots of gnarled and twisted trees writhed across the rocky surface, clinging for a foothold on the precipitous incline. The walls closed around them, shutting off the sunlight and plunging them into a cool, twilight gloom. Carl pushed his way into the lead when they reached the cindery floor of the chasm.

The zombie sprang from behind the tree, and Wendy let out a small shriek. She leaped sideways, keeping her balance only by grabbing at a bush whose thorns pricked her palm. The creature's face glowed with fluorescence, and it groaned mournfully as it swayed from side to side. Her nerve ends were still tingling moments after she realized the apparition was only a dummy.

Carl had turned around to watch her reaction, gloating over her discomfiture.

"Wha' fo' you do dat, mon?" Leon grumbled as he pushed the spring-loaded contraption back into its hiding place.

"Wendy likes a little joke, don't you, doll?" Carl gave a short bark of laughter. "There are playful little gadgets like this fellow scattered all over the island. Except most aren't as harmless. Just in case any strangers manage to make it through the reef and start poking around."

He glanced back over his shoulder at her. "Of course, anyone trying to escape from the island could blunder into one of the booby traps just as easy. Neat, eh?"

"Ah'll take de lead, mon." Leon sounded thoroughly disgusted.

The entrance to the cave was a hole in the ground hidden behind a large chunk of lava. Leon disappeared into it, then his head popped back into view and he guided Wendy's foot onto the top rung of a ladder. Dim sunlight filtered down through the hole, filling the interior of the cave with a pale greenish light. Water dripped from gray-white stalactites and splashed into the puddles of water that covered most of the floor.

Leon took her hand and guided her deeper into the rocky chamber, warning her not to turn her ankle on the round, slippery stones. He paused before an opening that was a darker circle of gray near the base of the far wall.

"Hab to go on hands an' knees for a bit." Leon's solicitude was nothing less than bizarre under the circumstances, but it sounded sincere enough. He squatted on his haunches and squirmed his way into a tunnel.

Carl's hands reached out and squeezed her rump painfully as she crawled into the opening. The walls were dank and sticky with salt and the blackness was absolute. Finally Wendy saw a faint glow of light spilling around a corner where the tunnel veered sharply to the left. The height of the roof gradually increased, and she was able to stand almost upright by the time they reached the bend.

The light was coming from a small cavern festooned with stalactite chandeliers and with rivulets of water running down the walls. A raised stone ledge ran along the middle of the floor. It was covered with palm fronds to make a crude couch. A sentry in green Mongoose fatigues emerged from behind a rock wall and silently stationed himself by the tunnel opening.

"I'm going to leave you for a while, dollface," Carl murmured. "But don't you worry, I'll be back!" He pointed to a basin of water and told her she could wash up if she liked.

Shivering in the damp air of the cave, Wendy dipped her hands in the soapy water and rinsed the salt from her face. She longed to strip off her clothes and wash all over, but the sentry's unblinking gaze scuppered that idea. Drying herself with the threadbare scrap of towel, she sat down on the palm fronds with her legs drawn up and arms locked defensively around her knees.

Her mind welcomed even the thought of Bartholomew as a means of holding her immediate future at bay. He had paid her a second visit late last night. When his brief and distasteful lovemaking was over, he asked her once again to name her rescuers. He shook his head sadly when she refused and told her she was to be interrogated.

"I beg you not to persist in your folly too long. It would be a shame to see such beauty disfigured." He spoke with the matter-of-factness of one whose power was absolute. "But I have instructed Carl he can do whatever is necessary." He sighed gustily. "That boy can be so impetuous at times."

She had dropped to her knees and seized his hands imploringly. They still gave off the icy chill of the grave. Scowling with what might have been embarrassment, he freed them with an abrupt jerk. But he seemed not to suspect her true motive. So the frigid stigmata was always with him. The small victory of

138

gaining this knowledge gave her morale a perceptible boost.

Uncrossing her legs, Wendy felt a sharp need to go to the bathroom. She hadn't been for hours, not since Carl had hustled her on board the launch, just as the sun was appearing on the horizon. The sentry didn't give her any argument. He took her to another cave, deeper in the labyrinth and where the slow surging hiss of the sea could be faintly heard through the rock walls. Wooden slats had been placed across a narrow fissure. It was obvious that a number of men were quartered in the system of caves.

With a gesture of his rifle, he indicated a pail of seawater that she could use for flushing. Wendy toyed with the idea of dashing its contents in his face and making a bolt for it, but he kept well out of range, his rifle at the ready and watching her relieve herself with an unblinking stare.

They must have been back in the main cave for almost an hour before Carl returned. He was carrying a black box the size of a small suitcase. Two young Mongoose thugs trailed after him.

"You sure made a big hit with the 'man,'" he said conversationally as he unsnapped the catches. "He'll be very pleased with both of us if you talk without getting yourself all messed up."

Slowly, using both hands, he removed the dark glasses. The poached-egg eyes stared down at her with unpitying malevolence, and Wendy saw the bitterness twist his lips as she shrank back in revulsion. Then he bent over the open case and carefully lifted out a set of electrodes and dangling black wires. She licked lips gone suddenly dry.

Then rough hands pressed her down on the slab, and Carl was removing her clothes. There was a sharp

139

intake of breath from one of the guards when her silky thatch of black pubic hair was exposed.

Wendy's brain was on fire with the waves of unbearable pain pulsing deep inside her skull. Carl's face was a fuzzy white and blue balloon looming over her, yelling at her to talk and stop being such a bloody fool. Then his fingers were moving over her body, and she began to scream. Although the electrodes were attached to her nipples and inserted in her vagina, the real white-hot pain was in her head, searing across the synapses and threatening to blow her mind apart. Finally it subsided and she could hear her own screams echoing around the vaulted dome. She choked them off and turned her face away. The rock slab was slick with the sweat that had poured from her body. Carl cupped his hands around her cheeks and turned her head to face him.

"You got guts, dollface, I'll say that. But all you're doing is making things tougher for yourself.

"Look at this." He reached into the case and held up a shiny black rheostat. "If I turn this thing up high enough it will overload your circuits permanent-like. Your headspace will be nothing but a mess of blown fuses."

He removed the electrodes from her private parts, wiping them on the same cloth Wendy had dried herself with. Then, while she whimpered with fear and struggled in the brutal grip of the guards, he taped two metal disks to her forehead, one on each side. With helpless fascination Wendy watched his thumb and forefinger slowly turn the rheostat knob to the right.

Her body arced until she felt her spine would snap. Then the convulsions hit her. As though she were looking on from a great distance, she watched her legs thrash the air. She knew she was screaming, although no outside sound could penetrate the roaring inside her skull. She fought to hold out until a merciful oblivion would strike, but her lips were begging for the torment to stop, crying out that she would tell him whatever he wanted to know.

For a moment Carl let her float in a pain-free world. Then he said, "Let's hear it, dollface."

"I was picked up by a schooner."

"The name?"

"*Antilles Rose.*"

"Who was on board?"

"Just the crew. I . . . I don't know their names. Except for the captain—they called him Capt'n Johnny." As she spoke the name, she realized that she had betrayed Colin. It would be a simple matter for them to check out the schooner and discover that he had been on board that trip. But that would take time. . . .

Carl's rough voice broke into her misery. "Does this Capt'n Johnny know about me?"

She rolled her head from side to side while those unfinished eyes studied her. Finally, he muttered, "Okay, I'll buy that. But you're holding something back on Carl, baby. And that ain't nice."

He gave the rheostat knob a quick twist, and once more the pain stabbed deep inside her skull. After a few seconds he turned off the power and her writhing body fell back on the stone ledge. She smelt the pungent odor of urine and knew it was her own.

"There was a white man there, too," she whispered.

"Are you going to make me tear this out of you, word by fucking word? His name, for Christ's sake."

"Colin. Colin . . . Townsend." She wondered if she would ever be able to forgive herself.

"Sweet Jesus!" Carl breathed. The hotshot pilot that Mallabone preened himself on recruiting, was a goddamned spy. Wait till Bartholomew got a load of this!

But Carl had second thoughts almost immediately. The homosexual Englishman was too dangerous to fool with. The safest course would be to report directly to Mallabone and give him a chance to clean up his own mess.

The swift tropic dusk was poised to fall when Carl stepped outside the principal entrance of the network of caves. It was on the windward side of the small island, screened from the sea by a jumble of rocks. He paused for a moment to take a few deep breaths of fresh air before beginning the scramble up the volcanic cone. Leon kept his sideband radio transmitter up there; near the peak to be above any obstructing land mass.

The air was suddenly filled with the unmistakable whine of turbo engines which quickly built to a straining crescendo. Carl stopped climbing and stood rigid as though transfixed by the earsplitting scream. Silently he mouthed "Shit! Shit! Shit!" in a venomous litany.

That interfering bastard Townsend was taking off for South America! Maybe the son of a bitch would crash. But there was only the sound of engines being throttled back and then gradually fading in the distance.

Chapter Fourteen

The bottom edge of the sun was touching the sea when Colin trimmed the Otter for level flight at twenty meters. He was flying directly into it, but its orange glow had lost its burning glare. The sky was free of clouds and the horizon was clear and distinct. Colin pulled off his Bausch & Lomb glasses and stared directly at the rapidly descending sun, trying not to blink.

The light was turning yellow as the last slice of the sun fell below the horizon and then he saw it—the quick flash of light that was greener than emerald and gone in the blink of an eye. The last time he had seen the green flash must have been before his family had lost High Trees and moved to Albertstown. There was a hill behind the house he used to climb at dusk when conditions were just right; no clouds and a crystal clarity to the air.

Six hours of nerve-wracking flying at wavetop level stretched in front of him, yet Colin felt more relaxed than at any time since Jill had told him about Wendy's capture. Trying to act natural around Mallabone and his cronies had taxed his acting abilities to the limit. But from a remark that Tony dropped he realized his strained behavior was being put down to the shock of discovering that he was up to his eyeballs in the hazardous occupation of dope smuggling. He hadn't managed to pick up so much as a whisper about a beautiful Chinese girl being held captive. Christ, she could be dead by now. Grisly images of what might have happened to her tumbled through his mind as the black airplane droned on through the night.

This time his route took him over the northern part of Venezuela. Climbing to 600 meters to clear a hump of land, he caught a fleeting glimpse of distant lights that could only be the Lake Maracaibo oil fields. The balloon-tired wheels were practically brushing the tree-tops, but he had learned to trust his instructions. Within the specified five minutes the land fell away and he put the Otter in a shallow dive before swinging north to home in on the beacon. The flarepots flickered to life only when the sound of his engines was almost overhead.

The same English speaking *mestizo* clambered aboard when the Otter rolled to a stop on the sandy soil. And there was the same long wait through the broiling heat of the day for the contraband caravan to appear. Colin kept to himself, sweating profusely, and unsuccessfully trying not to think of what might be happening to Wendy. A fat lot of help he was, sitting it out on this sun-blasted wasteland, nearly 1800 kilometers away from Soufriere.

He forced himself to lie down for a few hours in the afternoon. He awoke sticky and hot, but at least he had a reserve of sleep to get him through the return flight.

The cargo was the same assortment of wooden boxes and wicker baskets, including two long crates that took the combined effort of all the *mestizos* to get aboard. Colin had no doubt that if he pried the cover off, the grotesque face of a pagan idol would leer up at him. But inside the hollow shell of that idol there was bound to be a fortune in refined heroin. He had only the haziest notion of what it would bring, but, cut for the street, he was probably toting a million-dollar load.

A cooling onshore breeze had begun to blow by the time the laborious chore of refueling by hand was completed, and he had received the sealed instructions for the return leg from the *mestizo* leader. The Twin Otter trundled over the rough terrain, gradually picking up speed and bumping heavily into the air.

Colin found himself vaguely disappointed when he jumped down from the cabin and Leon made no comment about the landing. This time he had brought the airplane to a halt a full five meters from the barrier and without throwing it into an incipient ground loop. Made it look too easy, I guess. He grinned to himself at the thought, still feeling a sense of elation. If nothing else, this crazy business was sharpening his flying skills.

"What's eating on you, Leon?" he finally asked as the last crate was safely lowered to the ground.

"Nuttin', boss. Jes' got work to do," Leon grunted as he watched his squad of laborers disappear into the night with the crate suspended between two long poles. Accidentally or not, the muzzle of his Armalite always seemed to be pointed in Colin's direction.

"Well done, old chap." Mallabone's unmistakable drawl came from the shadows of the palm grove.

An unpleasant chill ran along Colin's spine, but he kept his voice casual as he slowly turned around. "Visiting the front lines, are you Tony?"

He was not reassured to see a revolver dangling from Mallabone's hand. The fastidious Englishman held the butt of the Smith & Wesson .38 between his thumb and index finger as if to have the least possible contact with the distasteful object.

"It seems we have a bit of a problem, old sod." Tony

stopped a few meters in front of Colin. The laborers were returning to push the black airplane under the canopy of trees, and Tony paused to watch them for a few moments before continuing. "The delectable Ms. Wong has been telling us all about her dramatic rescue at sea."

"So?" The sound of Colin swallowing was clearly audible.

"So we have to wonder about your motives in joining our merry little band."

"Money. What else?" Colin made a halfhearted attempt to bluff it out, knowing within himself that he would never be allowed to walk away with his life.

Mallabone saw the realization sink home. He spread out his hands in a half-regretful gesture and murmured, "Apologies and all that. But you can see that we can't have you toddling about on your own."

"Where is Wendy? I want to see her."

"That can be arranged." Mallabone's ready acquiescence took Colin by surprise until the Englishman added, "We are aware that she is vital to your continued cooperation."

Colin thought that one over as they scrambled down the steep slope to sea level. It could only mean that they intended him to complete the flights. The haunting calls of night birds followed their descent, and Colin realized that they were under constant surveillance. Bartholomew could have a bloody army stashed away here on Jumbie for all he knew.

Inside the first cave Leon fished out a flashlight from behind a rock and led the way into the dungeonlike blackness. Brown anemones hastily withdrew their waving tentacles as the light struck the shallow pools where they lived. Then the route angled upward through a smooth-walled lava tube. Halfway along, the tunnel abruptly narrowed, forcing them to crawl on their hands and knees. The gray lava walls were replaced with a layer of limestone which lasted until once more they were able to walk upright. Ahead of them, light seeped around the edges of a tarpaulin blocking the end of the passage.

"She's expecting you," Mallabone announced with the air of a gracious host. He brushed past to take up the head of their little column and drew back the tarp with a flourish.

Battery-powered lanterns lit up a scene of unearthly beauty. Chandeliers of translucent, milky-white stalactites, delicately tinged with green and vermilion, hung from the vaulted roof, and oily white and orange stalagmites rose from the floor like giant candles.

"Do be careful," Tony urged in playfully mincing tones. "We don't want to damage any of these precious things, do we?"

Colin ignored him. He was too busy searching the spectacular chamber for Wendy. Finally he spotted her, sitting motionless on a stone bench along the far wall. Her beautiful features were unmarked, and her movements were smooth and fluid as she rose to her feet. But her expression of abject misery stopped Colin in his tracks.

"I gave you away, Colin," she whispered in a voice bitter with self-loathing. "You save my life, and then I betray you." She touched her forehead. "They did something terrible to my head."

"You had no choice, Wendy. I know that." He reached out to hold her, but a guard made a warning sound in his throat and interposed his rifle between them. It was to be look but don't touch.

"You can see for yourself that she has come to no harm," Mallabone murmured.

Colin saw the look of incredulous contempt cross Wendy's face. There was nothing he could do about that at the moment, however.

"And she better not," he gritted. "If you expect any cooperation from me."

"Just so. Well, now that you've seen her, you better catch up on your sleep. You are going to need it before you're finished. I promise you that."

Once more Leon led the way, with an Armalite-toting guard bringing up the rear. Colin's sleeping quarters turned out to be a small cave with a roof that barely cleared his head. The walls were covered with a strange-looking white substance. He touched it gingerly and his finger sank into its spongy surface.

"Moonmilk." Leon told him.

Good God, is the man trying to seduce me? Colin kept his expression noncommittal as Mallabone flashed another smile. The Englishman had shared a late breakfast with Colin, then lingered on to chatter interminably in his piping voice.

Colin's bafflement grew as it became increasingly apparent that Mallabone was doing his best to charm him. The Englishman was practically *squirming,* and, as though unconscious of what he was doing, began to edge closer. Colin rewarded one of his verbal sallies with a grudging smile, which emboldened Tony to reach out and give his knee a playful pat.

Colin's right hand closed on the homosexual's slender wrist while he batted at the gun with his left. Tony let out a small shriek, and the Smith & Wesson clattered to the floor. Colin heard the sound of the guard's footsteps running along the passageway. The leather soles of his boots were slipping and sliding on the rocky surface as he pounded around the corner.

Without releasing his grip on the helpless Mallabone, Colin scooped up the pistol, his left hand fumbling awkwardly with the safety switch. He managed it somehow; the firearms course he had taken as part of the flying school's antihijacking precautions had insisted on the use of either hand. The guard slid to a halt at the sight of his boss with a blue-black pistol pressed against the back of his head.

"Tell him to drop the rifle and stand aside, Tony." Colin waited for the count of three, then added with quiet menace, "Do it, man. Or I'll blow your head off."

He felt the tremor run through Mallabone's thin frame, then Tony cleared his throat and croaked, "Do as he says."

Relief flooded through Colin as the guard, after a long moment's hesitation, finally shrugged and placed his weapon on the ground. Everything depended on Mallabone having enough clout so that his subordinates wouldn't dare try anything that might endanger his life.

"Now you're going to take me to Wendy." Colin backed up his command with a sharp twist of Mallabone's arm behind his back, bringing a gasp of pain from the homosexual.

Colin could sense the scrutiny of unseen eyes and the pressure of pent-up breaths as he and his prisoner made their way through the labyrinth. Somewhere behind them a small boulder rolled down from the wall, caroming off its fellows with a series of clinks. Hair stirred on the nape of his neck as he imagined a sharpshooter bracing himself for the shot.

"By the way, Tony," he said conversationally, "I've got the hammer cocked with my thumb. If that pressure is released for any reason, *any* reason at all, your head comes off. I just thought you should know that. In case you want to tell your men anything."

Despite the clammy dankness of the cave, Mallabone's *guayabera* shirt was splotched with dark patches of sweat, and he gave off the sharp reek of fear. The quaver in his voice was amplified by the echo. "Don't shoot. Stay back. That is an order!"

"That's telling them," Colin approved, then tensed as he spotted the tarpaulin curtain up ahead. It moved slightly and there was obviously someone standing right behind it. "Tell them to open it, Tony. All the way."

It was the same vaulted chamber with the breathtaking display of stalactites and stalagmites. Several lanterns still burned, their beams diffused by shafts of weak daylight that filtered down through cracks and fissures and bathed the grotto in a pale mauve color, unexpectedly making Colin think of Jill's eyes at nightfall.

He saw Leon first, then Wendy standing almost behind him, hand at her mouth and a look of incredulous hope dawning on her face.

"Ah admire your style, mon. Ah purely do." Leon shook his head with a small rueful smile.

"The airplane is refueled?"

Leon hesitated, then nodded affirmatively.

"Good. Now I want you to go up there and get your men rolling those boulders off the runway."

"You neber make it wit' two passengers, mon."

"You let me worry about that." Colin couldn't repress a quick grin at the terrified gasp that escaped from Mallabone's lips.

His arm was beginning to ache from the strain of keeping the pistol against Tony's skull. He prodded the Englishman into motion with another jerk of his wrist and told Wendy to follow. He had a bad moment wondering if someone would try and force a stalemate by grabbing her, but they must have decided he would never give up his chance to escape for a mere woman. There was no doubt they knew exactly what would happen to them if any harm befell Bartholomew's chief adviser.

Colin called a halt when they came to the narrow section of the volcanic tube.

"We'll have to crawl for a bit," he told Wendy. "I want you to go first. Can you hack it?"

She drew in a deep breath and nodded. Then Colin whispered fiercely in Mallabone's ear, "This gun won't be pointing at your head when we're in there, but you'll be every bit as dead with a bullet up your asshole. Understood?"

"Look, Townsend. *Nobody* is going to try anything. Believe me."

"Oh, I believe you, Tony." Colin grinned. "I just like hearing you say it. Tell you men one more time."

Once more the walls echoed with Mallabone's voice, ordering his men not to try any stunts.

The soles of Wendy's sandals disappeared into the mouth of the tunnel, and Colin ordered Mallabone to crawl in after her. At one point Wendy stopped and lay on her stomach, blocking their progress. Colin breathed in the musty smell of moist limestone and was just about to call out to her when he heard the scraping sounds that told him she was struggling forward once more.

The ladder, already in place, that led up to the mouth of the cave was the next spot where they might be vulnerable to an ambush. Colin solved that by climbing up the rungs backward and making Mallabone follow him, with the muzzle of the revolver staring him in the face all the way.

The sheer walls of the ravine loomed over them, blocking out the sun, but the air was wondrously fresh after the darkness of the caves.

"They've got booby traps all over the place," Wendy said. "You know, things that go bump in the night. To scare strangers off."

"Beautiful," Colin muttered. "Well, our friend here better make sure that we don't blunder into any, or my trigger finger may slip."

"Good lord, man, *I* don't know where they are," Mallabone expostulated.

"Seems like you better get us an escort then. Unarmed. To steer us around any traps."

With a Mongoose guide up front they began to scramble up the volcanic slope. They paused halfway up to give themselves a breather. Holding the gun pressed against Mallabone's skull, Colin switched hands and lowered his aching left arm. He shot a quick, anxious glance at Wendy.

She said, "I'm okay. Really." Again her hand went up to her forehead. "I get little blank spells every now and then, but even they seem to be passing."

Colin knew there was something wrong the moment they stepped onto the airstrip, but it took him a couple of seconds to pinpoint the trouble. The bloody wind had changed! The faithful trades had deserted them, and a dirty little gale was gusting in from the west.

Chapter Fifteen

Colin twisted in his seat and glanced back into the cabin. Mallabone was crouched against the bulkhead beside the rear door, his face ashen with shock. Colin had just told him he was to bail out during the takeoff run. He was so terror-struck at the prospect that he didn't seem the slightest bit aware of the gun Wendy was holding on him.

Leon was standing on the ground with his arms folded, looking for all the world like a man seeing off departing guests. Colin raised his hands in a half-salute and then firewalled the power levers. He was taking off downwind, figuring the extra altitude of the cliff gave him a marginally better chance than trying to clear the palm trees at the upwind end. But "marginal" was the operative word.

He had no idea what was going on behind him; the dicey takeoff demanded his full attention. He was pretty confident he had convinced Mallabone that they would crash for sure if he didn't jump. It would be that and not the gun in Wendy's hand that would make him go through with it. Colin hadn't felt any extra drag from the open door, but that didn't mean a thing when they were pulling this much power.

God, it was like they were *glued* to the ground. The wind was pushing them along, hurrying them toward the cliff. Without any conscious thought on his part, he began to move the yoke back and forth. Through the seat of his pants he felt the wheels straightening up as the weight pressing down on the undercarriage eased. Then the nose tilted ever so slightly forward. The old girl was telling him what to do! He was pumping the control like an Olympic sculler and she was lifting, sweet Jesus, she was lifting! His face was split with an exultant grin as the turboprop shook free of the earth and sprang into the air with three meters of runway to spare. Airplane jockeys who made a career of flying the Twin Otter boasted that she always had something new to teach them about herself. Now he knew what they meant.

With the turbos purring contentedly in a normal climb out he had a chance to check out the cabin. Mallabone was gone and the slipstream had forced the door closed. Wendy was crawling forward on her hands and knees. Engaging the autopilot, he went back to help her.

"Did we really get away?" she asked as he buckled her into the copilot's seat.

"For damn sure. And we've got enough fuel to leave them far behind."

"There's not enough fuel in the world to do that." She leaned back against the headrest with a small sigh.

Colin heard her all right but he made no reply. He concentrated on tuning the ADF, trying to find a radio station that would guide them north. He decided to head for Puerto Rico where they would have the best chance of contacting the U.S. authorities.

The airwaves were filled with broad West Indian accents going on about some cricket match. Colin twirled the dial, hoping to pick up a station that would identify itself.

"What th . . ." he stared in disbelief at the cracks radiating out from the small round hole in the windshield. The slipstream whistled in through the shattered side window, tearing and bending the broken strips of plexiglass.

He squinted under the port wing to try and pinpoint where the shot had come from, at the same time pulling the power levers back to flight idle and deploying full flaps. The manual said never to lower the flaps at cruising speed because it could bend the rods. To hell with that! Just as he threw the Otter into a tight right-hand turn, he caught a fleeting glimpse of his attacker.

It was a shabby Cessna 180 with great patches of metal showing through the paint. Only one man flew a crate that looked like that—Joshua Todd, the Koramantee. Leon must have radioed Todd to take off from Soufriere and intercept the escapers. Now Colin's own wing tip was blocking his view of the other craft.

Where was that bloody Cessna? Leaning forward with his face pressed against the pierced windshield, he strained to see under the wing. His own turning radius was so tight there wasn't another plane in the world that could get inside him, but that wouldn't stop the Cessna from zooming in from the outside and shooting up through his belly.

He rolled out of the turn just in time to see the 180 diving in from the west, a black shape against the sun. Colin slammed on power and pulled into a steep climbing turn. The Cessna flashed harmlessly by underneath, but then it was turning and climbing after him. The copilot's seat was empty which meant the rifleman was in the rear and free to shoot from either side.

Colin spared a quick glance at his passenger. Wendy

was pressed against the back of the seat with her arms tucked against her sides to stay out of the way of the yoke's violent movements. Beneath him the Cessna was turning to the left to put the sharpshooter in position for an upward shot. He dropped a wing and the Twin Otter plunged down toward the sea.

The Cessna dived after him, and the two monoplanes skimmed above the water like courting dragonflies. They should have been evenly matched, but Colin saw that his pursuer was slowly gaining. He remembered thinking the motor had a special note to it that day at the Soufriere airport. The only thing to do was to knock that damn Koramantee out of the sky.

Colin's heart beat faster as he checked the clearance between the wheels and the spinning propellers. Enough room to fit over the Cessna's rudder. He had the bigger and sturdier aircraft, but how often did *anyone* survive a midair collision?

Another star of cracks suddenly blossomed in the windshield on Wendy's side, making up his mind for him. He pulled back on the yoke and they shot skyward like an express elevator.

Todd had turned sideways to let the marksman get off his shot and had lost some ground as a result. But now he was climbing after them. Probably smacking his lips, too, thought Colin.

"Hang on," he shouted at Wendy and dumped the yoke forward, sending them screaming back down toward the Cessna.

"Do something, damn you!" he muttered through clenched teeth as the Cessna's sharklike snout grew larger in his shattered windshield.

"Got you!" he shouted when Todd finally turned to one side. Still diving, Colin flung the Otter into a gut-wrenching turn. When he pulled out halfway

156

through, the Cessna was just below and in front of the blur of his starboard prop. With the speed built up in the dive, the Otter's balloon tires drew level with the 180's tail fin, and Colin eased on right rudder to skid sideways. If he could bump their tail with the wheel he could disable the Cessna and maybe not inflict any fatal damage on his own airplane.

Too late he saw the Cessna bank to the left. The shriek of tortured metal overrode the noise of the engines as the propeller bit into the Cessna. Colin saw its tail disintegrate in a shower of fragments, and then the other plane dropped from sight. He felt a violent bucking of the yoke in his hands, and the Otter was vibrating at a rate which would tear her to pieces in seconds. Colin shut off the fuel to the starboard engine and the mad pounding eased. As the whirling propeller slowed, he saw one of its blades had been snapped off.

With the vibration temporarily under control, he looked around for the Cessna. It was going down in a flat spin, trailing its broken tail behind it as it drifted earthward in a series of lazy spirals.

It looked like it was going to be the kind of crash where there could be survivors. Colin trimmed the Twin Otter for single engine flight and watched the Cessna's death plunge. He saw its propeller suddenly stop spinning as Todd shut off power. Then it pancaked in, throwing up a great geyser of white water. It came to rest almost immediately, lying spread-eagled on the surface like a crippled seabird.

The figure of a man heaved itself out of the sea and climbed onto the wing. Then he crawled over to crouch on the almost submerged roof of the cabin. He kept glancing up at the low-flying Otter. It was the Koramantee and it looked like he was the sole survivor. The

157

Cessna's rudderless tail canted out of the water as its nose dipped further beneath the surface.

"That plane won't float much longer, will it?" Wendy asked.

Colin shook his head wordlessly. Their own situation was much more critical than he had first realized. The vibration had torn the engine right off its mounts, and it slumped alarmingly in the bottom of the cowling. The drag was something fierce, and there was no telling how much damage had been done to the wing structure itself. Well, they were still airborne. Gingerly he increased the power in the port engine and switched on the autopilot. Unsnapping his seat belt, he turned to face Wendy.

She was staring at him with an incredulous look. "You're going to help him, aren't you?"

He gave a sheepish grin. "He'd just be shark bait down there when night comes."

Kneeling beside the rear door, Colin made a final check of the rope knotted around Wendy's waist and told her, "When I raise my right hand you open the door and use your feet to push the life raft against it just hard enough to keep it open. When I drop my hand you kick it out with both feet. Okay?"

Disengaging the autopilot, Colin eased into a shallow 180-degree turn. She was one sick bird. Slowly he straightened her out and began his run.

The water was up to Todd's crotch now, and he was shaking his fist at the approaching airplane. Colin looked back over his shoulder and raised his hand. He saw Wendy gritting her teeth but she managed to get the door open and the rolled-up life raft kept it ajar.

The Koramantee dove head first into the water when he spotted the open door. Figures we're going to shoot him, Colin smiled grimly, and dropped his hand. The raft splashed into the water within ten meters of the downed airman's head. Banking for a final backward look, Colin saw that Todd had swum over to the raft and already had it half-inflated.

"Does that light mean anything?" Wendy pointed at the amber glow in the center of the control panel.

Colin jerked his gaze away from the disabled engine and swore helplessly. "Christ, yes. It means we're losing fuel. Fast. That propeller blade must have punctured the forward fuel cell."

He switched over to the aft cell. "It's bad but it's not the end of the world. We still have at least three hours' flying time."

They both stared in frozen disbelief as the second amber light blinked on. The low-level fuel lights were activated when there was only twenty minutes at maximum power remaining, but at the rate they were losing fuel that twenty minutes could become twenty seconds.

The jutting headland that marked the northern tip of Soufriere lay off their starboard wing. Another minute and he spotted a familiar landmark, the rusting hulk of *The Southern Cross,* a cruise ship that had gone aground one dark night more than twenty years ago. He and Robbie and Pierre Demaret had occasionally bicycled up there to fool around the wreck. There was a black sand beach in the small cove that was almost blocked by the luckless ship. The beach had a fairly steep slope, but it was clear of any large boulders; he remembered that because they had played scrub soccer on it.

They were coming up on the wreck now, its brown skeleton looking like an extension of the reef itself. The change in the wind had kicked up a nasty chop that smashed against *The Southern Cross,* swirling around the jagged gaps in its hull in a froth of white water. There'd be no swimming on the Atlantic side today.

The high-pitched whine of the turbo died away. No preliminary coughing or stuttering, it just stopped. They were suddenly conscious of the wind rushing through the bullet holes and flapping the strips of torn plexiglass. Colin saw Wendy's knuckles whiten as she gripped the seat cushion, but she made no sound.

With no power to offset the drag of the broken propeller, the Twin Otter had a frightening pull to the right. He had no choice but to increase his angle of descent to maintain the airspeed.

A flock of brown pelicans flapped awkwardly into startled flight from the wreck's canted deck. Its gutted superstructure loomed like the battlements of a Moorish castle. They were heading directly for it, like some World War II kamikaze pilot, but there was no other way to reach the beach. He thought of turning aside and trying to ditch, but the reef would tear them apart. From the corner of his eye he saw Wendy's legs move as she braced herself for the crash.

Colin was staring at the gaping hole where the bow anchor had once been secured. It was dead level with the Otter's blunt snout. Now! He popped full STOL flaps and hauled back on the yoke. The airspeed dropped alarmingly, but she was responding to the extra lift. He felt the incipient stall rippling through the controls, and the warning light flashed ominously as their shadow swept across the ship's buckled deck plates. The railings had long since been removed by looters. Jesus! The right wing was going to hit! It was the old liner's rakishly pointed bow that saved them; it was cut away just enough to let the aileron slip by. Colin dropped the nose a few degrees and somehow the astonishing aircraft picked up its injured wing.

They hit the beach hard and at the wrong angle. The nosewheel crumpled when it struck the sharp upward slope, plowing a furrow through the black sand. The Otter stood on her nose and threatened to flip over onto her back. But the drag of the heavy sand slowed her down, and she came to rest still upright but tilted forward and over on her right wing.

"You okay?" The shoulder straps were pressing painfully against Colin's ribs.

Wendy nodded. She even mustered a faint smile.

"Let's get out of here. Smartly." Colin pulled the pilot's door open and half-dragged her out, making her run across the sand until they were well clear of the upended airplane.

"I don't think anything's going to happen. Not with empty tanks. But you never can be sure." Colin shaded his eyes against the lowering sun, relieved to see that the black plane was above the high-water mark. The only sound was the faint cracking noises the port engine made as it cooled. She wasn't going to burn.

"You know what?"

Wendy shook her head.

"*I* have just declared war, by God!"

Unexpectedly, she laughed. A real laugh. "Oh, Colin, you're something else! You really are. A guy does his best to kill you and you hand him back his life. It'll be some war! But count me in!"

Impulsively, Colin bent to kiss those luscious lips. She averted her face, and he ended up with a patch of thin air, and feeling incredibly gauche.

"Look, I'm . . ."

"Don't say anything, Colin. Let's just forget it, can't we?"

"Okay. Have it your way. But we've got to get off this beach." He knew that word of his forced landing would sweep through the island like a cane fire and bring the Mongoose boys swarming around.

Chapter Sixteen

They walked side by side in stiff silence across a long stretch of arid open country, the sandy soil riddled with the burrows of land crabs. It was nightfall by the time they reached the bottom of the mountain range and began the climb up its lush slopes. The coming of darkness was the signal for a whistling frog to commence its unmusical serenade. After a few strident calls, it suddenly stopped. Colin froze in mid-stride. He touched Wendy's arm and pulled her behind the trunk of a towering *immortelle*. The aroma of nutmeg wafted through the night air as though someone had brushed against the seed-laden branches.

A ripple ran through the leaves, silvered by the dim light, and the dark shape of a man appeared between the rows of banana plants. His face was hidden beneath the peak of a military cap, and he was armed with an assault rifle. His footsteps made no sound on the spongy floor of the rain forest.

If he did his job properly and searched all the way round the huge tree, they were for it. Colin didn't dare switch off the safety on the S & W; the noise would give them away. He held his breath until the soldier was almost abreast of their position, then he gave Wendy's hand a gentle squeeze and they sidled sideways around the tree trunk. The slightest sound and they would be cut in two with a burst of automatic fire. Standing with his back pressed against the cool bark, Colin felt the pistol grip grow sweaty in his palm. Any second now the soldier would peer around the corner.

As unexpectedly as it had stopped, the whistling frog resumed its distinctive *bleep bleep*. Colin exhaled a long sigh. But he knew the reprieve was only temporary; it looked like they were carrying out a systematic search of the area all the way back to the beach. And the next member of the search party might turn out to be a little more dedicated. He whispered to Wendy that they would stay in the shelter of the tree for a few more minutes. She nodded and he leaned back against the trunk trying to work out whether it was possible to reach Palm Hill before daybreak.

He tensed as the frog switched off once again. High above them, a gentle breeze toyed with the leaves and red blossoms of the *immortelle,* but here on the ground everything was still.

"Don' do nothin' hasty, Mistuh Townsend." The soft slurred whisper came from the darkness. "Ah'm heah to help you, mon."

"Who are you?" Colin hissed in the general direction of the voice.

"Dat don' matter none. Excep' dat ah'm not Mongoose trash." A pause, then a muttered, "Ah'm comin' out now, mon."

There was a faint rustle of leaves and then a hulking young black man stood before them, a murderous cutlass gripped in his right hand.

"You stay heah an' dem Mongoose find you fo' sure. Dey really on de prowl tonight."

"And you can help us?" By now Colin had decided he was dealing with a member of the Soufriere Freedom Union. Throughout his stay in Soufriere he had heard

164

guarded whispers about the existence of the insurgent group.

"Yar," the newcomer answered, clearly relieved at the note of acceptance in Colin's voice. He whispered, "Follow me, an' don' make no din," and set off without a backward glance.

The Mongoose Gang was on the move, too. Three times the guerrilla guide, who at one point muttered that his name was Bob, motioned Colin and Wendy to remain hidden in the trees at the sound of trucks laboring up the hills in low gear. They were ready to dart across a narrow dirt road when they heard the fourth one coming. It pulled up with a squeal of brakes before a tightly shuttered, unpainted shack. A sergeant jumped down from the cab and hammered loudly at the door. The soft glow of a kerosene lantern leaked through the shutters and the door opened a crack. The burly sergeant kicked it wide open, sending the home owner reeling backward and dashing the lantern from his hand. Within seconds the straw stuffing of a burlap mattress burst into flames, and then the blaze was licking at the tinder-dry wooden walls.

The driver threw the truck into reverse and hastily backed it out of range while the troops, hooting with excitement, scrambled down from its box to watch the flames back-light the human forms scrambling out through the door. A naked boy, no more than five years old, came first, shooed along by his parents. Then a concerted whoop went up as an old woman tottered to the doorway, her cotton nightgown and crinkly white hair burning fiercely. Her limbs jerked in a macabre dance before she fell back into the inferno.

The daughter managed to open one of the shuttered windows and climbed out just as her denim shirt was beginning to smolder. She was running the instant she

165

touched the ground, trying to reach the safety of the woods. But the soldiers spotted her and they gave chase, their shouts blending into an animal-like roar. One, sprinting ahead of the pack with the speed of a trained athlete, brought her down in a flying tackle.

The mother was down on her knees, beseeching the sergeant to protect her daughter. Cowering next to Bob among the side bushes, Wendy almost gagged as the breeze carried the sickly sweet smell of the grandmother's burning flesh. Bob was testing the edge of the cutlass with his thumb, a look of helpless rage contorting his young face. The kneeling woman reached out to touch the sergeant, but he pushed her aside, sending her sprawling to the ground. The girl was naked now, brown skin gleaming in the light of the flames as she twisted and fought in a vain attempt to break free. She screamed only once, when they pinned her on the ground and the first man entered her. Wendy heard Bob's low groan of anguish and felt him tensing himself for a suicidal assault. She laid her hand on his rigid forearm and shook her head.

The sergeant ignored the gang rape, concentrating instead on the head of the unfortunate family. First he barked a question and then followed it with a blow of his open palm across the face. When the man kept shaking his head in mute agony, the sergeant began to pummel his midsection with hard chopping blows of his fist.

Nauseated with the mindless brutality, and helpless to intervene, Colin whispered, "We better move on while those sons of bitches are doing their thing."

Bob tried to reply but his voice choked in his throat, and Wendy saw the tears on his face before he turned away and crept along the ditch. Only the occasional spark still floated up from the dying fire by the time he

166

finally led them, crawling on their bellies, across the road.

Land crabs scuttled underfoot, rustling through the litter of fallen palm leaves. Bob held up his hand as a signal for them to halt at the edge of a copra-drying yard. The long wooden racks cast bands of deep shadow in the cold light of the stars. The unseen skittering of the crabs was the only sound. The racks were empty and looked as though they hadn't been used for a long time. Bob did something with his hands to make the *clack clack* of a cricket and was answered from the depths of the yard. Then Pierre Demaret emerged from under one of the racks, brushing pieces of dried coconut husk off his clothes.

"I see you have not lost your knack of getting into scrapes, old friend." A wide smile lighting his face, Pierre held out his hand. Colin grasped it warmly, feeling a surge of affection for his childhood companion.

Demaret bowed with a grace that was completely natural over Wendy's hand. Then he brushed off the last piece of husk clinging to his shirt and said, "I thought for sure they had me about an hour ago, Bob. And they would have, too, if they hadn't been too damn lazy to poke around in the trash."

He took a second, closer look at the youth. "What happened, Bob?" His tone was that of a man who has learned to expect the worst.

"Dey got me family." The young man was close to tears. "Burned down de house an' kill me ol' gran'mother. An' . . . ." he broke off, unable to complete the sentence. Finally he blurted, "An' I's couldn't do nothin' to halt dem. Not one fuckin' thing!"

"Bastards!" Pierre breathed, while Colin and Wendy gazed at each other, aghast.

167

"Jesus, Bob." Colin muttered. "We didn't realize . . ."

"I don' wan' talk about it no more." Bob turned away to hide the tears he could no longer hold back.

Pierre clasped his shoulder for a moment, shaking his head in silent sympathy, then turned back to Colin. "Where do you fit into all this?"

"Damned if I know," Colin muttered. They had moved into the trees, and their outlines were obscured by zebra shadows cast by the upright bare trunks. "I take it you have something to do with the S.F.U.?"

"You certainly can take it that we are not among Bartholomew's greatest admirers," Pierre replied. He paused, then continued thoughtfully. "I have a pretty good idea of what has happened to you and Miss Wong." He gave Wendy another courtly bow. "What I need to know now is what you intend to do from here on."

"Fight. There's no safety anywhere for either of us while that crew remains in power."

"That is what I was hoping to hear." Pierre cuffed Colin's arm then continued briskly, "Come, we have some hiking to do this night."

"Sorry about the field rations, but we can't risk a fire." Pierre handed Wendy a banana and then a wooden plate of cold rice, pigeon peas and a cold chicken leg. In the early morning sunlight Colin was shocked by his old friend's appearance. The good looks, so much like Pearl's, were still there, but they were spider-webbed with faint lines of strain and the several days' growth of stubble was flecked with gray.

Spooning a mouthful of rice, Colin glanced around the encampment. It was an abandoned cacao plantation with the small, circular trees spaced at regular intervals like so many beach umbrellas. The broken pattern of light and shadow provided an almost perfect concealment for the figures sprawled on the carpet of dead leaves.

"This reminds me of a tropical version of Robin Hood and his Merry Men," Colin said in an effort to dispel his concern over Pierre's appearance.

"Not so bloody merry," Pierre muttered.

Colin saw what he meant. As near as he could make out there were twenty guerrillas in the camp, including two busty, high-rumped black women cradling Uzi submachine guns equipped with banana clips. Most of the men wore their hair in the "dred" curls that were the emblem of the Marxist faction. All of them were in their late teens or early twenties. They were a sullen, unprepossessing lot, although there was no doubt they regarded Pierre as their leader. However, thought Colin, if they ever do succeed in knocking Bartholomew off, Pierre will have his hands full keeping this bunch in line.

Pierre's voice interrupted Colin's thoughts. "Have you heard anything about that thundering great statue Bartholomew has commissioned?"

"Only a few whispered jokes on the cocktail party circuit."

"Can you feature it? The country is bankrupt and he spends a million U.S. dollars on a statue of himself. On horseback, yet. And the man can't ride anything livelier than the back seat of a Mercedes."

"When's the unveiling?"

"Any time now. Would you believe Bartholomew wanted to have it when that American senator comes here on his state visit? Tony Mallabone had a hell of a time persuading him that the senator would not be impressed with aid money being used for such purposes."

169

"You seem to be pretty well informed."

"We have a few sources." Abruptly Pierre got up and took his empty plate over to rinse it in a plastic bucket. He returned to the subject later that morning when he and Colin were alone.

"We've already lost five men trying to knock over that monument," he remarked conversationally.

"You figure it's that important?"

"I do. Not only is it a symbol of Bartholomew's blind arrogance, but if it *were* to be toppled, the people would take it as a sign that *he* could be too. And I'm convinced it would have a real impact on Bartholomew himself. He's superstitious as hell."

"How were your people killed?"

"We made two attempts to destroy it. Both times they were caught by the guards who, incidentally, are the cream of the Mongoose Gang. The two who weren't shot in the course of the raids were pitched over the cliff." He plucked a ripe cacao pod and frowned at it absently. "So much in this bloody island is just going to waste." Dropping the pod on the ground, he continued, "If nothing else, we've proved that the statue is impregnable to a ground attack. And it can't be got at by water, except maybe by a band of expert mountaineers. It's at the top of a cliff that rises straight out of the sea. So that passing ships will have a good view of His Excellency."

"You haven't mentioned an air attack."

"No. I haven't, have I?" Pierre murmured. "And, of course, that's the only way it could be brought off. Want me to tell you about it?"

"You mean I have a choice?" Colin grinned down at his mulatto friend. For a moment it was as though the years had rolled back and they were planning one of their youthful escapades. Growing up on a Caribbean island like Soufriere provided plenty of scope for that kind of action.

"You might start with the airplane," he went on. "If you were thinking of the Twin Otter, forget it. She's bent pretty badly."

"Not to mention that she'll be under constant guard. But not to worry, we have access to a plane that is ideal for the purpose. A Taylorcraft. Very quiet."

Colin raised an eyebrow. The Taylorcraft was an interesting piece of equipment, a replica of an old-fashioned high-wing monoplane. The last original was built in 1949, but the basic concept was so valid that somebody had gotten hold of the dies and forms and started manufacturing replicas.

"It would have to be a night mission," Pierre was saying. "The idea is you would dive in without power, completely blacked out, drop the bomb and disappear over the cliff. With any luck it'll all be over before the guards figure out what's coming down."

"Yeah, sure," Colin grunted skeptically. Pierre waited in silence and finally Colin asked, "Who would handle the bomb?"

"An expert." Pierre's smile was sardonic. "A graduate of the Cuban school for foreign national agents, no less. They taught her all there is to know about terrorist bombing methods."

Colin did a double take at the "her," but swallowed his surprise and asked, "How do we do this without blowing ourselves up? We'd be right on top of the target and the airplane will practically be standing still."

"Seems like it's time to consult the expert." Pierre jerked his head and one of the machine-gun-toting girls sauntered over to them. She was dressed in crotch-tight jeans, and her heavy breasts moved under a coarse khaki sweater. Her features were broad and rounded, and her skin was the color of chocolate fudge.

Her name was Carla; Colin guessed to himself that it had been something else before she went to Cuba, and he was right.

"Fuse," she said laconically when Colin repeated his question. "We figure out how much time we need and set the fuse. But it's got to be damn short, so some hero-type bastard can't pick it up and heave it over the cliff. You tell me our approximate speed and I'll take it from there."

"Our speed will not be less than one hundred kilometers per hour. How low do we have to be for you to make the drop?"

"In order to make sure of hitting the target, no higher than ten meters."

"Jesus on a crutch!" Colin exploded. "What are you planning to do? Lay a wreath on the damn thing?"

A faint look of contempt crossed the guerrilla's young face. Then she shrugged and turned away. "I'll start putting things together."

The monument site was a pinprick of light on the edge of the curving line that divided the dark land from the leaden sheen of the sea. There was no moon. Colin cut the power, feeling the jagged crack in the throttle knob with his thumb, briefly amused at his own naivete in automatically assuming that he would be flying a replica of the Taylorcraft. This ancient bird was one of the originals, and she showed every year of her age.

"How long before we're over the target?" Unconsciously Carla was whispering as though those on the ground could hear her voice. It was eerily silent, with the monoplane gliding down through the night like a monstrous bat.

"Four minutes." He raised the nose a fraction to keep the airspeed from building up. The instrument lights were extinguished, but you didn't need instruments to fly this baby. She told you everything you needed to know through your fingertips.

Carla was counting under her breath. With two minutes to go she reached down and picked up the homemade bomb at her feet. It was a crude affair; dark woollen blankets wrapped around sticks of dynamite and taped together.

Colin peered through the windscreen for any sign of human activity around the statue. He was damned if he would blow up innocent workmen. But the lighted area looked to be deserted. Pierre had been right about them only working in daylight and that the lights were merely used to discourage prowlers. The monument, foreshortened from this angle, was surrounded by plywood and canvas screens. The gigantic bronze horse reared on its rear feet, and Bartholomew's right arm was raised in an imperial salute.

There was a rush of wind as Carla forced the door open on her side. The bomb was cradled in her lap, and she held what looked like an electric cigar lighter in her right hand. The sharp stink of cordite stung Colin's nostrils, and he saw a dull red glow at the end of the fuse. Suddenly there was an orange flash from the ground as someone opened fire on them. Another orange flash stabbed the darkness, and Carla made a strangled, wheezing sound and a thick gush of her blood splashed against the windscreen.

Colin could hear the fuse hissing like a venomous snake as it smoldered on Carla's lap. She was dead; he knew that from the way she slumped in her seat.

173

Visions of the bomb getting stuck in the door or lodged in the undercarriage raced through his mind, but he had to get rid of it before it blew up right beside him. He reached over and gave it a mighty push, sending it tumbling into the night. Then he hit the switches, praying that the aged engine would turn over.

The concussion from the explosion tossed the light plane like a toy, blowing it away from the cliff face. There was nothing to do but ride it out and hope that the force of the explosion wouldn't rip the wings off the frail craft. The motor burped blue smoke and caught. He power-dived straight down to the sea, picking up the shelter of the cliff and finally breaking free of the turbulent air. Leveling out, he took stock of his situation.

The airstream was holding the door closed, but it wasn't latched. He reached over Carla's body and secured it. The cabin reeked with the warm smell of her blood. She had been a fanatic Marxist, and maybe she was happy to die like that, pressing home the attack against the fascist enemy.

There was a fire on the cliff. Through the binoculars he made out the remains of the canvas and wooden screens burning briskly. The flickering light illuminated the broken statue lying on its side, and Colin's lips tightened with grim satisfaction when he saw that Bartholomew had been decapitated.

Chapter Seventeen

The real-life Bartholomew was throwing a tantrum. He ripped a black and white photograph of the shattered statue into small pieces and flung them in Mallabone's face.

"Imbecile! Fool!" he stormed. "The whole world will be laughing at Bartholomew."

Mallabone bore the tirade without flinching, carefully refraining from brushing off the bits of paper. It was not unknown for Bartholomew's rages to end in the death of the unfortunates who were the cause of his displeasure. Mallabone wasn't worried about that happening to him. Not this time. The dictator still needed him too much. But Bartholomew was getting less tractable of late.

"And as for you!" Bartholomew hawked and spat in Joshua Todd's face. A knot of small muscles suddenly bunched at the corner of the Koramantee's jaw, but he held himself rigidly motionless.

"You don't belong in the same sky with Townsend," Bartholomew sneered. He turned back to Mallabone. "Where the hell is Carl? I need him to hunt these bastards down."

Mallabone detected the slight change in the dictator's voice. The dressing down had been going on for half an hour, and Bartholomew's wrath was abating.

"He's due back here tonight. The capture of the yacht

175

went very smoothly," Tony added, eager to give Bartholomew something positive to think about. "She's on her way north with a full load."

"Any survivors this time?" Bartholomew asked and gave a small grunt of satisfaction when Mallabone smilingly shook his head.

Todd surreptitiously wiped the sputum from his face, keeping his lids lowered to hide the murderous rage in his eyes.

"We don't know for sure it was Townsend driving that airplane," he muttered.

"It was Townsend," Bartholomew said with finality. "Somehow he's managed to link up with those S.F.U. traitors."

"You want Townsend, I can deliver him," Todd grated.

Mallabone shot him a bright, speculative glance, started to say something then checked himself.

"I would like that very, very much," Bartholomew said softly. "Alive. Understand?"

A red light flashed and Mallabone pressed the intercom switch. Bartholomew frowned at the interruption, but Tony assured him it must be important or Pearl wouldn't have put it through.

Pearl's voice was saying, "Colonel Stroud is here. Says he must see His Excellency."

"Send him in," Tony ordered, at the same time dismissing Todd with a curt, "That will be all for the moment, Joshua." The pilot and the mercenary commander passed each other in the open doorway.

The colonel's gaze went directly to Bartholomew, and an expression of relief flitted across his face. He snapped off a salute.

"Well, Colonel?" Bartholomew studied the polished tip of his swagger stick.

"We ... we received a report that you had been assassinated, Excellency."

For the next few seconds the only sound was the muted whine of the air conditioner. Then Bartholomew's laugh boomed out. "As you can see, the report of my death is greatly exaggerated."

Overcome with his own humor, he doubled over the desk, his shrewd eyes covertly checking to make sure his audience appreciated the joke properly. Mallabone was making a big production out of it, placing his hand over his mouth as though to choke back gales of laughter.

"Where did it happen?" Bartholomew's voice was suddenly icy.

"At the Fineberg yacht christening."

"I see." Bartholomew fell silent for a moment. Aaron Fineberg was one of a small colony of expatriates who found refuge on Soufriere from the jail terms that awaited them at home. But the cost of the dictator's hospitality came high. Nine months ago he had ordered Fineberg to have a yacht built to make it look like Soulfriere's ship-building trade was recovering.

"Which one was it?" The question was directed at Mallabone.

"Number three."

"There's only one left, now."

"Right. The best one as it happens. And the clinic is processing two more." Mallabone was referring to the only enterprise that still prospered under Bartholomew's regime—a medical school where students who couldn't meet the entrance requirements of the American universities could, by paying exorbitant fees, obtain a degree. A busy and very lucrative plastic surgery clinic had developed as an offshoot of the facility.

"How did it happen?" Mallabone asked the colonel, almost idly.

"He was shot. Twice. With a high-powered rifle."

Bartholomew's temper suddenly exploded. "So your Mickey Mouse security force can't even protect me from a goddamn rifle!"

"The sniper died within minutes," Colonel Stroud said lamely. Mallabone stiffened slightly at that, but Bartholomew didn't notice. "And what bloody good is that?" he was thundering.

"This could work to our advantage," Mallabone murmured.

Bartholomew scowled at him, then his brow cleared. "You mean . . . ?"

"A reincarnation, no less. Everyone believes you are dead, then you suddenly appear in their midst. A miracle."

"And people will forget about the statue?"

"Exactly," purred Mallabone.

"I wouldn't put it past you to have engineered the whole thing." He beamed fondly at his white adviser and murmured, "My old fox."

Pearl's voice was on the intercom again, telling them that a crowd was gathering outside the gates.

"That is to be expected," Mallabone replied. "What is their mood?"

"Quiet. So far. It seems there's a rumor that the president is dead."

"It's time for you to show yourself, Excellency." Mallabone paused and added with the ghost of a sardonic smile. "To reassure your loyal subjects."

Bartholomew hesitated. "This could be dangerous This is the *real* me, you know."

"No harm will come to you. Is Baron Samedi not the Chief of the Legion of the Dead?"

Bartholomew gave an evil little chuckle. "It'll sure scare the hell out of some of those geeks. Let's go."

An awestruck murmur rippled through the crowd when Bartholomew made his appearance. He stood for a moment on the porch before slowly descending the stairs. Whispers of "Baron Samedi" could be heard on all sides. Then the hand-clapping started, scattered at first, but rapidly growing in volume as the hapless citizens outdid each other to prove their unswerving loyalty to the tyrant. Men and women fell to their knees, and many banged their foreheads on the hot pavement in abject supplication.

Bartholomew stopped a few meters from the iron fence and stood with his hands on his hips.

"I say to my enemies, who are also the enemies of Soufriere—" he paused for effect and was rewarded with a chorus of "Amens." "I say to them that Bartholomew will not be cast down. If he falls, it is only to rise again."

A chorus of "praise be's!" and "hallelujahs" greeted this pronouncement. By now all the people were on their knees and the eyes of some were beginning to roll up until only the white showed. Bartholomew glanced back to where Mallabone stood beside the Administration Building's entrance and got a quick negative shake of his head.

"Pass the word, my children," he was wrapping it up quickly, "that Bartholomew lives so that he may continue his work for his country and his people."

"First rate." Mallabone congratulated him as a sentry clanged the metal door shut and the crowd began to disperse, muttering excitedly among themselves.

Pearl met them in the long cool hallway. "Senator Nesbitt's secretary is on the line. He sounds very upset."

Mallabone scooped up the white phone. After a few seconds he covered the mouthpiece and whispered to Bartholomew, "The wire services have picked up the assassination story."

Then he was murmuring unctuously into the mouthpiece. "I assure you, His Excellency is standing right next to me at this very moment. In the absolute pink of condition. As His Excellency himself said," Mallabone paused for an appreciative chuckle, "reports of his demise have been greatly exaggerated."

The conversation went on for another five minutes with Mallabone doing most of the listening and uttering soothing reassurances from time to time.

"They're still coming," he said as he replaced the receiver. "They'll be flying in from Barbados late this afternoon. That secretary chap sounds like he's ready to shit his pants. He has visions of them all being massacred as soon as they stepped off the plane."

"You should have let them stay away," Bartholomew grumbled.

"I don't think you realize just how important this visit is to us. If the senator doesn't show because of the threat of violence, the appropriation will be stopped. You can count on that. And his visit has to go off perfectly. With absolutely no incidents. Remember, it's only for three days."

"There are a lot of things we should be doing in those three days," Bartholomew objected.

"I know. But they'll just have to be postponed. Everything must be absolutely cool while the senator is on the island. And don't forget you're hosting a big jump up for him on the final night."

Bartholomew's gloomy expression brightened at the

mention of the fête, and he clapped his hands with childish glee. "That old goat will think he's in paradise when the jump up starts and those honey girls rub their little bellies up against his whanger."

Chapter Eighteen

At the same time as Bartholomew was playing his resurrection scene, Colin and Pierre finally made it back to the insurgents' encampment deep in the rain forest. They had been toiling up and down the pathless hills for more than three hours, and the physical exertion, coupled with an almost total lack of sleep during the last few days, was getting to Colin. But the stunning success of the mission still gave him a rush of adrenalin that kept him going.

As always it was difficult to pick out the human shapes in the mixture of light and shadow. It wasn't until Wendy jumped to her feet that Colin saw her. Then she was running, reaching out with her arms and calling his name. He held her close and she clung to him, half-crying and half-laughing as the words tumbled out.

"Oh, Colin. Darling! I love you so much and I was so afraid I had lost you forever."

A feeling of delirious happiness swept over Colin as their lips met. He was holding the love of his life in his arms and suddenly, magically, she seemed to love him as well.

"I want to explain about the other day," she murmured as they finally broke apart.

"No explanations needed." He kissed her again. "Just that you love me."

"I do Colin. So terribly much."

He was only vaguely aware of the other people as they walked through the camp, his arm around her shoulder, both of them wrapped in the wondering glow of new love. The young guerrillas, only too conscious of how fleeting and rare were such moments in the life of a freedom fighter, drifted away to hear details of the bombing from Pierre. Colin heard an excited cheer go up, but paid it no attention. He and Wendy sat down on a log and he tenderly kissed the corners of her eyes.

"You have no idea how I've wanted to do that ever since the very first night on board *Antilles Rose*," he whispered.

She traced the outline of his lips with her fingers. "When I was so awful to you on the beach, it wasn't because I didn't love you. I loved you so much it was tearing me apart. But, Colin, some terrible things have been done to me . . . things that made me feel . . . well, soiled."

She swallowed and he interjected softly, "You've got it right. They were *done* to you. They're not part of you. They're not part of *us*, my love."

"I finally realized that when you went off on that crazy mission and I was sure I would never see you again. I promised myself that if I ever had another chance, I wouldn't let anything, *anything*, stand between us."

As the late afternoon shadows lengthened, Colin fell asleep with his head cradled in her lap. Wendy smiled down at him, fingers gently stroking his hair. Such a tall, blond WASP was her lover. Not what she had expected from life at all.

"It's been a long time since they've had anything to celebrate." Pierre smiled in the direction of the figures grouped around the campfire. Since they were in a remote part of the rain forest, he decided to let them have a small fire, and they had dug a small pit to shield it from view. Chunks of goat meat roasted in the coals, and bottles of the fiery local rum were circulating, although Colin noted that the consumption was fairly moderate. Pierre had been at pains to explain that the two goats had been paid for, not "appropriated" in Mongoose style.

A guerrilla jubilantly brandished his machete as he went by and called out, "First the statue, now the man!"

"It's done bloody wonders for their morale," Pierre said.

"I'm glad. For Carla's sake," Colin replied, and Wendy squeezed his hand in sympathy.

"She would have gone on that mission even if she had known beforehand exactly what was going to happen," Pierre murmured.

"What's behind all these assassination rumors?" Colin changed the subject; the memory of lifting the girl's limp body out of the cockpit was still disturbingly vivid. "They didn't really knock the guy off, did they?"

"No such luck," Pierre snorted. "They got one of his stand-ins. He uses them all the time. Mallabone's idea originally. Clever bastard."

"I didn't realize it at the time, but I ran into one at the Administration Building. I remember thinking that Bartholomew was acting kinda strange," Colin mused.

"It's impossible to keep score, but his supply of doubles has got to be running low. In that sense, the shooting may be a good thing, although it gave the S.O.B. a chance to do his reincarnation routine. Incidentally," Pierre accepted a bottle from one of the men and took a thoughtful swallow, "we had nothing to do with that caper."

"Then who did?" Colin reached across Wendy for the rum.

"Damned if I know. But I intend to find out." Pierre stood up. "That goat is starting to smell pretty good. Let's grab some."

The group around the fire companionably made room for Colin and Wendy, and one of the women fished out pieces of meat from the coals for them. The guerrillas seemed surprisingly indifferent to the killing of Bartholomew's double but were elated over the destruction of the monument.

"You're fast becoming part of the folklore of revolution," Pierre joked. "Right up there with Ché."

"Go to hell," Colin grunted amiably, and took a bite of the surprisingly tender meat.

A few minutes later Pierre left them for an earnest conference with someone on the far side of the fire. He was frowning and listening intently. Finally he nodded and came over to kneel beside Colin.

"Talk to you for a minute, mon?"

Colin followed him to the perimeter of the group and waited for him to speak.

"We just got word that Jill Powell wants to see you. Urgently."

Colin started to ask how the message had been sent, then realized that all Jill would have to do was mention it to one of the plantation workers. There were bound to be S.F.U. supporters among them, and she would likely know who they were.

"Did she say what about?"

Pierre shook his head. "No. Just that it was important." He glanced back at the group around the fire. "You and Wendy have something going. Right?"

186

Colin blinked then replied tersely, "Right. I take it there's a reason for that question?"

"And Jill is just a friend?"

"A good friend," Colin replied quietly. "What are you getting at, Pierre?"

"She and that Koramantee pilot are lovers."

Pierre spoke with such matter-of-fact certainty that Colin accepted the truth of what he was saying without question. "Christ on his cross!" he finally breathed. "It'll destroy her parents. They don't know about it?"

"They haven't the slightest idea. We only ran across it because we've had Todd under surveillance. Those two have done a first class job of keeping the affair secret. Even used you, mon."

"Of course. I was the perfect 'beard.' They must have had some good laughs about that." There was no anger in Colin's voice, only sorrow that Jill had gotten involved with a no-good prick like Todd. It didn't matter so much that he was black, although that would drive the Powells-senior right up the wall, but Todd was such a stupid, egotistical bastard he was bound to break her heart.

"She's stark mad for him," Pierre murmured. "I gather he's a real stud."

Colin gestured with his hand as though he didn't want to hear any more.

Pierre sighed. "Put it all together and it adds up to a trap. For you."

"It sure reads that way." Colin was still coming to grips with the idea of Jill having an affair with Todd. Except it went much deeper than just a casual affair, if what Pierre said was right. He shook his head as though to clear it. "So, what do we do?"

"The *sensible* thing would be to forget about it and stay well clear."

"Agreed. But that wasn't my question."

"Well," Pierre said slowly, "it sure would help if we could take that pilot out of play."

"Did she say when this rendezvous is supposed to take place?"

"Tonight if possible, if not, then tomorrow night. It has to be at night, it seems."

"Any particular place?"

"The Cotton Tower."

"Interesting."

"Very. I think it can only mean they plan on taking you prisoner. It's for sure Todd and a couple of the Mongoose goons will be hidden inside, ready to pounce."

"Todd may not show."

"I reckon he's got to," said Pierre. "To keep Jill in line. She won't be any too thrilled about pulling this on you."

"Can we make it there tonight?"

"Easy. But, mon, you're overdue for some shut-eye."

"I got in a couple of hours this afternoon. That'll do."

"Okay. But we gotta come up with a *plan,* mon."

"We'll do that on the way."

Wearing an apron of cloud, the moon rose in the west, bathing the Cotton Tower in its silvery rays.

"It's lit up like a bloody stage," Pierre whispered, but he didn't sound particularly concerned about it.

Colin was lying next to him in the trash of a harvested cane field. He was still impressed by the way they had arrived there. A Toyota Land Cruiser, the yellow insignia of the Soufriere Forest Service painted on its door, had carried them along with five guerrillas over the steep, rolling hills of the rain forest. The Forest Service emblem had shaken Colin at first, but Pierre, clinging to a handhold as they ground up a precipitous slope in

188

four-wheel drive, explained that the driver was one of an increasing number of Bartholomew's govermental employees who had switched sides. The Toyota dropped them at the edge of the plateau where the dense forest gave way to rippling cane fields.

Anytime now," Pierre breathed, and, as if on cue, Jill appeared in one of the upper windows.

Even from a distance and in the pale light of the waning moon, her wide-shouldered and rather hippy figure was unmistakable. Colin felt a stab of disappointment; she was going through with it, after all. The memory of Wendy's face in the flickering firelight came back to steady him.

Jill's presence narrowed their options considerably. Pierre hadn't come right out and said it, but Colin sensed that if she hadn't been there, the guerrillas would have launched an all out firefight against the tower.

Jill had gone to show herself at the window on the opposite side, facing east. Now she was back and it was time to make their play. Colin rose up from the litter of dead sugarcane leaves and began to walk toward the tower.

Jill was waiting for him just inside the doorway. It was on the dark side of the narrow building, and he smelled her musky perfume before he saw her. That was unlike Jill; she usually wore a delicate, flowery fragrance. She must have put it on for her black lover. For the first time Colin knew for certain that Joshua Todd was in there with her.

She was sobbing as she flung herself into his arms. He held her, nerves crawling over his skin as he waited for the shot that would blast him into eternity. He was staking his life on Pierre's judgment that Bartholomew would insist on having him captured alive.

189

"There is only one fate in store for the man who knocked over Bartholomew's monument," Pierre had declared as they bounced around in the Land Cruiser. "The volcano. Bartholomew will settle for nothing less." Sudden tears glistened in Pierre's eyes, and he had hastily averted his face.

Now Jill was mumbling something against Colin's shirt. He took her elbows and gently pushed her away from his chest. She looked up at him, her full lower lip trembling as she fought for control. "You've got to leave this island, Colin. Everyone says that you were the one who bombed that awful statue and that Bartholomew won't rest until he has his revenge."

Despite the night breeze drifting in through the observation ports, it was dry and musty inside the tower, and the ancient boards still retained the heat of the day. Moonlight streamed in to illuminate the middle of the octagonal floor, but left the corners in deep shadow. A ladder, its rungs worn thin with use, led up to the second floor through an open trapdoor.

Jill was still talking, almost babbling; the words tumbling out, never looking directly at him but somewhere over his head. Straining to hear the other sounds that would presage an attack, Colin wasn't really listening to her. His attention was caught, however, when she mentioned Capt'n Johnny, saying that he could get Colin off in the *Antilles Rose*. She was backing slowly toward the middle of the room, away from the doorway. He was still holding her arms, so he moved with her, the sweat an ice cold band across his forehead.

"Freeze, Townsend. Else you dead meat!" Colin had been expecting it, but still his head jerked when the hoarse voice grated down through the trapdoor. Jill tore herself from his unresisting grasp and ran over to lean against the wall and burst into anguished weeping.

The booted feet of a Mongoose sergeant were coming down the ladder, the black automatic in his left hand aimed at Colin's head. He was followed by a second trooper and then Joshua Todd slid down, jumping off a few rungs from the bottom and landing beside Colin with a triumphant sneer.

The sergeant frisked Colin expertly, giving a low grunt of satisfaction when he came up with Mallabone's S & W. Jill's heaving sobs broke off abruptly when Todd gave her a stinging slap across the face. She looked up at him in bewilderment, fingertips touching her burning cheek as she whimpered, "But I did everything you asked. I did it for you, Josh."

"You did just fine, baby. Now pull your act together and leave off this wailing. It gets on my nerves."

The hurt in those violet eyes made Colin want to comfort her. She was just a kid, and she was just beginning to find out what she had let herself in for.

"Bring the girl," the sergeant hissed. "We gotta get back to the car."

"Okay, okay," Todd grumbled, not relishing being ordered about. Then he showed his even white teeth in a wide grin. "The president is going to be mighty pleased with this night's work. Mighty pleased."

"Yar," the sergeant assented, mud-brown eyes suddenly agleam with the thought of the perks that could come his way. Maybe a free night out at Bartholomew's night-club with one of them classy milk-chocolate broads.

They went in single file along the edge of the cane field with the trooper in the lead and the sergeant pressing the muzzle of the automatic into the small of Colin's back. Todd, half-carrying Jill, brought up the rear. He cursed her as she stumbled over the cane stalks lying on the ground; she seemed to have fallen into a numbed trance.

The small procession crossed a country road and entered a straggling patch of woods. So far Pierre was batting one thousand; he had been right on about the prisoner-taking bit. The thought comforted Colin, but the tricky part was just starting.

"Hey. The car. It's not there!" The trooper came to a sudden halt as he rounded a bend and stared down the faint trail.

"It's got to . . ." the sergeant involuntarily took a half step forward and died instantly as the blade slid into his throat just above the larynx and was pushed home to the hilt.

"Nobody moves!" Pierre barked from the darkness.

"You double-crossing bitch! You sold me out!" Todd screamed at Jill. He was throttling her, lifting her off her feet as his hands squeezed her neck. A rifle cracked from somewhere in the trees, and his handsome, furious face exploded.

"Hey. No more of that shooting," the trooper cried. "See, I'm putting my gun down." Moving with exaggerated care, he laid his rifle on the ground and straightened up, hands clasped over his head.

Everything stood still for a frozen moment, then Jill fell to her knees beside Joshua. When she saw the bloody wreckage of his face, she screamed, a long keening wail that lifted the hairs on Colin's neck.

"Oh, God," she sobbed. "He thought I set him up. He died thinking it!"

"That's right, Jill." Colin put his hands under her arms and lifted her to her feet. "And he was doing his best to kill you. Don't forget that."

"Get her out of here," Pierre hissed. "This man," he tapped one of the guerrillas on the shoulder, "will take you back to the truck. We'll catch up to you there." He handed the S & W back to Colin. "Hurry, mon."

"I heard a shot," the driver of the Toyota whispered. "That'll bring them Mongeese buzzing around like flies. What went down back there anyway?"

Colin was just starting to tell him when Pierre and his guerrilla band loped into view. Colin watched Jill wilt when she saw they had left Todd's body behind. Only the Mongoose survivor, arms tied behind his back and doing his best not to stumble on the uneven ground, was with them.

"Now what are we going to do with you?" Pierre looked dispassionately at the forlorn figure of Jill.

"I don't care," she mumbled.

"We can get you back to Palm Hill if you like."

She shook her head vehemently. "I couldn't face my parents right now. Besides I told them I was staying in town tonight. With a girl friend."

Pierre shrugged. It was plain he did not consider her to be a threat, mainly because he knew the other side had already identified him as the leader of the S.F.U. Jill told him where she had left her car, and he dispatched one of his men to get it out of sight. Then they clambered into the Land Cruiser and the Forest Service officer, frantic to get back into the safety of the hills, rammed it into gear.

"Wendy, you've been with Jill for hours. How do you read her?" asked Pierre.

Wendy placed her half-eaten breakfast of cold beans and salted chunks of red snapper on the ground. "Heartbroken," she said slowly, adding with a glance at Colin, "and feeling guilty as hell."

"Guilty enough to want to help us?" Pierre probed in his mouth for a fishbone.

193

Wendy took her time over that one. "Well, she's definitely not part of Bartholomew's inner circle, if that helps. It was just Todd. She really loved the guy. Which makes me feel a little better about what she did. A little." She gave Colin a sudden unexpected smile, and his heart turned over.

Pierre glanced across to where Jill, finally succumbing to exhaustion, slept in the dappled shade of the trees.

"It would mean telling her something about our plans. Just enough so that it could undo everything if she ratted."

"Oh, I don't think she'd do that," Wendy said. "Not deliberately anyway. She might tell you and your plans to go to hell, but that's all."

"That's my view, too." Pierre heaved a small sigh of satisfaction. "We'll let her sleep for another hour. I think you should be there, Colin, when I make my pitch. Prod her conscience a bit."

They didn't have to wait out the hour. It wasn't more than twenty minutes before Jill cried out and sat bolt upright. She blinked at her surroundings, and then a grimace of pain settled on her face as the memories came crowding back. Pierre signaled Colin and casually sauntered over to her.

She looked puzzled then nodded indifferently when Pierre asked if her family had been invited to Bartholomew's big jump up. He was sure they would have been. The dictator loved to display his aristocratic white planters, and the Powells were at the top of the heap. And Bartholomew's invitations weren't the kind you refused.

"But I'm not going," she was saying. "Not now. I'll just say I'm sick."

"Jill." Pierre reached out and held her hand. "We want you to go. It's very important."

Her lower lip pouted rebelliously, then she flushed and looked up at Colin. "Do *you* want me to?"

"Yes, I do, Jill. Like Pierre says, it's damn important."

Pierre straightened up, murmuring, "Think it over for a little while. Then maybe we'll talk some more."

The insurgent band was breaking camp, an exercise which consisted of little more than packing duffel bags and backpacks. That afternoon they would filter through the forest to another temporary resting place. Even though the Mongoose ruffians seldom ventured into the depths of the green jungle where sudden death lurked behind every clump of lush foliage, the first rule of guerrilla warfare was to keep on the move.

"Do you think she'll go along?" asked Pierre as he watched two men scattering the dead ashes of the fire. It seemed incredible to Colin that it was just last night they had roasted the goat meat.

"Yes. If we don't push her too hard." Colin shot a curious look at his companion. "What's so bloody special about her going to the jump up?"

"Because," Pierre replied slowly. "She knows every nook and cranny of Government House. The Powells were real cronies of old Burstall, the last governor before independence, and she practically lived there as a child."

Jill and Wendy were standing together, not saying much, when the two men approached.

"I really do feel rotten about what I did to you last night, Colin." Jill scuffed her sandals through the dead leaves underfoot.

"I think I can understand what made you do it."

A wan smile trembled briefly on her lips. "I'm glad for that, at least." She blew her nose and turned to

Pierre. "Okay. I'll go to that damn party. What do you want me to do?"

He took her by the elbow and walked her away, speaking in a low urgent voice. In a few minutes he brought her back, saying, "Jill's going to be leaving us now."

He and Colin stood at the edge of the overgrown cacao field and watched Jill disappear into the jungle with her escort of two guerrillas. They would take her to where her car was hidden.

"Then she's going to drive to her friend's place to freshen up before returning home," Pierre murmured.

"I take it her friend will not be surprised at her being out all night," remarked Colin wryly.

"One gathers she is used to it."

"A fellow 'beard.' You won't believe this, Pierre, but I was actually trying to think of a tactful way to cool things without hurting her." He shook his head in wonder, then asked, "Do you really think it's safe for her to be driving openly around Albertstown?"

"Yeah. In the first place I'm not sure whether Bartholomew actually knows about her and Todd. I have a feeling that last night was Todd's own little caper. Mallabone was probably in on it, but he doesn't tell his boss everything. Not by a long shot. Anyway Bartholomew has his hands full with the distinguished senator. And he's got to be on his best behavior. It's probably killing him."

Chapter Nineteen

"I don't give a shit how important the senator thinks he is," Bartholomew roared. "I'm not going to trail around after him and get myself shot."

"Senator Nesbitt is most anxious to have a tour of our industries and I'm sure he would feel slighted if you did not accompany him," Mallabone purred.

"Use a fucking double, then. Which one is left? Number ten?"

Mallabone nodded and Bartholomew said with a baleful leer, "All right, let *him* watch old ladies peel mace from nutmeg shells and weave their blasted straw rugs. Nesbitt's so goddamned scared he'll never notice the difference."

"But, Excellency, you sat next to the senator at dinner last night. It's true number ten bears a particularly strong physical resemblance to you, but he doesn't have your conversational abilities or your air of assurance."

Bartholomew preened for a moment before growling, "You'll just have to do the talking then. Take Carl along; it'll make Nesbitt feel safer to see some white faces." He frowned suddenly. "Where the hell is Joshua? That Koramantee is some kind of crazy, but he really sounded like he had a handle on Townsend."

"We all know how Josh is inclined to exaggerate his own importance, Excellency. Somebody hired him to fly a charter over to Barbados. I'll question him personally when he returns. I do hope," he added with a smirk, "that he brings their plane back in one piece. Well," Mallabone gave a slight, resigned shrug, "if you're determined not to go on the tour, I'll have number ten brought down here. It will be best if he is seen leaving from this room."

"Give me a chance to slip out the side door first. You know I don't like looking at them. It gives me the creeps."

Thinking it was time to put the dictator in a better mood, Mallabone murmured, "While we're gone perhaps you might think about your costume for the carnival."

"Right on!" Bartholomew whacked the desk with his swagger stick. "Maybe Baron Samedi will come callin'."

The man gets full marks for his diagnosis of Nesbitt's state of mind, Mallabone admitted to himself as he followed the senator down the circular stone stairs to the roasting ovens. Nesbitt, looking faintly nauseated by the sweet cloying smell, was paying no attention to what the guide had to say about the cacao factory. His bony shoulders were hunched protectively around his turkey-gobbler neck, and his hooded eyes were never still in their furtive search for hidden snipers.

"That old bag of shit *would* have to pick Soufriere for his winter holiday at the taxpayers' expense," Carl Dykstra grumbled in Mallabone's ear. "We got things that need to be done, man."

Mallabone shushed him angrily and hurried after the senatorial party into the sunlight and the waiting cavalcade of black Mercedes. He and Nesbitt were riding in the same vehicle. The senator had nodded eager assent when Mallabone suggested it might be better "from a security point of view" if he and

Bartholomew used different cars. That part had worked out rather well. Nesbitt was so terrified of being struck by a stray bullet meant for the dictator that he had shied away from him throughout the tour.

The black cars cautiously inched their way through the narrow streets rapidly filling with excited carnival celebrants. Some were already dressed in costume and beginning to jump up and down to the beat of a distant steel band. Normally the presidential cavalcade would have bulled its way through with horns blaring, scattering pedestrians in all directions. But the idea was to show Nesbitt how benign and benevolent a despot Bartholomew really was.

"Your visit is very popular with the people of Soufriere, Norbert." Mallabone repressed a shudder at the senator's incredible given name. Norbert Nesbitt. What *could* his mother have been thinking of? "They dearly love a carnival, and His Excellency has laid on a bang-up fête in your honor."

"Very nice," Nesbitt smiled weakly. "Are these windows bulletproof by any chance?"

"Heavens, no. We have no need for such precautions. His subjects worship the president."

Mallabone didn't bother to add that Bartholomew's regular limousine now occupied by his stand-in *was* bulletproof.

Andrew Powell looked around to make sure none of the house servants were within earshot. "Trust Bartholomew," he sighed, "to have a carnival right in the middle of the crop. Even the foremen have taken off for Albertstown."

Mary tucked a heart-shaped anthurium in the middle of a floral arrangement and stood back to appraise the result. "They'll all be back next week," she consoled him. "Partied out and ready to work. By the way, I've got the most smashing buccaneer costume for you."

Andrew shot her a long-suffering look and crossed over to the sideboard to pour the sherry. "Jill dining with us tonight?" He handed his wife a glass of Bristol Cream.

"She's having a tray in her room. She looked absolutely done in."

"Uhmm." Andrew took a thoughtful sip. "You don't suppose she's still tangled up with Townsend, do you?"

"Andrew Powell, you know perfectly well the boy's name is Colin. His parents were among our closest friends. 'Townsend,' indeed!" She paused after this mock outburst and wrinkled her snub nose at her husband. "No, I don't think it's Colin she's seeing. He seems to have dropped right out of sight."

"With good reason from what I hear. I gather he's managed to get crossways with Bartholomew. That young man has a real talent for trouble."

"Andrew." Mary studied the sherry in her glass. "Have you ever thought what it would be like if Soufriere were free of that tyrant?"

Andrew went back to the sideboard and splashed whiskey into the tumbler. He took a long swallow before replying. "There are days when I think of little else. But the damnable thing is, if Bartholomew is overthrown, the white plantocracy—meaning us—will go down with him."

"The new regime wouldn't accept whites owning the plantations, is that it?"

He nodded glumly and she whispered, "But that's the way it's been for centuries. Our families built the plantations. They're *ours!*"

"You're flying in the face of history, my dear. Wherever a revolutionary black regime has come to power,

the whites have been dispossessed. It's almost an arti-
cle of faith with them. On the other hand," he sighed
and took another pull at his drink, "Bartholomew
doesn't have to worry about things like that. He's
content to leave us alone as long as we don't make
waves and pay up without complaint."

"I'm not sure I could bear leaving Palm Hill. Not at
this stage of our life."

"I know," he muttered miserably. "But it may come
to that if Bartholomew falls. And yet, to be subject to
the whim of a bloody madman . . ." Andrew patted his
wife's hand. "The times do seem to be out of joint for
people like us, my love."

Leave Palm Hill? Transfixed, Jill stood outside the
doorway, bright artificial smile still in place while her
world crumbled about her. She had decided to make
the effort and join her parents for dinner if only to allay
her mother's obvious suspicions about where she had
spent the last twenty-four hours. But to think they
might be driven off the land and forced to drift from
place to place like homeless refugees. Penniless, too.
They wouldn't be allowed to take a thing with them.
With these dismaying thoughts churning through her
mind, Jill slowly turned and tiptoed across the gleaming
parquet floor to the staircase.

She opened the bedroom door to the maid's knock
and accepted a supper tray. But it remained untouched
while she leaned out the open window, gazing down at
the courtyard and beyond to the slumbering stables.
The dogs had already left for the mahogany grove and
their nightly skirmish with the monkeys.

She realized with a slightly ashamed feeling that the
threat to Palm Hill was affecting her more deeply than
losing Josh. Maybe it was because death was so final
and irrevocable, while the other thing was only a

horrid possibility. Josh could never hurt her now, as she knew he would have eventually. In a way it was a release. But if Pierre Demaret and his damn S.F.U. thought they were going to take Palm Hill away from her . . . she'd bargain with the devil himself to prevent that.

A dog howled and the rest of the pack immediately joined in. The unearthly baying of the giant hounds was an omen. She would see Bartholomew tomorrow.

Chapter Twenty

Jill was thoughtful as she stepped out of the fragrant tub and wrapped herself in the softness of a bath towel. She had a lot to offer Bartholomew, but was it enough to guarantee the safety of Palm Hill? If she only knew enough to be able to promise the total destruction of the S.F.U. She was so immersed in thought as she sat down at her dressing table that it took her a moment to notice the envelope propped against a bottle of toilet water.

Frowning, she extracted a single sheet of paper and read the terse message. It was from Colin, saying that another meeting was imperative. "Imperative" was just the sort of word he would use; he had a funny, almost professorial manner at times. She was to drive out to the main gate at eight-thirty and follow a tan Hillman traveling north.

At first the delay infuriated her. It was going to be hard enough to get through to Bartholomew as it was because of the carnival. Still, there was always the magic of the Powell name. And the meeting meant another chance to learn something more about the S.F.U.'s plans. Some hard information she could bring to the bargaining table. She was humming softly to herself as she finished dressing.

The driver of the small, nondescript sedan looked straight ahead as he went by the gate. Jill dawdled along behind him, staying just close enough not to lose him at the innumerable crossroads. At this hour of the morning, the road should have been jammed with sugarcane traffic, but even the sugar factories had closed down for Bartholomew's carnival.

Finding the envelope among her toilet things hadn't really surprised her. The house staff was undoubtedly riddled with S.F.U. supporters. Someday when she was mistress of Palm Hill ... Up ahead, the Hillman's brake lights glowed briefly as it turned off the road onto a narrow strip of brown stubble bordering an unbroken row of bamboo trees. It slowed almost to a standstill, waiting for her to catch up, then surged forward, straight at the dense, impassable wall of tree trunks.

"You bloody . . ." the words died in Jill's throat as the bamboo parted and the Hillman plunged through. Then she was bouncing over the rough ground toward the narrow opening, seeing the white slashes where a machete had cut through the slender trunks.

The Hillman reversed back out through the opening as soon as her own car was inside the protective screen. Three men, naked to the waist, dragged an upright wooden framework with the severed bamboo stems lashed to it, across the entrance. Jill felt trapped and had to remind herself that there was no way the insurgents could possibly know her intention to betray them. She recognized the guerrilla who stepped into view from a thicket; it was the same one who had guided her back to her car the night Josh had been killed. He signaled her to kill the engine.

"This better not take long," she muttered crossly as she climbed out of the car.

He ignored her show of irritation and slipped deeper into the forest, motioning her to follow. She was per spiring and fuming with impatience by the time they reached the flagpole-straight *gommier* tree where Pierre and Colin waited.

Pierre saw the anger in her imperious little face and said placatingly, "Sorry to bother you like this, Jill, but there are a couple of things you need to know."

Jill smoothed the scowl from her forehead. She glanced at Colin who was strangely silent, then she turned back to Pierre and made an apologetic face.

"Look, I was so upset by what happened to Josh that I'm afraid I wasn't really listening yesterday. Maybe you better start all over again."

"Sure, Jill, I understand. Anyway there's been a change . . ."

Pierre broke off when Colin said, "Talk to you a sec, Pierre?" and moved a short distance away.

"We got trouble, Colin? It was you who wanted this meet."

"Because I was having second thoughts. I know the lady and it's just not like her to be this interested in any cause but her own. I'm getting bad vibes. Very bad. I think she means to sell us out, Pierre."

"Jesus!" Demaret breathed, but he didn't argue the point. He had been in too many situations when one's instinct was the only guide. "This sure plays hell with our plans."

"We'll just have to improvise." Colin walked back to where Jill was standing. She brushed a strand of hair back from her eyes and smiled uncertainly.

"We have a little problem, Jill. We think you're going to double-cross us."

"What?" Her hand flew to her mouth and the gray eyes turned mauve. Then she spun around and began to run.

Colin caught up to her in four long strides. He held

her while Pierre did a rapid frisk and came up empty.

Despite his anger, Colin felt an odd sense of relief when Jill finally broke down and admitted her scheme to save Palm Hill. He had acted on little more than a hunch, and she probably could have bluffed it through if she hadn't been so strung out by everything that had happened to her in the past couple of days.

They had reached the escarpment that sheltered the new guerrilla camp by the time he got around to asking her whether she had told anyone about the costume she had planned to wear that night. Belatedly, she clammed up and shook her head rebelliously.

"This is no time to start acting stubborn," he grunted as he clambered after her up the rocky outcrop. "The S.F.U. stopped playing games a long time ago and they will not be amused when Pierre tells them what you had in mind."

"Only mother and the dressmaker know about it," she mumbled reluctantly.

"Good. What were you going as?"

"A highwayman."

"Couldn't be better," Colin grunted, thinking of the concealment such a costume would provide.

Pierre stood in plain view on the ridge and held up his left hand. The shape of two guerrilla sentries materialized among the trees below.

"Hello, Jill. I didn't realize you were to come back here." Wendy looked a little uncertain as she came forward to meet them.

"There's been a slight change of plans," Colin muttered. "Jill thought it would be more fun if we were met by a reception committee tonight. Laid on by Bartholomew, no less."

Wendy's eyes widened, then she sighed, "Well, she did her best to betray you once before." She looked at

Pierre. "You were counting on her pretty heavily for tonight, weren't you?"

He nodded mutely, his dejection in sharp contrast to Colin who seemed almost jaunty as he said, "Bartholomew uses ringers. Why not us?"

"Like me, for instance?" Wendy struck a pose with her hands on her hips.

"Come off it, you two," Pierre protested. "You're a living doll, Wendy, but you're not exactly Jill's twin."

"It's a costume party, remember? They're both the same height and with some padding in the right places . . ." Colin paused and spoke directly to Wendy. "What do you think? Jill was going dressed as a highwayman."

"They always hid their faces behind scarves and masks, didn't they? That part should be okay. But how do I crash the party in the first place?"

"You drive in with your loving parents, of course," replied Colin.

"What? Oh, you mean they'll cooperate because we've got Jill?"

"Like lambs." Colin glanced at Jill. "I hate the thought of putting your parents through this, but I think even you can see we have no choice."

A curl of her lip was his only answer.

"What happens once I'm inside?" Wendy directed the question at Pierre. "You were all enthused about her knowing Government House so well and I've never laid eyes on the place."

"That's true," Pierre spoke with rising excitement, "but it just might be possible to bring it off all the same. There's time enough for you to memorize the details. If you're game, I say let's give it a shot.

"The first thing is to make you completely familiar with the layout," he went on after Jill had been led

207

away. "The main ballroom will be your starting point. It's to your left as you come through the main entrance. There's a marble foyer . . ." He closed his eyes to help himself concentrate, and his voice dropped almost to a whisper.

Two hours later, Wendy finished with a quick rush of words, "I turn right at the end of the third corridor and there's a blank wall in front of me, but it's false. There's a mahogany table in front of it with a heavily carved border. I push the button which is the center of the fourth rose from the left." She took a breath and looked triumphantly at Pierre.

"Bravo," he beamed at her. "Now take a break and let it all sink in."

"It's about time for you to make that phone call," Colin said.

"*Me* make the phone call?" Pierre put on a face of mock outrage, then added quietly, "You're right, of course. It has to be me. But I'm not looking forward to it. I think the world of Mr. and Mrs. Powell."

Wendy was muttering, ". . . go down the second corridor past the washroom . . ." under her breath as the two men walked away.

"It might help if you told the Powells her daughter was going to turn us in," Colin said. "And that she thought she was protecting them and Palm Hill. That's made me wonder about what really will happen if you take over. The straight Marxist line? Grab all the land and distribute it among the peasants? That's what Jill thinks."

"You know me better than that, Colin," Pierre spoke slowly, weighing every word. "I'm a moderate. I have come to believe that the best approach to the Caribbean economy is to use a mixture of government and private enterprise. We will work with the planters and businessmen to improve the lot of our people. Of course," he shrugged, "if they refuse to join with us, we will have to take other measures. But I am confident that will not be necessary. Men like your friend David Henderson for instance . . ." he paused and looked interrogatively at Colin.

"Uh uh. I know David would like nothing better than to operate under a stable regime."

"And there are others just like him. Maybe not as enterprising, but capable and knowledgeable. That is what this island needs."

"Makes sense to me. But I have an idea that it won't go down too well with some of your supporters. They look like gung-ho little commies to me."

"I can't deny that. But there are others who are true moderates. I have given a great deal of thought to this and I do not intend to abandon my stand. In fact I have been counting on your assistance when the time comes."

"Me? Come back to Soufriere to live?"

"Why not, my friend? Is it not your land as well?"

"I don't really know the answer to that," Colin replied, then added more briskly, "Anyway, we're getting ahead of ourselves. There remains the small matter of dumping Bartholomew."

They paused just below the lip of the escarpment.

"Do you have a safe place to call from?" Colin asked.

"There's a village not far from here with a small general store. The proprietor is one of ours. One of our moderates," Pierre couldn't resist adding. Then he climbed over the top of the ridgeback and disappeared from Colin's view.

"Mistah Powell not heah. Mebbe you wan' speak wid Mistress?"

Pierre scowled at the old-fashioned wall phone. The

back part of the little store was redolent with the smell of smoked fish, and through a crack in the door he could see the owner displaying a bolt of colorful cotton prints to a well-upholstered brown lady.

"You still yere, sah?" The soft voice of the Palm Hill maid came over the wire.

"I'll speak with Mrs. Powell," he said reluctantly, comforting himself with the thought that Mary Powell was a brisk, no-nonsense woman.

"You bring Jill back here this instant, Pierre Demaret," she commanded when the full import of what he was saying finally got through to her.

"I can't do that, Mrs. Powell, and you know it." Pierre was dismayed by the nervous tremor in his voice. He was still in awe of the Powells and all they represented. "She was going to lead us into a trap. But I promise that if you and Mr. Powell do as we say, you'll get her back safe and sound."

"All right, Pierre." Mary knew there was no point in further argument. "Tell me exactly what you have in mind."

She listened without interruption while he explained about Wendy going with them masquerading as Jill.

"You realize it means a ghastly death for the three of us if we're found out," she said when he had finished.

"I do. But we're desperate, Mrs. Powell, and I have to tell you that you will never see Jill alive unless you do as we say."

"It's all wrong, Pierre, but you have a deal. How do we join up with this girl? Are you bringing her here? You can't wait till dark, you know. The jump up starts at seven-thirty sharp and it's a long drive into town."

"You often order breadfruit from old Joe Williams at this time of year, don't you?"

"To feed the field hands. Yes."

"He'll deliver a load around five this afternoon."

"I see. Be careful, Pierre. I understand roadblocks have been set up on the back roads."

"Thanks, Mrs. Powell." Pierre hesitated then said softly, "I can't help feeling you're on our side. I like that."

"You just take care of my daughter." She rang off and Pierre, startled by the jangling of the bell that announced the arrival of another customer, did likewise without noticing the connection was still open. There was no one to hear the click of the second Palm Hill receiver being replaced.

Chapter Twenty-one

The ancient pickup lurched forward with a death rattle of gears, making Wendy slip backward on the splintery floorboards. The guerrillas had constructed a makeshift crate for her to lie in and then stacked the yellowish-green globes of fruit around it. They had been careful to leave air spaces, but panicky twinges of claustrophobia nibbled at the edges of her mind.

Her cheeks were still hot from what Pierre had said while they waited for her hiding place to be finished. He had brought up the subject of Bartholomew's doubles and how difficult it was to cope with them. "You can never really be sure you're zeroing in on the right target," he had said. "We know that with the really attractive women he carries out a certain part of the interrogation personally. Know what I mean?" He was looking everywhere but at her.

"I know what you mean," she replied. His obvious discomfiture made her feel better about what he was trying to say. And at least he had the decency to wait until Colin was out of the way before bringing it up.

"That means you're one of the very few people on our side who can be sure they have encountered the genuine Bartholomew. In the flesh, so to speak."

"Altogether too much in the flesh," she muttered and told him about the icy hands.

He had heard about that, but said it was something lots of people had.

"You may be right," she conceded. "But I'll never forget that touch. Never."

"I believe you," he murmured. "Anyway, if you do happen to make a positive identification of Bartholomew, alive or dead, I need to know about it immediately." Then he added that on no account was she to allow it to jeopardize her primary objective.

She felt herself sliding forward as they began to descend a steep hill in low gear. They were moving very slowly, almost at a walking pace. Dear God, there must be a checkpoint up ahead. Wendy flinched as though the probing cutlasses were already plunging into her flesh.

The truck driver kept his foot on the pedal and yanked on the hand brake, with a prayer that the worn linings would hold. The checkpoint had been set up at the foot of a long hill. His hands tightened on the steering wheel when he saw the Mongoose bullies hassling the natives. An ancient crone scrabbled in the dust to retrieve the scattered bunch of plantain that had been knocked from her head. A wizened old man held his burro's halter and gazed stoically into the distance as the corporal slashed the panier straps and dumped the load of papaya onto the ground.

Finally the driver heard the sound he had been waiting for—the frantic blaring of a horn. The small crowd at the barricades looked up the hill and scattered wildly in all directions as the runaway bus bore down on them. Although he had been expecting it, the driver of Wendy's pick up was still unnerved as the careening vehicle swept past. Like all buses on Soufriere, it was simply a truck chassis with a homemade wooden body mounted on it. Stained glass windows surrounded the windshield, and its name, NO PROBLEM, was painted across the rear. Its driver was wrestling desperately with the wheel and leaning on the horn button while the few passengers clung in terror to the wooden uprights of its open sides. A crate of chickens tumbled from the roof and smashed on the roadway sending the frightened fowl flapping in all directions. It was obvious that the brakes of the ancient vehicle had failed, and its only hope lay in staying on the road until it reached the level ground beyond the barricades.

A soldier raised his automatic rifle to spray the onrushing bus with bullets, but the corporal knocked his gun aside. Then the air was filled with broken slabs of wood as it smashed through the barrier and sped on. A Jeep loaded with wildly gesticulating troops took off in pursuit of the quarry, now obscured by a billowing cloud of dust.

Wendy felt the truck rolling forward as the driver released the brakes and let it coast down to the shattered barricades. Two private soldiers had been left behind to man the checkpoint, but their attention was riveted on the chase. The taller one helped himself to a ripe breadfruit and waved the truck through.

The driver's heart was knocking against his ribs as they approached the Jeep and the now stationary bus. One of the male passengers was retching violently into the ditch; another had flung himself on the ground and was kissing its dusty surface with fervor, while the others leaned weakly against the sides of the decrepit vehicle. The wild-eyed driver was shouting something at the corporal, pointing excitedly at the underside of the bus. The soldiers stood around, slapping dust from their uniforms and grinning hugely at the shaken passengers.

One of the soldiers standing next to the corporal

touched his arm and pointed at the breadfruit-laden truck pulling out to pass them. At that precise moment an enormously stout lady passenger let out a loud groan and swooned into the unfortunate corporal's arms, bearing him to the ground in a smothering welter of gingham and flesh. The bus driver and the soldier, the latter almost strangling with the effort of keeping a straight face, tugged mightily at the woman's unconscious bulk and finally managed to free the apoplectic corporal. By then the produce truck was well down the road, and the soldier, reasoning that it had already cleared the checkpoint and not wishing to further infuriate his superior, prudently decided to let the matter drop.

Mary Powell was waiting for the truck as it wheezed and banged up to the kitchen wing of the Great House. Bert, the only male house servant, had been sent over to a neighboring plantation to deliver a bouquet of exotic blooms. She had also dreamed up chores to keep the maids in other regions of the house and said she would supervise the unloading herself. The produce farmer was still so unnerved by his experience at the checkpoint that Mary had to do most of the work herself, feverishly piling the fruit on the floor of the cool limestone storeroom. Joe Williams recovered enough to prise off the top boards with a claw hammer, and they both helped Wendy climb to her feet. She was clutching a small cloth bag.

"Have you seen Jill?" Mrs. Powell demanded. "Is she all right?"

She stared intently at Wendy as she replied that Jill was fine, gave a curt nod of acknowledgment and rolled the door shut behind the departing pickup.

"I'll take you up to Jill's room. Follow me." Mary led

the way through the deserted butler's pantry and up the narrow back stairs.

Her husband, looking hot and annoyed, was just returning from a frustrating tour of the idle cane fields as she descended the main staircase.

"Pour us both a drink, Andrew. I have something to tell you."

Mallabone listened without interrupting as the orderly repeated the message telephoned in by the Palm Hill spy. "Very good," he said at its conclusion. "I will deal with the matter personally."

As soon as the door closed behind the man, Tony let out a whoop of pure glee. If he played things right, not only would he be master of Soufriere, he would also have eliminated the only effective opposition. He was still smiling as he pressed the intercom and ordered Colonel Stroud to report to his office.

"This is the moment we have been waiting for, Colonel." Tony gloated as he told the security chief about the substitution of the girls.

The mercenary regarded the gay Englishman with disfavor. "So we capture the Chinese cunt one more time. That's no big deal."

"You st ...." Tony checked himself then explained with sugary patience. "Demaret must have a reason for wanting her to attend the jump up. And what is that reason almost bound to be?" He paused for effect before answering his own question. "To let somebody in from the outside. Including almost certainly Demaret himself. He simply cannot afford to let a major S.F.U. operation take place without leading it personally."

"Could be," Stroud conceded grudgingly. "And if that's what it is, we'll grab them."

"Of course you will. But only when the time is exactly right, and I will be the judge of that."

"The president knows about this?"

"Naturally. We have His Excellency's full support. Go now and instruct your men not to interfere in any way until the word is given."

Alone once more in his office, Mallabone ran a final check on his plans, mentally testing each link. The S.F.U. invaders could best be dealt with in the confusion following the killing of the disguised true Bartholomew and the unveiling of Mallabone's own puppet. He discarded the idea that the S.F.U. might try a full scale assault. They were much too few and too lightly armed to tackle the Mongoose Gang head on. Besides, Government House would be packed with innocent outsiders, many of them American tourists, and Demaret wouldn't run the political risk of triggering an all-out massacre. No, it would be a small raid with a specific purpose. Probably another attempt to knock off Bartholomew.

His bland expression suddenly grew agitated—suppose they killed *his* Bartholomew. The frown disappeared from his high, smooth forehead as he realized that shouldn't prove hard to prevent. What could be more natural or praiseworthy than for Bartholomew's chief adviser to order that the president be completely shielded by his bodyguards during the floor show? The frown returned. Bartholomew was being childishly coy about his costume, and one could never really be sure what the black ape was up to. But he *was* sure about the shapeless green dress that had been delivered to the presidential suite only yesterday. And dressing in drag was one of the dictator's favorite pastimes.

Tony glanced at his slim, gold wristwatch. It was time to activate number ten.

Chapter Twenty-two

"I must say this is one elegant way to launch a revolution." Colin's appreciative gaze roamed around the luxurious interior of the room.

"We've used it before. A deluxe beach resort makes a surprisingly effective 'safe house.'" Pierre was opening closet doors in search of something. "The manager had a lovely daughter. A beautiful girl who was the joy of his life."

"I think I can guess the rest."

"I'm sure you can. Bartholomew got hold of her and now she is a hopeless heroin addict—no longer attractive enough for the palace guard, she services the worst scum in the Mongoose Gang. Ah, here we are." Pierre lifted the costumes down from the rack and laid them on the bed. "You're the friar."

"I hope they made it long enough," Colin grunted as he shrugged himself into the voluminous black folds. The gown fell to within a few centimeters of the floor. "There are times when this organization of yours strikes me as pretty damn efficient."

"We're improving." Pierre was climbing into the tight-fitting pants of a harlequin. "But we have a long way to go. All we can do at the moment is to strike whenever an opportunity presents itself. Like tonight."

High up on the white wall a night lizard darted round a picture frame and startled a whistling frog into a prodigious leap. The tiny amphibian landed on the front of Colin's costume and clung there, throat pouch pulsating rapidly. Colin squinted down at the terrified creature. No more than two centimeters long, it was perfect in every detail and put him in mind of a gold charm from a woman's bracelet.

"In all the years I spent in California it was the memory of this little fellow's call that reminded me most of Soufriere." Colin kept his voice low, so as not to further frighten his unexpected visitor.

"It's the most typical Caribbean sound there is," Pierre agreed, smiling at the little golden animal, still pretending to be invisible against Colin's robe. "Why not have a gold frog on a black background as Soufriere's new flag?"

The whistling frog made a lightning leap to a bureau and disappeared from view.

"About tonight." Pierre's tone grew suddenly brisk. Colin tensed, waiting for him to continue. The fatigued look had lifted from Pierre's face, making him look younger and even more like his sister.

"We'll have to play it by ear. Much more than I want. But there are so damn many variables. Bartholomew and his bloody look-alikes. At a *costume* party, yet. He might not even be there, for all we know."

"He might not even exist," Colin interrupted quietly. "Have you ever thought of that?"

Pierre's left eyebrow arched. "He exists. Unfortunately. And that precious Mallabone has some scheme afoot. We know that but we haven't a clue what it is. It'll be blindman's buff all the way. Anyway our two objectives are clear. To eliminate Bartholomew if possible and . . . to bring Pearl out. We know Mallabone is all set to denounce her as a double agent."

"And is she?"

"Yes. And, as you can imagine, she's been invaluable. She's the sole reason my identity remained unknown for so long. She couldn't save our kid brother, but . . ." he faltered then took a deep breath and went on, "that'll be your mission—to help her escape."

"She'll be in costume. How am I supposed to recognize her?"

"There are two scenarios. She'll start out the evening by being easily recognizable. Bartholomew dotes on these carnivals and insists that everybody be completely disguised until the great unmasking at midnight. But he's so vain about having a Miss World around that he wants everybody at the gala to know exactly who she is. So you'll spot her right away. The other thing is that Wendy will be smuggling in a black cat costume for her."

Colin drew in his breath sharply, and Pierre paused to look steadily at him before continuing. "She's wearing it next her skin under Jill's costume, and she'll give it to Pearl if she gets a chance. So it's either Pearl or a black cat you're after."

There was a faint rapping on the other side of the wall, and he sprang to his feet. "The others are ready. Put on your mask and let's go."

Two costumed figures waited for them in the shadow of the sea almonds that screened the hotel villa from the beach. One, considerably shorter than the other, was dressed in a baggy clown costume. Most likely one of the women guerrillas, Colin thought but couldn't be sure. The other was dressed in dark, nondescript tramp clothes. No one spoke. A taxi started its motor and crept toward them as they moved out from the shelter of the building. They climbed in like so many ghosts enroute to a haunting, and it bore them off in the direction of the downtown area.

221

Once they reached the outskirts of Albertstown, their progress was reduced to a crawl. The streets were incongruously bedecked with Christmas lights that Bartholomew had borrowed from London's Regents Park for the Independence celebrations and then neglected to return.

A steel band, playing a spirited calypso, marched out of a side street and brought the taxi to a complete halt. The band was followed by a throng of costumed dancers, all of them masked, jumping up and down and rotating their rumps with frenetic energy. Another band and its followers, heading down the hill, broke ranks and flowed along both sides of the line of stalled automobiles without missing a beat. The dancers carried flaming torches which bathed the interiors of the cars with a flickering orange glow. Although he realized he was completely hidden behind his lifelike plastic mask, Colin instinctively faced away from the window until the revelers had passed.

Bartholomew was clearly out to give the people a real bash. It was right in the middle of Lent, and once it would have been unthinkable to have held such a bacchanal during the religious period. But the dictator never lost an opportunity to undermine the Christian religion and flaunt its traditions.

The cars were crawling forward once again, through a river of black humanity brandishing bottles of rum and shouting harsh, guttural cries. Craning his neck to peer up through the window, Colin caught a glimpse of their destination lit by the bright glare of floodlights.

Government House was a Victorian monstrosity perched on the highest hill overlooking the city. It had been built by the British during the 1840s to put the final stamp of their authority on the island which had changed hands so many times in its turbulent history

The first story was of limestone coral, but the remaining three floors were wood, painted white and decorated with elaborate curlicues and fretwork. It was hung with long verandas that made it look like a giant wedding cake.

"One final point." Pierre touched Colin's arm. "The *Antilles Rose* will be at Hurricane Hole from midnight on. Just in case everything goes to ratshit and we need a means of escape."

"That old pirate!" Colin exulted. "He gave them the slip."

"You don't work the 'bubble trade' for thirty years without learning how to do that," Pierre said drily.

"I honestly never knew Capt'n Johnny was one of you."

"He isn't. He's simply looking after you. To him you will always be a Townsend of High Trees."

"Maybe that's what I always will be," Colin said as if thinking out loud.

The mention of Hurricane Hole revived a sudden memory of the night they had sailed the schooner into the intricate labyrinth of mangrove-choked channels in the lee of a high, protective headland. A hurricane, rare this far south, was heading for Soufriere, and he would always remember the purple sky and the strange steely taste to the air as they fled before the storm.

The taxi's engine coughed and died as they encountered a solid wall of merrymakers sambaing in the wake of a steel band.

They were swept up Market Hill by the jiggling press of people. Colin accepted a rum bottle that was thrust into his hand and raised it to his mouth, pretending to drink deeply. His samba was more a sort of swaying shuffle, but that was true of many of the dancers. The real experts were in the front, right up there with the band. He kept his knees bent to disguise his real height and never took his eyes off the red and blue diamonds of Pierre's costume bobbing in front of him. The narrow, cobbled street was made even narrower by the rows of parked cars on either side. It ended in a T intersection in front of the whitewashed stone wall that encircled the grounds of Government House.

The sentries at the ornate iron gate were attired in the dress uniform of the old Soufriere police force, white pith helmets with brass spikes and starched white tunics cinched with black leather belts. It was like a scene from the glory days of the British Empire. A few stragglers were still arriving; their invitations were meticulously checked against a master list before they were permitted to walk up the long driveway lined with poinsettias. The reluctant gait of some plump, middle-aged figures revealed a lack of enthusiasm for the festivities, but Bartholomew's whims were not to be disobeyed.

Without missing a beat, Pierre disengaged himself from their original group and joined another band of marchers streaming past the front of the palace. Exhausted revelers dropped out from time to time to catch their breath or rest aching feet, so no one took any notice when a harlequin and three companions hobbled over to the curb as the procession went by a dark side street.

The rear of Government House was almost as brightly lighted as the main entrance, but the guard was in battle fatigues and carried a modern automatic rifle. Pierre and Colin crouched in the shadow of a lean-to garage across the street and waited. The taller guerrilla, the one dressed as a tramp, staggered into view singing in a cracked voice and almost falling as he took a long swig from the rum bottle. The sentry watched

224

him impassively, but his hand tightened on the rifle barrel. It was clear that if the drunk ventured within range, he would be clubbed unconscious. But the victim was blissfully unaware. Crooning with intoxicated good-fellowship, he lurched ever closer, proffering the bottle in his outstretched hand.

He overreached himself and stumbled forward, recovering with an unsteady lunge that sent him reeling back. Eager for his sport, the sentry took a short step forward. The clown spurted around the corner of the wall on sneakered feet with a garrote stretched taut between raised hands. The sentry's larynx made a faint splintering sound as the wire cut through it, but otherwise he died silently. The drunk reached out to catch his rifle before it struck the pavement. Grasping the lifeless body by the legs and under the armpits, the S.F.U. commandos carted it across the still empty street and deposited it inside the lean-to.

Pierre was already at the wall, throwing a line with a grappling hook over the top. In his haste to scramble after him, Colin's long flapping robe caught on a spike, and too late he heard the sound of ripping cloth. A telltale strip of the black material remained behind, in plain view against the white stones. Before he could even curse his own clumsiness, the two guerrillas came swarming over after them, and the clown deftly plucked the offending rag from the spike.

The spacious grounds were dotted with huge old trees and clumps of shrubbery that offered ample cover to the intruders. Canine patrols normally covered that chink in the security, but the killer dogs were off duty that night for fear they would attack some guest innocently wandering about the garden. Pierre led his group across the grass, darting from one pool of shadow to the next until they were within a few meters of the limestone wall of Government House itself. The steel shutters that covered the rear, ground-floor windows had been opened just enough to permit the air to circulate. The noise filtering through made it possible to talk without fear of being overheard.

Pierre touched the metal butt of the revolver under his belt. "I'm going to do everything I can to take Bartholomew out tonight. Regardless of anything else. Without him, this whole rotten regime will collapse. So I want you to concentrate on getting Pearl out of there. Deal?"

"You got it. But remember you're the one who has to put this country back on its feet." Pierre acknowledged that with a somber nod, and they fell silent in the scented darkness. Finally Colin shifted his position and whispered, "What happens next?"

"We watch the wall and wait for Wendy to do her stuff."

Standing on the sidelines, Wendy glanced up at the entrance hall. It was alive with swirling color as the guests streamed through two decorated archways and down the short flight of marble stairs to the ballroom. There was no receiving line; that would have given away the identity of the host and guests of honor. Not that there was much doubt as to who the host was. Hidden behind their masks, the eyes of the guests peered with surreptitious fascination at the dread figure of Baron Samedi. The skull mask under the top hat completely obscured the wearer's face, but no one else would have dared to appear as the dictator's personal *loa*.

Bartholomew was light on his feet, swooping his partner in graceful circles to the music of the police band. As they twirled closer, Wendy recognized Baron

Samedi's partner. It was Pierre's sister Pearl, the same woman who had tried to comfort her after she had been raped by Bartholomew. Pearl's small eye-mask accentuated rather than hid the delicate perfection of her features, and the low-cut bodice of the Marie Antoinette dress revealed the tattoo on her breast that Pierre had described.

"They say that's Miss World. Isn't it just *too* thrilling, Walter?" the pudgy *houri* standing next to Wendy gushed in a ripe Georgia accent.

A waiter nudged Wendy's elbow, offering a tray of champagne glasses. She took one and raised it to her lips, feeling the rolled-up headpiece of the cat costume scratching the skin between her breasts. But she would have to put up with it for at least another hour; the switch wasn't to be made until just before the floor show.

"Jill?" The young man swept off his cavalier's hat and bowed extravagantly. He must have recognized the Powells somehow when the three of them came in together.

She quickly handed him the half-empty glass of champagne, mumbled something about suddenly not feeling well and fled. She skirted the floor of the packed dance floor until she caught sight of the temporary LADIES sign that had been pasted over a door at the end of a short hallway. She would wait in there until it was time to make her move.

The band had swung into a Latin American beat by the time she emerged. She was pretty sure she had pinpointed the location of the washroom in the diagram that Pierre had sketched and made her memorize. If she was right, there should be an alcove with empty bookshelves a short distance down the hall on her left. Carefully refraining from even a glance in the direction of the ballroom, she walked purposefully along the corridor. The alcove was there, all right. In fact it looked rather cozy with a couple of low armchairs and end tables. And the shelves were bare, except for a few tattered magazines.

Mallabone watched the figure of the highwayman disappearing down the hall with a sardonic smile under his Mephistophelian mask. The swirling cape by itself was pretty effective camouflage, and it would have been a simple matter to pad the Chinese girl's slim shoulders. Jill Powell did tend to be a trifle wide in the shoulders and hips. Tony swished the tails of his own coat and glided away in the opposite direction.

Wendy's pulse raced as a flash of bright orange cloth disappeared into a doorway. She kept on, unconsciously holding her breath as she drew abreast of the door. It was closed, but each moment she expected it to fly open and someone leap out at her. Then it was behind her and she was desperately trying to remember what came next. The strain of forcing herself to creep past that doorway had temporarily driven everything else from her mind.

The corridor dead-ended, and she knew she was to go left. That was okay, and then there was a door she was supposed to open. But was it right after the turn? Or was there another interconnecting hallway first? It was so hard to visualize things from just a diagram. What *had* Pierre said?

She spotted the door as soon as she turned the corner. She paused and tried to recall Pierre's voice. "Then you turn to your left and . . ." There was someone walking down the passage behind her, heels clicking on the bare floor. She couldn't just stand there! She tiptoed across to the door and turned the knob.

The man looked at her incuriously then returned his

full attention to urinating in the toilet bowl. He even moved companionably to one side to make room for her. It suddenly dawned on her that he assumed she was a man. Without uttering a word, she closed the door and scuttled further down the hall. The sound of clicking heels receded; whoever it was must have turned off somewhere in the rabbit warren of corridors and small rooms that made up the back part of the palace.

The next one *had* to be the right door. Wendy's palm was slippery with perspiration as she reached for the knob. She exhaled a sigh of relief when she saw the narrow stairs, carpeted in a faded floral design. Pulling the door shut behind her, she crept down the stairs, hanging on to the wooden bannister. A long, sparsely furnished room, covered with the same floral carpet, stretched in front of her.

The feeling of being observed was overwhelmingly strong as she stood at the bottom of the stairs. She made herself look in all directions, her inner costume scratching her skin as she turned her neck. There was no one to be seen, but the feeling persisted. She shook it off and began to walk across the worn carpet.

The room was really a huge central hall with numerous corridors branching off from it. Fortunately they were all on the left. She followed the third one until it ended and then paused for a second before looking quickly to the right.

The blank wall was there and so was the carved mahogany table. And so was the slim, sinister figure of Mephistopheles, complete with white tie and tails.

"Is this what you wanted, my dear?" Mallabone asked in his languid drawl and reached across to press the center of the fourth rose.

Chapter Twenty-three

"She's done it! "Look." Pierre grasped Colin's wrist. A section of the stone wall was moving, accompanied by the rumble of wheels on metal tracks. The slab was no more than a meter wide and slightly less than two high. It had been installed by a jittery governor at a time when it was thought that Napoleon III might try to restore the former glory of France in the Caribbean. Bartholomew found it useful on occasion.

"We have less than two minutes to get inside," Pierre warned.

The four figures flitted across the last remaining strip of grass and filed through the opening, carefully stepping over the heavy iron rails. Once inside they waited until, with a clanking of gears and rumbling wheels, the opening was sealed. Pierre switched on a flashlight. The passageway, its floor covered with a thick coating of dust showing faint footprints, none of them recent, curved along the inside of the wall whose rough stones formed one side with the other being made of unpainted boards. Pierre covered the lens of the flashlight with a handkerchief and they crept forward.

Mallabone held the transceiver to his ear, the modern instrument looking out of place with his formal attire. "They're inside," he murmured as he released the switch.

"What were you supposed to do next?" He studied Wendy's face as he spoke. The Mongoose guard was holding both her scarf and mask in his hands. "Were you supposed to rendezvous with them somewhere? I thought not," he said after a pause when she showed not the slightest flicker of expression. "Scatter and lose yourselves among the guests. That's what I would do. Now we must find you an escort for the evening. How about that charming Carl Dykstra? You've met before, I believe?"

Back in the ballroom, Mallabone gestured imperiously at a masked man in a naval commander's uniform who was chatting up a bird over by the bandstand.

"That outfit is a bit of wish fulfillment on Carl's part, I'm afraid," he sniggered as the naval figure swaggered over to them. "He'd never be accepted in the regular navy with those eyes of his. By the way, my dear, there's no need to reveal your identity. Much more fun to remain a lady of mystery, don't you think?"

As he drew nearer, Wendy saw it wasn't Carl's face under the braided visor of the commander's cap. The mask, with the handsome features of a Hollywood male lead, was so lifelike that it was only the failure of the lips to move when Carl spoke that gave it away.

It was almost pathetic, thought Mallabone, the way the man stood rigidly at attention while receiving his orders. Tony's normal drawl took on a crisper note as he instructed Carl to stay beside the girl and not let her make contact with anyone until after the floor show. He added that he wanted the white mercenary to station himself near the stage during the show. Then he gave Wendy an ironic bow and left them.

It was time for a last private chat with his tame

fire-eater. He would identify the target and assure the assassin once again that he would be allowed to escape unharmed after he had done his work. Pelé might be a superb fire-eater, but he was as gullible as he was greedy.

The band started up again, and Carl muttered, "Let's shake it, doll. Might as well have some fun."

At first he tried hard to place her; there was something tantalizingly familiar about her. But she refused to speak, and there wasn't a square centimeter of bare skin showing through her costume. He shrugged and placed his hand against the small of her back, pulling her to him. She resisted but he only squeezed harder, forcing his leg between hers. A shiver of revulsion went through her as his breathing quickened and his erection pressed against her body.

Raw jealousy stabbed through Colin when he saw Wendy dancing with the naval officer. They were practically making out on the dance floor! With an effort he looked away and tried to case the security.

He soon realized it was a hopeless task. There were a few uniformed police stationed in the archways, looking as though they were meant to serve as decoration rather than protection. But God only knew how many bodyguards circulated in disguise among the four hundred or so guests. On the surface, however, everything looked very laid back and cool.

Carefully avoiding the area where Wendy and her partner swayed together, Colin's gaze lighted on Pearl. She was on the opposite side of the room, her hand lightly resting on Baron Samedi's arm as she smiled her dazzling smile up at a tall, stooping Uncle Sam. He seemed oblivious to her charms, his white chin whiskers bobbing as his head moved nervously from side to side. That could only be Senator Nesbitt waiting to be struck down by an assassin's bullet. Then the orchestra switched to a waltz, and Pearl moved into Uncle Sam's arms. He danced clumsily, stumbling over his own feet, but Pearl's smile stayed in place. Colin wondered sourly if she was meant to be the senator's little treat for the night.

If Wendy was going to do anything about the costume switch, she'd have to make her move right after this dance. Reluctantly he looked for her and then it hit him. He had been so blinded by his schoolboy jealousy that he had jumped to a totally false conclusion. Wendy wasn't going through that sexy exhibition willingly. She wouldn't put up with it—unless she had to. She probably felt she couldn't create a scene at any cost. Or maybe, it meant the other side had made her and put the grab on her. But surely they wouldn't let her loose on the dance floor like that. It definitely called for a word with Pierre.

The red and blue harlequin was some distance back from the dance floor, bowing slightly as he accepted a glass of champagne. Colin began to thread his way through the crowd toward him. He heard a rich mixture of tongues as he sidled along: slurred West Indian vowels interspersed with snatches of French and one brief burst of staccato Spanish. But the nasal accents of the American midwest predominated. Colin wondered sardonically if the good senator felt suitably flattered. One positive thing about the presence of so many American tourists was that it should lessen the chance of an outbreak of violence.

Pierre sipped his champagne as he listened to Colin's whispered report. "She certainly doesn't seem to be enjoying herself," he murmured after an unobstrusive glance at the dancing couples. "I'm inclined to think your first explanation is correct and that she simply cannot make a scene. Anyway, we're inside and we have no choice except to see it through. But it looks like we're running out of time for the costume switch and that I don't like. The best thing you can do is to have a dance with the clown and blend into the background."

It was hard going with the clown. Despite her agility in scaling walls, she was awkward and uncooperative on the dance floor. Doubtless regards it as a bourgeois frivolity, Colin thought as he almost dragged her around the floor. Nor did she encourage any idle banter; her answers were monosyllabic and her voice was grating. She was even more formidable than Carla. These lady guerrillas might be great warriors, but they were definitely lacking in the social graces. Now he understood why Pierre had never considered using one of them as a substitute for Jill.

With no need to make conversation, Colin was free to let his eyes roam. Whatever else, Pearl was destined to be the belle of this particular ball. She danced with a constantly changing stream of partners, laughing gaily as the men cut in on each other for the thrill of dancing with a certified beauty queen. Mephistopheles seemed to be controlling the traffic, lightly fingering his curling mustache as he smiled and bowed, dispatching a favored guest for his turn with Miss World. Looking at the tall, diabolic figure, Colin knew he had pinpointed Mallabone. The Englishman never got out of character.

The illumination of the ballroom was growing steadily and almost imperceptibly dimmer as midnight approached. It was done so smoothly that the elaborate chandeliers must have been fitted with rheostats. Colin tripped over the feet of his reluctant and clumsy partner and bumped into a solidly built man in a hairy gorilla suit. He murmured a hasty apology and looked around for Wendy, but he had lost her in the swirl of dancers. "Let's sit this one out," he gritted through his teeth and headed for the sidelines. The clown angrily shook off his guiding hand at her elbow, but she stamped along in his wake.

It was nearly time for the floor show to get underway. Pearl, still in her Marie Antoinette costume, was impossible to miss. She was seated between Baron Samedi and Senator Nesbitt, a few meters back from the part of the dance floor that was being marked off with velvet ropes to make an impromptu stage. Unless Colin was very much mistaken, the security had suddenly grown very tight around Baron Samedi's little circle. They were in the middle of a jam of bodies, most of whom took no part in the social hubbub around them but concentrated on systematically surveying the scene from behind their masks.

The dancing had come to a stop, and the guests, most by now well lubricated with Bartholomew's champagne, began to gather around the stage. Colin, not caring whether his guerrilla companion followed him or not, eased himself into the stream of people. Pierre was ahead of him, worming his way through the crowd until he was two rows from the stage and diagonally across from Baron Samedi. Colin edged to the left; he wanted to be directly in line with Pearl.

It was the woman wearing the shapeless, garish green gown that caught his eye first. Her mask appeared to have been cut from a flour sack, and she had crammed a frightful brassy wig on her head. Then he saw Wendy, the subdued earth tones of her highwayman outfit almost invisible among the other costumes, standing beside the stout lady in the green dress. And that damned naval commander was on her right. They had found a place in the front row.

There was a sudden roll of drums and a young man in a white tuxedo sprang into the spotlight. He crooned typical M.C. patter into the microphone, cracked one or two jokes that fell flat, then, with a nervous glance in Baron Samedi's direction, said, "but we know you came here tonight to jump up and have yourselves a ball. So we'll keep it short and very, very snappy."

Then he introduced the first act. "The lovely calypso dancers performing one of Soufriere's traditional dances!"

The women dancers were thoroughly modest in the demure head scarves and long print dresses of a bygone era, and the dance, as the couples pranced close together then coquettishly drew apart, was innocent, charming and very sexual. The troupe were scurrying off the floor to an enthusiastic burst of applause when Colin saw Mallabone change position. Unobtrusively, with people making room for him, he drifted from his place behind Baron Samedi to stand, arms folded in a Mephistophelian pose, a few rows in from the top corner of the stage.

"And now, ladies and gentlemen . . ." the youthful M.C. was giving it his all, "the Flaming Limbo with the Great Pelé—King of the Fire-Eaters!"

Steel drums pounded out the stirring beat of the limbo, and a gasp rippled through the crowd as the dancers leapt onto the floor. There was nothing demure about this group. Four nubile, brown-skinned maidens, naked to the waist, writhed and dipped in sensuous abandon. Next, a male dancer bounded onto center stage brandishing a flaming torch. The tempo of the drums increased as he thrust it into a pot of kerosene sitting on an iron tripod, setting it alight. Hips rotating to the insistent rhythm, he returned to the shad-

237

owy rear of the stage where he arranged the limbo bar and other props while the women undulated their pelvises toward the blaze, making love to the licking flames.

The big drum suddenly spoke and the Great Pelé made his entrance, slithering horizontally, his back inches from the floor. The oiled skin of his torso glistened in the light of two flaming machetes that twirled daringly close to his face. The drum changed rhythm and the dancer effortlessly flowed upright until he was standing erect with the burning blades crossed in front of his chest. He was tall, with a graceful muscular build, wearing only skin-tight pants with a well-filled crotch. All the hair had been shaved from his head and body. He sank to his knees in supplication before the blazing kerosene, then went into his fire-eating routine, stuffing swords tipped with flaming wads of cotton into his mouth, letting the flames linger over his face until it seemed they would sear his very eyeballs.

The Great Pelé waited for the applause to subside then made a couple of easy passes under the limbo bar, sliding under with a half-naked girl perched on his knees. Now the drumbeat was building to a crescendo, signaling the climax was at hand. While the fire-eater leaped about the stage to work himself into a fever pitch, two of the dancers stretched out on the floor with the flaming bar supported on their firm young breasts. The audience was totally absorbed. Surely he wasn't going to try and go under *that?* Sweat was flying from the Great Pelé, spraying the stage and some of the ringside viewers with a fine mist. Suddenly he snatched two machetes from the fire, running them lovingly along his chest, the droplets of sweat sizzling with the heat. Then he was spinning the blades in two fiery arcs, his lips mouthing an incantation to the god of fire

238

The smell of kerosene and smoke permeated the ballroom.

With a sudden tingle of premonition, Colin looked across the floor to see if Bartholomew was still there. The skull mask of Baron Samedi, luminous in the semidark, leered evilly from the middle of the bodyguards. No ringside seat for you, you wily old bastard, thought Colin. Not with cutlasses flying around.

His attention had just returned to the fire-eater when it happened. A machete, its blade still dully glowing with the heat, sang through the air and buried itself in the breast of the black woman standing next to Wendy.

For an incredibly long moment the victim stayed erect, pawing at the terrible blade that impaled her. Then she tottered a few steps backward and began to go down. Instinctively, Wendy reached out to save her from falling. Their hands touched then slid apart as the woman's weight sent her sprawling to the floor with the voluminous skirt bunched over her hips. Wendy blinked in astonishment. The "woman" was completely naked under the dress and was unmistakably male. A long, thin penis, like a piece of black hose, dangled between the outspread thighs. Then Wendy's view was blocked by four men, bending over the body and reaching down as though they meant to carry it away.

Struggling to get over to Wendy, Colin saw a black revolver suddenly appear in the naval commander's hand. It was pointed at the fire-dancer, who was retreating across the stage in a low crouch, the scuffing of his bare feet clearly audible in the shocked silence. Two shots rang out, a woman began to scream and total pandemonium erupted. Both bullets smashed into the assassin, straightening him up, then slamming him sideways into the pot of kerosene.

Its flaming contents splashed onto the sheer pantaloons of the *houri* from Georgia. She felt the wetness first, then looked down in blank disbelief as her legs were enveloped in flames. A scream raw with terror was torn from her throat. She blundered blindly into the crowd, which hastily parted for her as people shrank back from the deadly flames. A man standing at the rear tugged frantically at the damask drapes until they fell free and ran toward the burning woman. He flung them over her in a desperate attempt to smother the fire, but the damask was dry and brittle with age. The drapes smoldered for a few seconds then ignited, engulfing the would-be rescuer and shooting an orange tongue up the wall.

Near the stage a rivulet of burning kerosene spread outward from the overturned pot, eating its way across the hardwood dance floor.

Chapter Twenty-Four

Mallabone seethed with furious despair as the flames fed the rising panic. This was the moment number ten was to have taken off his skull mask and declare himself to be Bartholomew. But Christ himself could make an appearance without attracting any attention from the fear-crazed mob. Cattle!

Suddenly he saw Baron Samedi standing rock still and frantically looking in all directions for his mentor. Agreeably surprised by this display of courage and good judgment on the part of his puppet, Mallabone raised his arm and beckoned him over.

Colin caught a brief glimpse of Baron Samedi fighting his way upstream against a flash flood of panicking guests. He seemed to be heading for Mallabone at the east end of the ballroom, opposite the main entrance. It was easier going for Colin now, as the main crush of people had passed by him to pile up at the archways. The floor was littered with discarded masks, some of them turning into miniature bonfires as they curled up in the heat and burst into flame.

He called Wendy's name, the acrid smoke burning his throat and sending him into a fit of coughing. She heard him and tugged desperately against the naval commander's grip on her wrist. He scarcely bothered to look at her as he pulled her forward; he seemed determined to keep the men carrying the victim's body in view. She was really fighting him now, leaning back and digging her heels into the floor. He was waving his gun, but Wendy either must have believed he wouldn't use it or she was past caring.

Completely forgetting that he himself was packing a gun, Colin dodged around an inebriated celebrant who was staring about in befuddled stupefaction and launched himself at Wendy's captor, kicking out at his gun hand. Colin's lunge was a flying body check, and it sent Dykstra sprawling and the revolver skittering out of reach. But Carl rolled smoothly to his feet and took up the defensive stance of an expert in martial arts. Colin hesitated, knowing that any attack he made would be turned against him.

"Hold it, Carl." Pearl stood beside Colin, both hands holding Dykstra's gun.

"Take off the mask, Carl." Her voice was almost a purr.

"For Chrissakes, Pearl!" he protested.

"Take it off." The gun barrel was unwavering.

"Shit!" He removed his cap and pulled off the plastic, matinee-idol mask. The poached-egg eyes regarded her balefully. He coughed and said, "Cut out the crap, Pearl. We'll be cremated if we don't get the hell out of here."

His look of exasperation changed to sudden alarm when she said, "This is for what you did to Tommy, Carl."

Then she shot him twice in the chest. He pitched forward, the impact of the bullets turning his body in a half spin, and landed on his back. A flow of bright red blood stained the white tunic and the rows of decorations. The phony bastard had awarded himself every medal in the book; the thought flitted irrelevantly through a corner of Colin's mind as he stared in aston-

242

ishment at Pearl. Her face was as devoid of feeling as though she had just stamped on a cockroach.

The sudden *whoosh* as another set of drapes went up in flames and the loud bang of an imploding window, followed by the tinkle of falling glass, snapped Colin back to reality. The density of the smoke was decreasing as the flames took over. The archways were choked with people, and most seemed to be getting through. A half-dozen blackened bodies, withered arms raised in grotesque supplication, lay on the floor.

"I saw Mallabone and Bartholomew heading that way." He pointed toward the east wall. It was adorned with an enormous oil portrait of Bartholomew, and a lacquered Chinese screen stood in one corner, but there was no sign of an exit.

"I know where they went. There's a panel behind the screen." Pearl began to move in that direction, shouting over her shoulder, "And that wasn't Bartholomew you saw. The *real* Bartholomew is dead. He was the woman in the green dress that the limbo dancer killed."

"Jesus on a crutch!" Colin swore. He ran ahead of Pearl, urging them to move faster. "Well, at least the son of a bitch is finished." The heat of the floorboards was seeping through the soles of his shoes. He struggled out of his flowing monk's costume, yelling at Wendy to get rid of her cape. Without breaking stride she gave the hasp a sharp tug and it dropped to the floor.

She was gasping for breath in the superheated air as she shouted over the roar of the flames, "That wasn't the *real* Bartholomew either."

"Oh, no!" Pearl sagged as though she might faint. "How can you be sure?"

Wendy glanced apologetically at Colin then said in a flat, matter-of-fact tone, "Bartholomew had been circumcised. The man under that dress wasn't. Besides, I touched his hands as he was falling and they were warm."

Pearl crossed herself. "The evil one still lives. He fooled them all."

With the sound of rolling thunder, the roof timbers began to crash down on the last of the guests still struggling to make it through the archways, crushing the life from some and pinning others under their weight. As the rumble of the falling beams slowly died away, a wild laugh rose above the screams of those trapped in the inferno.

The hairy figure of a gorilla capered about on the smoking floor. The headpiece had been thrown back and Bartholomew's broad face was lifted to the blazing roof, while peal after peal of laughter boomed out from his thick lips.

"My God, he's gone right over the flipping edge!" Colin muttered, although no one could hear him.

Pearl snapped off a quick shot, but the range was too great and it went wide. Bartholomew must have heard the sizzle of the bullet, for the demented laughter abruptly ceased and he scuttled backward, disappearing from view with startling speed.

"Forget him," Colin shouted in Pearl's ear. "We're running out of time."

She blinked, as if awakening from a trance, then spun around and raced over to the Chinese screen. The oil painting was beginning to burn, the flames devouring Bartholomew's features that the artist had labored to cast in a statesmanlike pose. Colin felt a tug at his arm and looked down. It was Pierre, his harlequin costume hanging in shreds and his face blackened with smoke and ash. He made a gesture indicating it was impossible to talk over the din and stared intently at Pearl as her fingertips explored the screen.

The wallpaper was curling away from the plaster, and any second now the entire wall would become an impassable curtain of fire. Colin ducked to one side to peer behind the screen. The wall was completely blank with no sign of any exit. Alarmed, he looked at Pearl. If she blew it now . . . She was frowning with concentration as she traced the sinuosities of a gilded serpent, then pressed the tip of one of its fangs. With a click that went unheard in the roar of the all-consuming fire, a section of the wall swung inward.

"Bartholomew has a passion for secret passages," she murmured in the sudden quiet as the panel closed behind them. "If he ever found out how much I know about them, I would have been put to death."

"He's still alive, Pearl," Pierre announced dejectedly. "They got the wrong man."

His companions made no reply. They were watching a tendril of smoke seeping through the thin cracks around the sliding panel. From the inside and without the camouflage of the striped wallpaper, the outline of the secret opening was easily discernible. With Colin in the lead, they began to edge their way down the corridor.

"Didn't you hear what I said?" Pierre cried, dumbfounded by their lack of reaction. "Bartholomew's not dead!"

"We already know that," Colin told him, then asked, "Where the devil did you come from? The last time I saw you, you were hightailing it after the men lugging the body away."

"That's right. We knew, or thought we knew, from Pearl what Bartholomew's disguise was going to be, and I wanted to make sure he was well and truly dead.

I got a glimpse of his face when they laid him out on the lawn and pulled off his mask. Apart from his build, he didn't even look like Bartholomew. So I slipped away and climbed back in through a window. He's around here somewhere and I'm going to get him. Once and for all."

A hoarse guffaw echoed through the walls. It seemed to be coming from all directions at once, and there was no way of telling how far away it was.

"There's your boy," Colin muttered. "All dressed up in a gorilla suit and completely around the bloody bend."

"Sweet Jesus," Pierre breathed. "There are more passages?" he asked Pearl.

"The place is honeycombed with them," she replied, adding with a shiver, "And he knows them all. I don't."

The floor shifted slightly under their feet, followed by the dull thump of an explosion. Wendy swallowed an involuntary gasp of fear and Colin said, "This place could be down around our ears any minute. Exactly where are we, Pearl?"

"This corridor leads directly to Bartholomew's main suite of offices. We have to go through them in order to reach the outside."

"Damn," Colin said. "There'll be guards all over the place."

"I doubt it," Pierre said. "Those hired guns won't hang around and run the risk of being roasted alive. You should have seen them outside, running around in a mad panic like a bunch of old women. Unless Bartholomew rallies them, the days of the Mongoose are finished."

The smoke was thickening and the temperature was rapidly climbing to the flash point. Pearl tapped her brother's arm. "See that door? His office is on the other side."

The knob turned in Pierre's hand. The fleeing Mallabone hadn't paused to lock it. Pierre kneeled and eased the door open an infinitesimal crack. The sound of a human voice, raspy with fear, was clearly audible.

"I don't feel so good about this, boss."

"Nonsense, dear boy. You'll be hailed as a ruddy god. Bartholomew risen from the ashes." Mallabone gave a fruity little giggle. "A bit more apt than I had really intended."

After a pause he went on in the same cajoling tone. "Remember you're the best of the lot. The chaps at the medical school did a bang-up job on you."

"And what happened to the others? They all dead, that's what."

"Things will be different when *I'm* running the show." Mallabone's voice sharpened with impatience. "Hurry up and get into that suit. We don't want to be trapped in here."

The raspy voice whimpered something that the others couldn't catch. Then Mallabone hissed, "Stop blubbering, you overgrown monkey. All you have to do is make an appearance. And that's the way it'll be in the future. Show yourself to the troops every now and then and in between all the dope and women you can handle. I'll give you a little fix when you finish changing. That make you feel better?"

Peering over Pierre's shoulder, Colin's eyes widened as he spotted the crack in the paneling on the opposite side of the large, brightly lit office. Mallabone's back was to it; he stood almost facing the door their own little group was hiding behind. He had taken off his mask, but the false beard was till pasted to his chin. Baron Samedi's skull mask and top hat lay on the desk, and Bartholomew was climbing into one of his white silk suits. Except, Colin corrected himself, it wasn't Bartholomew. It was Mallabone's stooge.

The crack in the paneling was slowly widening. Colin touched Pierre's shoulder and silently pointed to it. Then it was flung wide open and Bartholomew, with a howl of triumphant laughter, leaped into the room, holding a gun in his paw. The lights flickered, then came on again.

"You know what happens to those who betray me, Tony." Bartholomew sounded entirely sane.

Mallabone held up a hand. "Wait. Let me explain . . ." he began, then faltered, knowing it was hopeless. The false Bartholomew, with one leg halfway into the trousers of his white suit, gaped at the intruder and fell to his knees.

"You should be grateful I do not have the time to make your punishment as slow and painful as you deserve. But, even so . . ." Bartholomew took careful aim and shot Mallabone in the knee cap. The Englishman toppled sideways and then began to screech in agony. Bartholomew shifted his aim to the cowering number ten and his finger, still encased in the gorilla glove, tightened on the trigger. Then he let out a long sigh and lowered the gun. "I cannot do it. It is like shooting at myself."

Behind the door, Pierre was fuming with impatience. His .38 was in his hand, but the crack was too narrow to get off an accurate shot, and Bartholomew would immediately detect any attempt to widen it. Then Bartholomew glanced down at Mallabone writhing on the floor, and Pierre nudged the door with his fingertip. Suddenly the lights went out; the fire had reached the generator in the basement.

Two rapid shots reverberated inside the office, and

Mallabone's anguished screaming was silenced. Bartholomew's spine-chilling laugh rolled out in the darkness, and then somebody was bumping into furniture, followed by the sound of glass shattering and finally by the soft thud of a door closing. Had Bartholomew gone? Or was he still in there, waiting for them?

"We'll have to chance it," Colin whispered. "There's no other way out."

Pierre nodded and gave the door another nudge. Pearl leaned forward, her breast brushing against Colin's arm. "Let me go first," she whispered. "I'm the only one who knows the layout."

"As soon as we're inside," Pierre whispered back and crawled forward on his belly. Colin moved to one side to let Pearl slide past him and groped for Wendy's hand. There was a small involuntary gasp from Pearl as her fingers encountered a patch of wet stickiness on the rug. They froze, waiting for the blast of gunfire to rip into them. But the only sound was a sharp intake of breath from a corner of the room as the hapless number ten realized he had company.

They were all sweating profusely, but the stifling heat sucked up moisture like a desert wind and turned their throats to sandpaper. The room began to brighten with a diffuse orange glow. The flames had breached the wall and were flicking their tongues down the passageway. In the growing light they saw Mallabone's lifeless body slumped against the desk, long legs splayed out across the carpet. His wretched puppet was still on his knees, blubbering to himself. He submitted quietly while Pierre frisked him. Wordlessly, Pearl pointed to a narrow gun case. The glass front was broken and the single rifle rack was empty. Pierre swore under his breath, gave the room a final quick scan and opened the door.

The fire had outflanked them; the oak paneling in the outer office gave a mighty crack and split open, strewing bits of charred wood on the floor. Flames leapt up from the red hot embers.

"Run for it!" Colin shouted, hauling Wendy along as the flames raced across the floor. Pierre and Pearl made it through, but the terrified number ten jumped back, blocking the way. A hellish vision of a small sports car, overturned in a ditch while orange-red flames consumed Robbie Powell, shimmered before Colin's eyes. He hesitated and drew back, then yelled an explosive "No!" and barreled into the black man, shielding Wendy with his body as they crashed through the fiery gap. He landed in a heap on the floor and lay there, winded by the fall, smelling the sharp odor of singed hair and realizing it was his own. He struggled to his feet and they stumbled on, coughing, lungs seared with the heat. From somewhere up ahead came the faint sound of Bartholomew laughing.

"Traitor!" The word echoed like a thunderclap around the vaulted ceiling of the grandiose reception area, stopping them halfway across the tiled floor. "Bartholomew spares your life and you repay him by joining forces with his enemies."

The whites of number ten's eyes showed as he looked fearfully up at the balcony.

"The sentence is death." A rifle cracked and he crumpled, slowly folding inward on himself.

Bartholomew stepped out from behind a black marble pillar, brandishing his rifle over his head. The gorilla suit appeared to be miraculously unscathed by the fire.

"He'll pick us off one by one," Pierre whispered. The dictator was outside a handgun's effective range, and he knew it. He did a little victory dance on the balcony, pausing when the building shook with another rumbling explosion.

"It is time for the people to hail their Emperor!" he bellowed, baring his teeth in a ferocious grin.

"I will show them that Bartholomew lives." Suddenly he paused and peered down at the little group huddled in the middle of the rotunda. "Come with me, Pearl. You have always been my favorite and now I will make you my Empress. You look like a queen."

Pearl gave an ironic glance at the tattered remains of her Marie Antoniette costume, then stepped forward.

"For God's sake, Pearl, don't go!" Pierre hissed under his breath.

"I must," she answered quietly, then called out, "I will come with you, Your Majesty, but first you must promise to let my friends go. They will be our loyal subjects."

A tongue of flame licked under the door of the outer office.

"It is so ordered. But you must hurry. Come, Empress Pearl!"

"Good bye, Colin. Pierre, remember that Soufriere needs you." She walked toward the winding staircase, oddly regal in her torn and scorched gown.

They saw a hairy paw reach out for her at the top of the stairs and caught a fleeting glimpse of the gorilla's massive back. Then the balcony was empty.

It was Wendy who broke the spell, tugging at Colin's hand and crying at them to move. The bronze handle of the double doors was uncomfortably hot to the touch, but the heavy door swung open easily enough. The night air felt unbelievably cool and sweet as they staggered down the few stone steps and onto the manicured lawn.

A cheer went up from a small group of people, clearly illuminated in the lurid light of the fire. They were calling Pierre's name as they surged forward, some of them carrying submachine guns. All wore identical white armbands with three links of a chain stitched in blue thread. The middle link was broken apart. One of them slipped a band on Pierre's arm, but the guerrilla leader paid no attention.

"We must get round to the front," he gasped. "Right away."

"No problem." One of the men shoved a submachine gun into his hands. "The goons are running for cover. And leaving all kinds of goodies behind." He tapped the metal butt of the gun. "A Kalashnikov, no less. Bartholomew did well by his pet bullies." He paused for effect before announcing, "We've seized the radio station."

"Great," Pierre shouted. "But we still have to stop Bartholomew."

He was picking his way across the lawn, dodging through the people staring up at the doomed palace. Colin followed him, feeling the cooling trade winds on his face. It was the trades that had saved them, blowing the flames toward the front of the palace and delaying the spread of the fire to the rear. But dear God, it was positively *raining* fire on the city. A row of towering royal palms suddenly burst into flame, their lofty fronds burning with a sharp crackling noise and sending up a Vesuvius of sparks. Colin watched the wind carry the embers over the dry wooden homes and small commercial buildings of Albertstown. Down below, he guessed it was near the sprawling open-air market, the siren of a fire engine wailed and its bell clanged self-importantly.

The crowd, carnival costumes casting weird shadows

in the glare of the flames, was hushed, subdued by the sheer drama of the spectacle and the presence of death. Many had already fled down the hill into the lower town to try and save their own homes. A few scattered shots could be heard in the distance.

A concerted gasp went up when the beastlike shape appeared high above them. Bartholomew had broken one of the few remaining windows to clamber out on a third-floor veranda. He turned and peered back inside as though searching for someone, but a wave of heat sent him reeling back.

"It looks like Pearl didn't make it," Colin said with a catch in his voice.

Pierre's eyes were suddenly moist in the bright glare of the flames. "It's better that way. Now she is finally free of that monster's madness."

A woman standing beside Colin let out a small scream as Bartholomew loped, with a rolling gait that was eerily apelike, across to the corner of the veranda and began to speak. His words were lost in the crackling roar of the conflagration. He seemed to realize this and shook his head in baffled rage. Once again, the movement was uncannily simian.

Colin heard the snick of the safety catch as Pierre slowly raised the submachine gun.

"Don't, Pierre," he reached out and pushed the barrel down. "It would be a mistake."

A scowl momentarily darkened Pierre's face, then he relaxed and said, "You are right, my friend."

A long drawn out *oooh* from the crowd made them look up again. Bartholomew had climbed onto the wrought-iron railing of the veranda. Swaying precariously, he cupped his hands to his mouth, but still his words were carried away in the tumult.

The main wing of Government House was a pyramid

of fire, shooting sparks into the sky like a giant roman candle. Bartholomew turned around and shook a furious fist at the flames. Then he was climbing again, shinnying up the iron pillar with an agility that brought gasps of disbelief from his audience. The gloves must be protecting his hands from the heat, thought Colin. Either that, or he's become impervious to pain.

Bartholomew grasped an eaves trough and hung for a moment with both hands before he slowly chinned himself and grabbed the ornamental grille that decorated the veranda roof. It held firm as he pulled himself over and temporarily dropped from sight. Then he was standing up, both arms raised over his head, and this time the rushing wind carried faint echoes of his voice. There were no words, just a wild primordial howl.

Government House was collapsing, rocked with a series of explosions and caving in on itself amid billowing clouds of smoke and flame. The roof of Bartholomew's veranda tilted sickeningly, pitching him sideways and making him grab for support. He straightened up once more and the crowd cried out when they saw his costume was on fire. A fiery aura spread around him as he posed there, absolutely still. The roof buckled and slowly slid back into the inferno, bearing him wit' it.

A stunned silence settled over the throng of onlookers and then someone started to cheer. Others picked it up and soon it swelled to a chorus of relief and thanksgiving.

"I don't think you have to worry about Bartholomew's memory now," Colin shouted at Pierre.

"Pierre Demaret, what have you done with my daughter?"

Pierre blinked and looked away from the fire. Mary Powell's square, determined face, smudged with soot glared back at him.

"She is perfectly safe, Mrs. Powell," he assured her. "She will be back at Palm Hill in a few hours."

"Thank you for that." She paused then asked in a milder tone, "Are you going to do a proper job of running this country?"

"I'm certainly going to try, Mrs. Powell. With the help of people like yourself and your husband, I hope."

She nodded as though satisfied and looked past him to where Colin stood with his arm around Wendy. "And what about you, Colin Townsend? Have you come back home?"

Colin bent down and brushed his lips against Wendy's smoke-filled hair. She smiled up at him as he murmured, "I think we have. I really think we have."

GREAT ADVENTURES IN READING